A MORNING AT THE OFFICE

ALSO BY EDGAR MITTELHOLZER

Creole Chips
Corentyne Thunder
Shadows Move Among Them
Children of Kaywana
The Weather in Middenshot
The Life and Death of Sylvia
The Adding Machine
The Harrowing of Hubertus
My Bones and My Flute
Of Trees and the Sea
A Tale of Three Places
With a Carib Eye (nf)
Kaywana Blood
The Weather Family
A Tinkling in the Twilight
The Mad MacMullochs (as H. Austin Woodsley)
Eltonsbrody
Latticed Echoes
The Piling of Clouds
Thunder Returning
The Wounded and the Worried
A Swarthy Boy (nf)
Uncle Paul
The Aloneness of Mrs Chatham
The Jilkington Drama

A MORNING AT THE OFFICE

EDGAR MITTELHOLZER

INTRODUCTION BY RAYMOND RAMCHARITAR

PEEPAL TREE

First published by the Hogarth Press
in Great Britain in 1950
This new edition published in 2010 by
Peepal Tree Press Ltd
17 King's Avenue
Leeds LS6 1QS
England

ISBN13: 978 1 84523 121 7

Supported by
ARTS COUNCIL
ENGLAND

INTRODUCTION

THE MOMENT BEFORE THE DAWN IN TRINIDAD

RAYMOND RAMCHARITAR

A Morning at the Office, written by Edgar Mittelholzer during his sojourn in Trinidad between 1941 and 1948, and certainly completed before he left for the UK in 1948[1], is set in that island in the period between the war's end and the coming of Independence, which began with the emergence of Eric Williams in 1956. The period was an interregnum between two distinct eras: the agriculture-based, pre-industrial Trinidad of before the war, and the industrialized modern nation it has become.

Two generations later, a decade into the new century, Trinidad is a republic of immense wealth and a disproportionate amount of suffering – all of it self-inflicted – the result of an almost narcotic stupor arising from the nationalist project. The novel, published in 1950 by the distinguished Hogarth Press (set up by Leonard and Virginia Woolf), was written at a time when India's independence was very recent and the implications for the British colonial world would have only just begun to register, and give a tangible model upon which to base expectations of independence.

Mittelholzer's novel captures in miniature the prelapsarian moment before anything of the next sixty years was conceivable. But more than just capture an essential moment, Mittelholzer's novel realises a fundamentally moral purpose: indeed, for the believer, *A Morning at the Office* could be likened to one of the last enigmatic works of the Old Testament. It is almost a prophetic parable describing the nature of the destructive chaff history had sown with the wheat of the future. In this case, the chaff was an obsession with race and status that pervaded the society as the coloured and black inhabitants strove, from the early 19th century, to assert a claim to the land against the British colonial administration, and, later, from the early twentieth century, as the descendents of Indian indentured labourers began to compete for their share of the future prizes of independence. It was an obsession that no morally centred institution in Trinidad – in national culture, education or the arts – was able to mitigate.

But you would hardly know this upon first entering the novel. As parables do, it begins innocently enough: as an account of a morning at the Port of Spain offices of a colonial export firm, Essential Products. The characters are the office staff and a few guest stars – including an Indian vagabond, an overseer with a conscience and two thinly disguised versions of the author himself – and they seem to do little except make their way through the hours. In this quotidian ordinariness just one thing appears remarkable: that in thinking, planning, discussing their lives and work, in the inner narrative each person recites to him- or herself, almost every character seems to be obsessed with his or her racial extraction, and engaged in a constant battle to satisfy baser desires – lust, ambition, greed – all of which seem to be inextricably bound up with racial origins and their manifestation in physical appearance.

From the black office boy, Xavier, to the expatriate English assistant manager, Mr Murrain, and through the office-society hierarchy, representing various ethnic groups and subgroups (African, Indian, Chinese, European, mixed-race Afro-Euro), each individual treads through a virtual minefield of associations, potential insults, embarrassments, and a sensitivity at being either mis-categorized or, for those at the bottom of the scale, correctly categorized. Each character's happiness or anxiety is directly related to the colour of his or her skin (the lighter the better), the status of his/her family (the older and more possessed of eminent personages the better), the texture of his or her hair (the straighter the better) and, more pertinently, how every other person they interact with interprets these characteristics. The characters in the office include a sampling of the various groups present in the country at the time – in proportion not to numeric presence in Trinidad as a whole, but to urban social importance (as the author interprets the norms of the period): two white British managers; two Indians; two Africans; a young Chinese woman; six "coloured" people of various extractions (English, French, Portuguese) – two from good families, two from the lower orders whose brown skin had been attained through sordid incidents; one "Spanish" – of Venezuelan stock – and one character whose ethnicity, of all the characters, seems most irrelevant – a gay man, who is characterised with considerable sensitivity.

The event that incites these characters into action is, ironically, a love poem, copied from Shakespeare by Xavier, and left in the in-tray of the lovely, unattainable, high-caste, high-brown Nanette Hinckson as a token of his adoration. It is Xavier's suppositions about what is being said about his action – and the actual discussions of it that take place – that intensify, in witting and unwitting ways, each actor's movements and interactions during the morning in the office. It is Xavier's heightened consciousness of who he is and his place in the scheme of things that provides the morning's dramatic denoucment.

The terms of Xavier's defeat in his unrequited love for Nanette, and the absolute hopelessness of any possibility of salvation, place Mittelholzer's treatment of this central episode in the Romantic arena where truth to feeling and self-knowledge confront the realities of class identity and learnt prejudice in an oppressive social structure. Xavier is ambitious; he desires to get ahead in the world – he tortures himself to be a reader of Shakespeare and Dickens. Nanette, too, as she considers Xavier's attentions, locates herself at the heart of this Romantic conflict:

> The office-boy. Apart from his age, his social position and the fact that he was black made him an impossible candidate. But he was a human being – a male human being. He represented another Instance. He was the intellectual type. The serious, plodding, ambitious kind who studied at night and who had "noble" ideals. She admired and respected such men because,

ironically, she herself was an intellectual. She liked books, she liked to discuss philosophy and politics and all serious subjects. She liked to think that her life was governed by her reason rather than by her emotions. Yet she could not fall in love with men fashioned this way (p. 105: references are to this edition).

And here is the subtle central conflict of the book: can the love of the things that books and the mind value and cultivate save their interlocutors from self-destruction? Sadly, Mittelholzer thinks not. Later in the book, Nanette catches a glimpse of one of the author's alter egos, Mortimer Barnett, and is struck by love at first sight. Barnett has come to the office to seek an advertisement for a literary publication. Nanette stares after him in wonderment: he appears to be the perfect union of the masculine animal and the intellectual. But in a moment of existential ennui, she decides she is unworthy of him, and succumbs to the unwholesome attentions of the predatory Pat Lorry, the coloured clerk whose lightness of skin, despite his inauspicious origins, allows him to exploit the island's absurd, hierarchic colour codes.

It is the fate of Xavier's love poem and the relayed transmission through the office of talk about it that is Mittelholzer's main structural device – an instance of what he describes, in the guise of the character Mortimer Barnett, as "telescopic objectivity".

"Telescopic objectivity" allows Mittelholzer to use a dent in the office's outside door, for example, to recall a roistering romp enjoyed by a drunken English sailor and his two new local friends, one Indian, one African, both blackguards, some years before. The sailor despoils his friendship by misidentifying his new Indian friend's ethnicity by insulting him with a derogatory name applied to Africans, which causes the Indian to attack him with a hatchet, dealing a glancing blow which dents the door. That incident fits into the thematic scheme of the book, but it (and other similar object-related incidents) also allows a shift of space and time from the confines of the office, to locate the novel's themes in the wider world.

The device also allows the selection of metonymic detail that reveals character, and purposeful digression from the main narrative line. In this way, we are introduced to Mr Benson's illegal, extra-office practices; Miss Henery's adulterous designs on her cousin's husband; Mr Murrain's domestic frustrations and the scar tissue of wartime memory; Mr Reynolds's torments over his homosexuality (nearly unspeakable at the time); and the obsequious assistant accountant Jagabir's fears at being fired at the slightest excuse.

What Mittelholzer calls "telescopic objectivity" is by no means an original technique in the fiction writer's repertoire; Dickens, for instance used comparable devices to propel his complicated, densely populated plots and Joyce and other modernists had used such techniques more self-reflexively, and this is perhaps Mittelholzer's inspiration in foregrounding the device in this novel. (At a pinch, one can see in it an imaginative anticipation of Robbe-Grillet's theory of "pure surface" in the Noveau Roman (a device further explored by the Guyanese novelist, Denis Williams in *The Third Temptation* (1968).) It is possible, too, that Mittelholzer's motive in foregrounding the device was, as well as a manifestation of a characteristic playfulness, intended as assistance to the relatively unsophisticated Caribbean reading public of the time, helping them to read his book to maximum effect.

This is plausible, since, from the evidence of his direct, almost earnest prose and his labouring to remove the potential barrier of ironic distraction between audience and message, Mittelholzer's purpose is at least partly moral – the narrative a device to expose the farrago of ethnic obsession which underlies and inhibits the characters' and the society's, strivings for self-realization. This becomes clear in the precise authorial explanations of the motivations of each character's racial neurosis. For example, introducing Miss Henery, the narrator explains:

> Miss Henery – like Mrs Hinckson – belonged to the coloured middle-class, and was very conscious of her background of gentility and her social superiority over the Negro, East Indian and Chinese elements which counted, in her estimation, as low-class. The whites debarred her from their society, but – like everyone in her class – she considered herself the equal of the whites in breeding and general culture. Her pride forbade her addressing a white man as "sir" (p.57).

Mittelholzer is equally frank about the quality of the expatriates, about whom, the narrator muses, the practice of hiring "was a good thing for the Old Country, for it provided employment for young men who were not too bright or who, for divers reasons, were *persona non grata* types at home" (p.42). (Apparently, if the political scandals that shook Trinidad in March 2010 in the aftermath of a commission of inquiry into the construction sector are any guide, some things never change.[2]) Within the office, Murrain, the chief accountant, is occasionally troubled by his idleness and the fact that Jagabir does his job for him – at one-third of his salary – but rationalises his idleness as a whiteman's privilege. There is, though, an exception: Sidney Whitmer, the young expatriate overseer who crashes drunkenly into the office to fulminate over his disgust with colonial society. He is even more direct in a letter to his mother:

> I'd hardly stepped ashore when I found myself being admitted to functions at the exclusive Country Club just outside Port of Spain – a club that considers you an aristocrat, and therefore eligible as a member, simply on the strength of your pink skin and your English accent. I've met chaps there who, in England, would be sniffed at by a Hoxton charwoman (p.42).

But if the office is a microcosm, it is not a complete one, as Mittelholzer acknowledges in a brief reference to striking marchers on the streets outside the office, quite late in the book. Their story is different from those in the office. Much of the African part of this group was in thrall to the American armed forces, providing labour – and entertainment, liquor, and flesh to satiate the vices of soldiers unleashed on a relatively naïve and impoverished population. This story is told elsewhere, for instance in Ralph de Boissière's novel *Rum and Coca Cola* (1954).[3] A substantial part of the Indian masses – glimpsed in Jagabir's nightmares of return to the canefields – was in parallel thrall to the Tate and Lyle owned West Indies Sugar Company.

The later phenomenon of Trinidadians of African and Indian origins moving in different directions, being influenced by different forces, providing yet another schizophrenic rift in Trinidad's social fabric, had to await the fictions of V.S. Naipaul and Earl Lovelace for attention.

But Mittelholzer understood that at the point in time at which he was writing – before the emergence of mass political parties – it was the people who had the luxury of self-reflection in matters other than their most immediate needs – food, shelter, safety – who were most crucial in a society's self-realization: these are the people in his office. Inside this crucible, various types and archetypes, who are still immediately recognizable to anyone who has lived in Trinidad, interact, intrigue, fulminate, scheme and in some cases are defeated by their own demons. And whilst Mittelholzer shows that a number of the characters have an embryonic sense that there was a cultural as well as a political struggle to be waged against colonialism – Nanette Hinckson is most explicit in this respect – what he portrays in the novel is an attachment to the minutiae of status that would sink all such nobler ambitions.

It is reasonable to ask – not as a judgment on what is legitimate in fiction, but as an assessment of the novel's fidelity as social realism – how close to reality was all this. Was Mittelholzer overstating the case? Did his alleged obsession with the facts of his own racial mixture result in a distorting of reality, rather than a reordering and manipulating an observable reality for artistic effect?

I am of the opinion that Mittelholzer was correct: if he was masochistically obsessed with his racial origins, (and as a Guyanese he wrote penetratingly about his own society's colour/class obsessions), I think he found in Trinidad a dungeon of ethnic sadism, and for this there are other articles of proof. The British novelist, Arthur Calder Marshall, visiting Trinidad before the War, records an identical racial obsession pervading the society in his *Glory Dead* (1939). L.E. Brathwaite's sociological essay, *Social Stratification in Trinidad: A Preliminary Analysis* (1953), outlines in some detail the racial neurosis of the coloured middle class, which largely conforms to Mittelholzer's description. And more than a decade after *A Morning at the Office* was published, Vidia Naipaul's chapter on Trinidad in his *Middle Passage* (1962), describes a society much like the one Mittelholzer described, and

11

Naipaul's later novel, *The Mimic Men* (1969), explores the shadows that these obsessions can cast. Sadly, one of the things that make *A Morning at the Office* relevant today is that, to paraphrase Ezra Pound, its content is news that has remained news. This would be obvious to anyone who has lived in Trinidad for longer than a tourist trip,

There are limits to Mittelholzer's perceptions. He does not examine Indian Trinidadians' racial neuroses with similar inwardness and depth to his portrayal of Creole characters; his two office Indians are types in the urban "Creole" hierarchy and their concerns are with their places in it. What was going on inside the Indian Trinidadian world is found elsewhere. There are hints of Indian cultural confusion in Seepersad Naipaul's *Gurudeva and Other Indian Tales* (1943), stories composed from his experience as a journalist working for the *Trinidad Guardian* in the 1930s. There are his son, Vidia's more extensive examinations in his novels, *The Mystic Masseur* (1957), *The Suffrage of Elvira* (1958) and *The Mimic Men* (1967). But it is in Yogendra Malik's political study, *East Indians in Trinidad* (1971), and Harold Sonny Ladoo's novels, *No Pain like this Body* (1971) and *Yesterdays* (1973), that the painful truth emerges. The story these works tell is of caste prejudice seasoned with racial prejudice, creating another, similar hierarchy among Indians – and remarkably similar opinions on status and aspirations to whiteness as in the urban "creole" world.

Nevertheless, Mittelholzer's portrayal of the two Indian characters is worthy of note, and the contrasts between Edna Bisnauth and Jagabir reveal how he attempts to distinguish between racial and cultural values (and in the process says more about his own biases).

Throughout the novel Mittelholzer insists that his notion of "civilisation" rests on cultural rather than racial criteria. Yet his falling back on ethnic stereotypes in the description of Jagabir and the ambiguities in the portrayal of Horace Xavier, suggest that he did not find it so easy to separate the two. The portrayal of Edna Bisnauth, the novel's most fluid, developed and inwardly drawn character, suggests otherwise, but in fact proves this point. Her judgement on the revelations of human absurdity at the office ("we ought to see ourselves with ironic eyes, but we should revere the humanity in us" (p.209)) is, indeed, very much Mittelholzer's postscript to the novel, and we can be reasonably sure that she is intended as the only character through whom we see others without distortion. Her view of life remains benign and only very gently ironic:

> ... It was a tinkling laugh but restrained and entirely lacking in maliciousness, and it produced in her an effect as though she were emitting rays of good nature, vital and saturating – a good nature the warmth and naivety of which gave the impression of surrounding her personality with an aura of insulation proof against the invasion of evil. For this particular instant she had a transfigured, spiritual air (p. 74).

The portrayal only just escapes being made too inconceivably sensitive and sympathetic, thanks to the gentle satire of her sincere but bad verse-writing, and her slightly ludicrous vulnerability:

> She wrote rapidly, then paused, biting her lower lip.
> The next two lines came.
> *"Oh, I wish it were mine, this flower,*
> *Just to hold to myself for an hour..."*
> She stopped writing, breathing fast, her eyes half closed, the lids quivering slightly. She did not seem at all ridiculous, for her mien was too earnest, too intensely sincere; there was almost anguish in her sincerity (p.79).

Because of his brown skin, straight hair and the skills he possesses, Jagabir ought to belong to the coloured middle class. He does not, because he still carries with him the stigma of his sugar estate background. Even the urbane Mrs Hinckson detests him, and Mary, the black cleaner at the bottom of the office hierarchy, sustains solace from her contempt for Jagabir as a "cheap coolie". Jagabir himself is acutely conscious of how others feel about him and it seems, at first, that Mittelholzer locates the responses to Jagabir in prejudice. When Miss Henery insists that, "It was not that she hated East Indians... But this man Jagabir made her sick in every way. His dissembling, his slyness, and prying habits, his sycophancy, his ingratiating…" (p.64), she rehearses a list of traits drawn from stereotypes employed in the nineteenth century racist rhetoric of justifying the harshness of indenture. Mittelholzer adds authorially that Miss Henery's response is a conditioned one:

> In her social sphere, a child was from an early age made to feel that the East Indians were inferior, contemptible people. They were dirty coolies, you learnt, … they were low filthy people who wore *dhotis* and smelly rags… lived in stinking tenement barracks, hoarded their pennies in mattresses (p. 64).

However, everything that Jagabir does supports the stereotype. He is obsequious to his superiors, bullies Horace, is deceitful and paranoiacally anxious to know everything that is going on. His hearing is "preternaturally acute". As an intruder in the office, his awkwardness is sharply imaged in the grease stain in his coat-pocket from the roti he always carries to work with him.

There *are* elements of sympathy in the portrayal; we are clearly intended to read Jagabir's behaviour as motivated by his permanent insecurity, his fear of being sent back to a life of hardship and humiliation in the canefields, the feeling that he does not belong in the white people's office. But Mittelholzer's portrayal also suggests that he, too, sees Jagabir as a coolie, still part of an alien, uncivilized culture, whereas Miss Bisnauth, civilized and sensitive, has rejected all aspects of her Indian past. She has the advantage, Mittelholzer implies, of parents who are wealthy and, despite a regrettable clannishness, "thoroughly Christian and Western in outlook…", who "spoke not a word of Hindustani" (p81). Their clannishness resides in their inability to accept the "coloured" Arthur Lamby (another of Mittelholzer's proxies in the novel) as prospective son-in-law, whilst for Edna Bisnauth: "Arthur was the best man in existence; the different bloods of which he was composed meant nothing to her" (p.81).

We must not, however, judge Mittelholzer too harshly for these portrayals. Indeed, there is an admirably ruthless detachment in them, a fidelity to reality: these types exist to the present day, and are clearly identifiable in Trinidad in 2010.

Even so, the elision of race into culture in the case of Jagabir is, perhaps, also at the heart of what is equivocal in Mittelholzer's portrayal of Horace Xavier. Horace is shown as trying to escape from the disorder of the black proletarian world to achieve the security and order represented by the office. He despises the world of his upbringing for reasons that Mittelholzer would seem to endorse. Yet Mittelholzer also seems to be mocking Horace as a black man in white face, who is attempting to become part of the white world: talcum-powdering his armpits to impress the "bacra people", forcing himself to read unrewardingly through *A Tale of Two Cities* as "necessary for his betterment", and his hopeless infatuation for Mrs Hinckson, for whom he has conceived an hopeless infatuation because she has "genuine white-people hair, not kinky hair straightened with a hot comb." At one level, Mittelholzer appears to satirize Horace's embarkation on the "weary road to whiteness", yet in the perspective of the novel as a whole, Horace's commitment to the values and culture of the White/European world can only be approved. And again, these details – the talcum powder, the futile wrestling with the classics – reveal a fidelity to reality, and affirm Mittelholzer's skill in constructing a fictive world where such details fit so perfectly.

The contradictions in the portrayal of Horace only make sense in relationship to the world outside the novel. Universal suffrage meant that, in the 1950s at least, the political leadership of the country would inevitably be dominated by Black Trinidadians. In the office, all are agreed, with varying degrees of alarm, that Horace must "rise in the world". Mittelholzer's empathy for Horace's pain at the barriers still facing him is there in the description of the "burning in the chest as though grains of sand were slowly trickling through his lungs" (p.78). Yet, as a member of a cultural and ethnic minority likely to be swept away politically, Mittelholzer's description of Horace's eruption in a paroxysm of pent-up passion at the end of the novel is, perhaps, inevitably ambiguous. It suggests both an act of revolt, a discovery of pride ("Because I black? You-all not better dan me!") but also an irruption of the emotional disorder which threatens civilised life.

Horace then leaves the office forever.

Nanette, watching Mortimer Barnett leave her life forever,

agrees to a sordid assignation with Lorry. The various characters return to their private dramas, and the business of the office drones on, endlessly, meaninglessly, to the present, where, with a few cosmetic alterations, the discourse and the preoccupations are the same, though perhaps the frankness with which they are articulated has changed.

Of course, *A Morning at the Office* is by no means the work of objective sociological fiction – or "mere social document (very necessary, however) in the guise of a novel", as Mittelholzer wrote to his friend A. J. Seymour – that its author may have set out to write. It is much more interesting than that, dramatising the conflicts, ambivalences and perceptions of a "swarthy" Euro-creole highly conscious of the social and cultural changes taking place in his contemporary world.

Mittelholzer acknowledges this subjectivity in the prominence of the fable of *The Jen*, Arthur Lamby's fairytale gift to Edna Bisnauth, in which he very explicitly foregrounds how he thinks the story of the Caribbean's emergence from colonialism should be told, and on what cultural foundations. Indeed, to minimize any possibility of misinterpretation, Mittelholzer/Lamby not only brings the Jen fable into the novel twice, but very explicitly interprets its significance.

Whatever he became later, the Mittelholzer of *A Morning at the Office* is committed to a Caribbean vision, but it is one that has its own emphases and oppositions. For Mittelholzer, the Caribbean writer has as much right to plunder the European literary tradition as any writer and, equally, should not become trapped in any monolithic definition of Caribbeanness.

As Edna Bisnauth reflects for the final time on the parable of the Jen, and what Arthur had discussed with her in relation to his artistic efforts, Mittelholzer has Lamby characterise the opposition as faddists, a description which, I believe, has unfortunate resonances beyond his time:

> Arthur said these faddists were trying to dig up everything they could pertaining to Negro folklore in the West Indies: the cumfa dance, shango, the nancy-story. They were glorifying the calypso and encouraging primitive institutions like the steel band.

16

They had purposely blinded themselves to the fact that if the West Indies was to evolve a culture individually West Indian, it could only come out of the whole hotch-potch of racial and national elements of which the West Indies was composed; it could not spring only from the Negro.

These faddists, Arthur had told her, were even trying to whip into life a spirit of aggressive nationalism, forgetful of the misery nationalism had already caused, and was still causing, in the world at large (p.205).

These were real people Mittelholzer was referring to here, to the activities, for instance, of Edric Connor, who, during the war had begun the movement unflatteringly described in the novel as "faddism". (More sympathetic accounts are to be found in Harvey Neptune's *Caliban and the Yankees* (2007), and Gordon Rohlehr's essay on Connor in his collection of essays, *Transgression, Transition, Transformation* (2007).) It is open to speculation how much Mittelholzer could have foreseen the trajectory of the movement whose genesis he had witnessed. Indeed, what he termed "faddism" became the overriding cultural theme of the independence movement in Trinidad (and elsewhere), which has persisted, intensifying with time, to today. Mittelholzer's objection to a single dimension to Caribbean cultural foundations was not unique. It puts him in company with Derek Walcott as expressed in his essays, "The Muse of History", and "What the Twilight Says: An Overture". Walcott, who lived in Trinidad from the late 1950s to the early 1980s, characterised this movement as "our pathetic African phase", with a contempt that surfaces in his autobiographical poem *Another Life* (1973), his plays *Dream on Monkey Mountain* (1970) and *Pantomime* (1980), and elsewhere.

It is my view that through the initial agency of Eric Williams, the mixing of ethnocentric culture and art with nationalism and politics has been at the expense of the development of genuinely national artistic institutions. This is not an original view; it echoes Rohlehr in his essay "The Culture of Williams: Context, Performance, Legacy", in his *A Scuffling of Islands* (2004), and the views of several other critics, such as Kevin Yelvington, in his introduction to the collection *Trinidad Ethnicity* (1993), and Peter van Koningsbruggen, in his *Trinidad Carnival, a Quest for National Identity* (1997).

Calypso and steelband, far from being considered, in Mittelholzer's words "primitive", are now, along with Carnival, considered the bastions of traditional national culture, and are a major topic of academic, populist and creative narratives. This remarkable and resilient growth has occurred apace with an equally remarkable decline in conventional literacy at all levels of the national school system: from the primary to the tertiary, a contempt for art and the consequent underdevelopment of artistic institutions and, most importantly, education. The faddists now hold high office, dictate policy, and write history.

But in the midst of all this, where are the characters from Mittelholzer's office? Most, I believe, can still be found in a typical Port of Spain office, in similar positions, but with a few subtle changes. At the head of the office, only one of Mr Waley or Mr Murrain would remain; one of the two senior executives would now be a black man, though there would still be a Xavier in place, but one whose ambition had been snuffed out. The other executive might well be an expatriate: ill-qualified, incompetent, who would, in Whitmer's words, still be sniffed at by a Hoxton charwoman, but would be not be sniffed at for country club membership or by many young Trinidadian women with designs on acquiring foreign residency. The colour bar has not been removed; it is now what architects now call a hidden line, or what biologists call a selectively permeable membrane.

Mrs Hinckson and Miss Henery would be better paid, and still have much the same feelings about the rest of the society. Of all the people in the office, they, perhaps with the "Spanish" Mr Lopez, would have remained most the same: obsessed with status, family, and contemptuous of those expatriates who consort with the locals.

Miss Bisnauth would be university educated, still afflicted with her nerves, but financially secure. Now, artistic ambitions aside, she would spurn someone like Arthur and be married to a young Indian lawyer or dentist, or have designs on the expatriate manager. Jagabir would not be there: he would have started his own business many years ago; as would the crooked Chief Clerk,

Mr Benson, who would have taken Mr Reynolds, the salesman, with him, or, if he had chosen to stay would be an executive. Lorry's complexion would have taken him out into the world into a far more lucrative job; and the reticent, secretive Mr Reynolds, wherever he was, would be more at ease with himself, but still guarded. Olga Yen Tip would have disappeared, either abroad, or into the professions, as would have Laura Laballe.

This leaves only Xavier and Mary, the cleaning woman. Mary would still be poor, worried about her son being sent to jail, but more truculent and angry, as opposed to distressed and hopeless. And Xavier: Xavier would still be there, looking at Nanette not with adoration but open lust – in addition to Miss Henery, Miss Bisnauth, and anyone else his mercurial attention could settle on. And would Shakespeare or Dickens now exist in his consciousness, or would his poetic sensibilities have been strangled by the most misanthropic, misogynistic American hip-hop or the gunplay of Jamaican dance-hall music? Perhaps he would still leave the office everyday thinking "Because I black? You-all not better than me!", only with rage and a desire for revenge, not passionate ambition.

But there would be one large, encompassing difference: all the characters would have another obsession, much more powerful than their ethnic preoccupations: they would all be a hundred times more enrapt in money and possessions, and treat each other with considerably less than the surface civility the imperial master insisted upon.

Endnotes:

1. A.J. Seymour, *Edgar Mittelholzer: The Man and his Work*. 1967 Edgar Mittelholzer Memorial Lectures, Georgetown, 1968, p. 13. Seymour thinks that an early draft of the novel was called "Caribbean Villa".
2. See guardian.co.tt/news/politics/2010/03/.../judge-dismisses-udecott-case, though these days expatriates are as likely to be North American as British.
3. See Harvey Neptune, *Caliban and the Yankees*, University of North Carolina Press, 2007.

CONTENTS

Part One

PERSONS · OBJECT · INCIDENTALS

Part Two

OTHER PERSONS · RECAPITULATIONS

LIST OF CHIEF CHARACTERS IN ORDER OF PORTRAYAL

Every character portrayed in this work is a creature of imagination, and bears no relation whatever to any living person in Trinidad or elsewhere

Horace Xavier:	Office boy; a Negro
Mary Barker:	Sweeper; also returned in the afternoon to prepare tea for the office staff; a Negress
Jagabir:	The Assistant Accountant; an East Indian
Everard Murrain:	Chief Accountant and assistant manager; an Englishman
Kathleen Henery:	The accounts typist; coloured
Edna Bisnauth:	The Manager's assistant stenotypist; an East Indian
Nanette Hinckson:	The Manager's secretary and chief stenographer; coloured
Patrick Lorry:	Customs Clerk; coloured
Eustace Benson:	The Chief Clerk; coloured
William Reynolds:	Salesman; coloured
George Waley:	The Manager; an Englishman
Olga Yen Tip:	The Chief Clerk's stenotypist; a Chinese
Laura Laballe:	Switchboard operator; French creole and Portuguese
Rafael Lopez:	Junior accountant; Spanish creole

PART ONE

PERSONS · OBJECTS · INCIDENTALS

The Office, the Key, the Office-Boy, the Door

Seen from directly opposite, on the southern side of Marine Square, the Office appeared at its most picturesque, because from this vantage-point it was visible through the foliage of the trees that grew in the square. From here it could be noted that the roof was a slated one and that the building which housed the Office was old – over a century, perhaps – for the slate had assumed that mellow, mossy look, dark green and purple in patches, which slate generally assumes after exposure to the weather for a great number of years. The brick walls had a pitted and seasoned mien. The pink paint that covered it, though fresh-looking, could not disguise the fact that it concealed many other layers. The style of architecture was not modern. Along the eaves and above and below each window ran a green iron fretwork of a design that featured leaves and fruit; the early French and Spanish creoles of Trinidad were fond of this kind of ornamentation.

The building was a two-storeyed one. The Office occupied the eastern half of the upper storey, the whole of the ground flat being taken up by a hardware store – Roalk's Hardware & Cycle Depot. The western half was let out to a dentist, a solicitor, a building contractor and the Trinidad Art & Straw Mat Company, a small industrial concern. Adjoining, on the west, stood another two-storeyed building of brick equally old in appearance, though the roof was of corrugated iron; on the east, a modern concrete three-storeyed structure – Rabat & Sons, a firm of Assyrian merchants.

The Office had black letters about a foot high painted on the wall beneath the windows, these letters combining to read: ESSENTIAL PRODUCTS LTD. Beneath these letters sloped an awning of corrugated iron painted green; it projected eight feet over the pavement, sheltering from the weather the people who passed outside the doors and show-windows of Roalk's Hardware & Cycle Depot.

The Office looked like many another office in Port of Spain.

At four minutes to seven on a dry, cloudless morning in April 1947, the office-boy stopped outside the door which opened on to the stairway that led up to the Office, and inserted the key into the lock...

The key was one manufactured by Petersen & Jason of Coventry.

Mr Petersen died in 1921, but Mr Jason was still alive in 1944, a white-haired, elderly Yorkshireman with shrewd, kindly blue-green eyes and a bluish, tufted wart low on his left cheek (the English travelling agent who had told all this to Mr Reynolds, the salesman, had had an eye for such descriptive details). Of Mr Jason's sons, Eric, the elder, had been a scholastic failure at Cambridge; Eric lived in London for some years where he dabbled in interior decoration, and moved in an artistic set; eventually he was successful as a sculptor.

Thomas had graduated, and was a promising executive in the firm, but showed no signs of marrying and producing an heir as his father wished. Thomas was killed (the travelling agent told Mr Reynolds) in a train smash in southern France in 1937, but the young man with delicately rouged cheeks and polished nails and wearing a green beret who had been in his company escaped with a broken left forearm and a bruise on his right hip...

This was the first morning Horace Xavier, the office-boy, would be opening the office. Formerly, it had been the duty of the Customs Clerk to open the office, but yesterday afternoon Mr Murrain, the assistant manager, had ruled: "In future I want you to open the office for us, Xavier. Mr Lorry says he finds it difficult to come out at seven. Mr Lopez, too. You've been with us over three months, and you seem a rather reliable fellow. You'll – ah – keep the key overnight, of course."

Horace felt that the bestowal upon him of this new duty represented an upward step in his career – a minor one but still an upward step. He felt triumphant, and proud of himself. Mr Murrain had admitted that he was a reliable fellow. He saw Mr Murrain's speech as a recognition of his efficient services during the past three months, and it gave him a sense of consolidation, made him feel he could now reckon himself beyond any doubt a member of the firm's office staff – a member who mattered.

He was a negro nineteen years old, five feet nine and thickset in build, with broad shoulders. Swimming and weightlifting had toughened his physique and given him well-developed arm muscles. Of a dark brown complexion, he kept his hair cut close to the skull so that when he had just come from the barber his skull gleamed like bronze and resembled a work of superior sculpture, for it was a well-shaped skull. For a negro, he had remarkably low cheekbones. His forehead was wide and domed; his eyebrows thick and frowning – again, remarkably so for a negro. He had a strong, firm chin.

He exuded an odour of talcum powder, for every morning after his bath he dusted his chest and armpits with Mennen's. His mother had always impressed upon him the need for smelling sweet and clean... "When you smell sweet and clean, people will respect you, and you will get on in de world, but when you smell sweaty and nasty de *bacra* people turn away from you and call you a stink nigger – and you punish and dead bad."

He respected his mother, and took heed of her pronouncements. She was a woman of fifty-one, and for the past thirteen years had been employed as a cook with the de Germains, a well-to-do French creole family resident in St Clair, the best residential district of Port of Spain.

When Horace was six, his father, a motor-mechanic given to gambling and drinking, had deserted his mother and left Trinidad on a schooner bound for Georgetown, British Guiana; his intention was to make good in the diamond fields of the Mazaruni River. But he had not made good, and for several years had wandered round the Caribbean, eventually returning to Trinidad; he was now a barman at a cheap hotel downtown, and still drank heavily, and gambled.

Rachel Xavier, his wife, had striven to get her son educated and equipped for an upright and creditable career – striven harder than she might normally have done, for the fear was always in her that her son might have inherited his father's tendencies for reckless and disreputable living. Horace had attended primary school until the age of seventeen. He had failed to win an exhibition which would have taken him to Queen's Royal College or St Mary's for five years' free schooling in the higher branches of education. His mother had lacked the means to pay for this more advanced tuition, so he had had to look for a job.

Roalk's Hardware & Cycle Depot had employed him as a messenger-boy at three dollars a week, and within a fortnight he was on terms of easy intimacy with George Joseph, the office-boy upstairs. He went swimming with George after work and on Saturday afternoons and Sundays – and George, though not interested in weightlifting, would drop round at the servants' quarters of the de Germain residence to watch Horace and two other friends indulge in feats of strength.

A little over three months ago, George had decided that he would become a postman. The Government wanted more postmen, and George had applied and been accepted. Before resigning as office-boy, George had told Horace about his intentions… "If you think you might like de job, apply. The pay is six dollars a week," said George. So Horace had applied and had got the job, and his mother had sighed and thanked the Lord. She told her mistress and her friends how her boy was getting on. He was actually working in an office. She saw him one day as Chief Accountant.

There was little that Horace kept from his mother. In her he confided his dreams and his hopes for the future. At eight, he had told her that he wanted to be a doctor and had been amazed to see her burst into tears. She had stroked his head and wailed: "Ah know you would mek a good doctor, me boy. You got it in you. But dat not for you. Dat not for you, Horace. Your skin black and you poor." But this had not discouraged him. If anything, it had flattered him; he was sure that every mother did not show such emotion over the confidences of her son; it heightened his belief in himself.

As he saw things today, no triumph of his would hold any savour were his mother not there for him to announce it to. No dream would appear rosy could he not dream it with his mother. Yet there was nothing of Oedipus in him; he regarded his mother as some successful actors regard their admiring publics. He was fond of her, but what concerned him mostly was her fondness

28

and high opinion of him; in her he had an audience which never failed to applaud his feats.

But within the past three or four weeks, a new factor had arisen to influence his outlook. He was puzzled to know how it had happened (for it had not yet occurred to him that despite a fairly well balanced temperament he was an imaginative and romantic young man), but he was infatuated with Mrs Nanette Hinckson, the chief stenographer and the Manager's secretary. Most of the time he could control himself – he was sure he had successfully concealed his feelings from everyone – but his condition caused him uneasiness, gave him a feeling of uncertainty and instability. Whenever he was in the presence of Mrs Hinckson he was aware of a tenseness and an unnatural inclination to take deep breaths; he felt an ache in his stomach; he stammered and felt his face going hot.

Towards his mother, these past weeks, he had felt a sense of guilt, because he had not been able to tell her of his infatuation; some intuition warned him that his audience would not applaud, that his audience would be unsympathetic, might even subject him to ridicule and contumely. It was a weakness which must be concealed from her, but the very concealment created guilt and a feeling of self-reproach.

He considered that it was foolish of him to have become enamoured of this lady. It was true that she was charming and attractive – physically as well as in manner – but he should have remembered that he was only a black boy, whereas she was a coloured lady of good family. His complexion was dark brown; hers was a pale olive. His hair was kinky; hers was full of large waves and gleaming. He was a poor boy with hardly any education, the son of a cook; she was well off and of good education and good breeding. He was low-class; she was middle-class.

Last night he had done something he considered daring – something which he even regarded as critical. From an old, battered copy of the *Complete Works of Shakespeare* – a volume passed on to him by Peter de Germain, the eldest son of the family – Horace had copied a passage from *As You Like It* which he deemed appropriate as an expression of his feelings.

It was in bed that the really daring idea had taken shape. Why couldn't he leave this quotation on Mrs Hinckson's desk? He would be the first to enter the office from tomorrow morning. No one would see him putting it on her desk. And if he got out of bed now and copied it on another piece of paper in block letters it would be perfectly anonymous. The thought that she would be reading something which his hand had written – words which, though not his own, represented his feelings – would be enough, he knew, to give him a deep satisfaction and relief.

He had tossed in indecision for hours, but had eventually made up his mind in favour of the scheme, and this morning the paper with the quotation nestled in the inside pocket of his khaki drill coat.

As he unlocked the door his feelings of triumph and pride at the knowledge that he was now a recognized and privileged member of the office staff were allied to a sensation of excitement and anticipation. He felt that the day ahead contained adventure. But even in this instant his emotions underwent a cooling, and he reflected in a spirit of calculation that this new privilege had already begun to yield advantages – dividends. Not only did it represent an upward step in his career but it was about to prove of use to him in a practical way; he saw it as a material perquisite.

His face took on a serious, earnest look, his excitement gone. He thought now of dividends. Opportunities and dividends. He envisaged himself rising to power, and the picture held him entranced. He must never miss a single opportunity. It was the men who grasped opportunities who eventually drew big dividends.

He pushed the door open...

The door was eight feet high, and painted pale green, with pink facings. Five or six inches to the left of the central facing design (a ball with two clubs branching away from it, one straight up, one straight down) there was a deep dent like a small lipless mouth.

This dent came into being on an evening of 1923.

A Cockney, James Fenwick, landed in Port of Spain on the afternoon of the twelfth of June. A member of the crew of the *Jasper*, a Pelham & Helfe cargo ship which had arrived at noon, Fenwick, before taking to the sea, had served several prison terms for petty larceny; he was an expert pickpocket. For the past four years he had led an exemplary life, though the captain and officers of the *Jasper* still kept a strict eye on him. On the whole, he was looked upon as a character who had definitely reformed.

In a downtown rum-shop he met Hervey Charles, a Negro, and Mungalsingh, an East Indian. He chummed up with them, and presently extracted a box of Venus lead pencils from Mungalsingh's hip-pocket without the East Indian being aware of the loss. When he held out the box and said: "'Ere naow, 'ow the 'ell did I come by this?" Mungalsingh was dismayed – but only for a moment. Mungalsingh winked at Hervey Charles, who winked back.

A few minutes later, Mungalsingh produced from inside his shirt a wallet which caused Fenwick to exclaim: "Screw me I'll eat my blooming 'at if that ain't mine!"

Mungalsingh told him it was, and confidences were exchanged. Fenwick slapped the East Indian on the back and bellowed: "Yer got talent, young feller! It ain't many 'oo can pinch my wallet and me not know when it 'appened."

For the rest of the evening Fenwick decided to teach Mungalsingh what he considered the finer points. As an Englishman, he could not admit a mere West Indian native as his superior in the art.

They wandered along the pavements of Marine Square, singing and stopping occasionally to pick each other's pockets while the "victim" turned away his face and shut his eyes. . .

"Naow, naow! That ain't no good. I could feel yer pulling my blinkin' guts out o' plyce. Do it agyn. Come on. Do it agyn, Ramjohnnie!"

Mungalsingh reminded him that his name was Mungalsingh, not Ramjohnnie, and Fenwick told him to kiss his ass.

They were within a few yards of the Door. On the pavement, a vendor of water-coconuts was chopping and trimming a green nut with a hatchet.

Hervey Charles suggested buying some nuts. He felt, he said, like drinking some coconut water for a change. Fenwick and Mungalsingh concurred, but Fenwick wanted to trim and cut open the nuts himself. Mungalsingh said no, he would do it himself. What did a Limey know about trimming and cutting open coconuts? There were no coconuts in England.

"I'll show yer if I can't do it, you bloody nigger!"

Mungalsingh objected to being called a nigger. "Watch me hair," he said. "Ah got smooth, straight hair. Nigger got crooked hair."

Fenwick asked him what difference did that make. An Indian or a nigger, it was all the same.

"Black nytives – every blimed one o' you dusky tropical blokes!"

Mungalsingh snatched the hatchet from the coconut vendor and dared Fenwick to call him a nigger again. He staggered drunkenly off the pavement while the vendor made a lunge at him to recover his hatchet.

Mungalsingh dodged and retreated.

Fenwick called from the pavement: "Trust a nigger to snatch a blarsted 'atchet!"

The hatchet caught Fenwick a glancing blow on the side of his head, chipping his ear, before it thudded dully on the Door, the blade burying itself in the woodwork.

Horace made his way upstairs, and passed through the gateway in the barrier – a rail and balusters – which separated the public section of the office from the section where the staff worked.

He went to Mrs Hinckson's desk, which stood near an eastern window within a few feet of the frosted glass door that gave into the Manager's sanctum. He took the slip of paper from his breast-pocket but hesitated to leave it. An incident of his childhood came alive in his memory... He was crouching on a shop awning watching the Carnival bands go past. Behind him were the windows of the dwelling situated above the shop. An urge to leap off the edge of the awning into the crowds came upon him. He knew it would be a foolish and dangerous thing to do, but the urge still gripped him. His body grew tense. He could hear a buzzing in his head... To jump or to remain where he was? To jump... He turned quickly and crawled up the awning back to the window and into the house...

So he felt now. As though he were faced with the decision to jump or to crawl back to safety.

If Mrs Hinckson discovered that it was he who had placed this paper on her desk his self-respect would be shattered; he would be so humiliated he would be unable to face her. The thought of her sniggering to herself would be unbearable. He would have to throw up his job.

He stood for a full minute reflecting; balancing his fears against the ecstasy of the knowledge that she would be handling this slip of paper which bore a message to her of his deep and sacred feelings.

He decided.

He placed the paper, folded across once, in the letter tray labelled *File*, shifting a brown phial of Vitamin B tablets on to it so that no chance gust of wind could blow it away. He wondered vaguely why Mrs Hinckson should have used a phial of Vitamin B tablets as a paperweight, but did not let the matter engage his thoughts seriously. Compared with what he had just done it seemed far too trivial a circumstance to trouble about.

He stood by the desk for a moment, regarding the black metal cover under which reposed the Royal typewriter. It was on this machine during the lunch hour that he practised his typing. About three weeks ago Mrs Hinckson had given him permission to use the machine while the staff was away for lunch. He thought of how he was progressing – and of his shorthand. Ambition made a swift glow inside him.

At the sound of footsteps on the stairs, he moved away from the desk.

It must be Mary, the woman who swept the office and who came back at three in the afternoon to make tea for the staff. She came in groaning, a look of misery on her black face. Surprise joined the misery when she saw him.

"What you doing here?" she wanted to know. 'Where Mr Lorry?'

"I'm opening the office in future – from dis morning. Not Mr Lorry no more." He could not keep the note of importance out of his voice.

But Mary seemed indifferent. She groaned again.

He gave her a glance of disapproval.

"What's the matter with you?"

"Troubles, boy. Troubles."

He was reluctant to question her further. The knowledge that he was her superior swamped his awareness. She was a mere sweeper – a menial. He was the office-boy. He had a desk of his own – on the public side of the barrier, it was true, but, nevertheless, it was a desk and meant that he was a person who counted. And then there were these new privileges which had been conferred on him. His inherent decency, however, triumphed.

"What happen? Why you groaning like this?"

She told him that it was her son Richard. The police had arrested him for disorderly behaviour. He belonged to a steel band, and last night there had been a clash between his band and another band at a dance in Charlotte Street. He was to appear before the magistrate this morning with eight others. She had just come from the police-station, and they had told her that they

34

could do nothing for her; the charge must go through. Perhaps if she attended the court she might be given the chance to appear before the magistrate so that she could ask for leniency as it was the boy's first offence. Richard, she said, was only seventeen.

He sympathized with her. He was genuinely sorry for her, because she was a good worker and very willing to do any little task outside her regular duties. For Richard, however, he experienced only contempt. His self-righteousness precluded any sympathy for the boy. The steel band, he felt, was a degrading institution and only encouraged the slum boys to be disorderly. At Carnival time it was all right, for everybody then was in a gay mood and wanted to jump about in the streets to the music of a band, but these slum idlers were trying to make the steel band an everyday feature.

"Why you don't keep him from dese steel bands?"

"Ow, boy! It's not for want o' trying. You know how often Ah talk to Richard! Oh, God! Ah weary talking. Weary, weary. And he leading his brudder astray – dat's de hurtful part. Peter only fourteen and he don't want to go to school. He only want to follow Richard to beat dis ole iron and pots and pans wid all dem worthless young men by de Dry River. Oh, God! Too much worries in dis world!"

Horace gave a shrug to indicate that the problem was one beyond him, and set about the task of opening the windows and jalousies.

On the southern side – that is, the street side – there were ten windows and eleven jalousies, spaced alternately. On the eastern side, eight windows and nine jalousies. Each window was provided with a Venetian blind which was never let down until the afternoon hours when the glare became unbearable.

His task completed, Horace settled down at his desk to pass the time by reading *A Tale of Two Cities*. It was a thumb-soiled and much-scribbled-upon copy. Like his *Complete Works of Shakespeare*, it had once belonged to Peter de Germain. He had been engaged in reading it for the past four or five weeks, and was barely halfway through, for he found it heavy going. It was only because he had heard it was a great work of literature, and had seen the film, that he persisted. It was something, he reasoned, like his typing and shorthand, necessary for his betterment; something that would help him to rise in the world. Before he went to bed tonight he would read solely for pleasure, and on this occasion the book would be Agatha Christie's *Murder In Three Acts*.

Mary Barker uttered a groan or a sigh as she swept. Sometimes she wagged her head without making any sound. She was plumply built. She lacked grace of movement, and walked with a slight up-and-down motion, the result of an injury to her left leg many years ago. Even had she not suffered this injury, she would still have been ungraceful, for she was flat-footed and possessed a large-boned and awkward frame.

Her dark brown face wore an expression of weariness, and every step she took seemed to call for a special effort of will. Not that this prevented her from doing a thorough job. She was a conscientious worker, and by no means lazy. As soon as she had finished sweeping the office she would trudge more than a mile to the two-roomed hovel on Gonzalez Hill which was her home, and set to work on her washing. The four dollars she got from the office was not enough to support her and her two sons, so she took in washing from well-off families in the city.

Peter, she was determined, must continue going to school. Other mothers often took their sons from school at fourteen and put them to work, but she wanted Peter to go on until he was at least sixteen. Richard, at seventeen, ought to have been working and contributing his share to the upkeep of the home, but since he had left school at sixteen he had done nothing but wander about the neighbourhood getting into trouble. His only interests were gambling – his favourite game was called *wappee*; it was a card game – and beating pots and pans in the steel band to which he belonged.

Mary's sons were both illegitimate. Richard's father, Boysie Lamb, a shoemaker, had lived with Mary and supported her for two years before deserting her for another woman.

In Mary's character there was a too-yielding, masochistic trait, and it had happened that Boysie was a similar type. He enjoyed being bullied by his women; it gave him a remote sexual satisfaction when a woman resisted him. He had been attracted to Mary because she had a strong, austere face, and he had subconsciously hoped that she would be stern with him. Living with her, however, soon revealed that, despite her outward mien, she was a meek, surrendering kind of woman very easily persuaded to his will on every occasion. He had gradually grown indifferent and contemptuous towards her – so much so that when he had met Susan McShine, a spirited, loud-mouthed girl who flared up on the slightest provocation, the day was lost for Mary.

Peter's father, Jason David, had been a quiet, fairly normal man. He had been faithful to Mary for eleven years and would have married her but for the fact that he was already married and his wife still alive. A stevedore, and, in his spare-time, a cabinet-maker, he had left his wife Roxane because of her infidelity with the Duke Challenger, a calypso-singer. In taking Mary to live with him as his mistress Jason had experienced no qualms of conscience because Roxane, with the two children, had at once, upon the quarrel which had caused the break, transferred herself to the home of the Duke Challenger who agreed to take her in and support her and the children.

Four years ago, Mary and Jason had been fairly happy. Then Jason decided that his work as a stevedore and a cabinet-maker was not bringing in enough money. He said he could do much better with the Americans. The Americans, at this time, were constructing their military bases and the island was more prosperous than it had ever been before. Mary disapproved of the venture, claiming that though things with them could be brighter, still they could not complain; they were struggling along all right; she even had a few cents put aside in the post office.

But Jason said he was tired of struggling along. When he looked around him and saw how many of his friends were in jobs with the Americans and what high wages they were getting he felt he had to do something for himself, too. He wanted a better place than this two-roomed cottage (it had taken him four years of hard saving and hard manual labour to build it, Mary pointed out). The roof was leaking, he said, and he was tired of repairing leaks. Soon the boards would be rotting because they had not been new when he secured them – and the place had never been painted.

His whole manner was filled with discontentment and surly

irresolution. He was not naturally an adventurous man; he loved security – and it was only that the success of his acquaintances had stirred up a deep envy in him and an unwholesome desire to possess an unlimited amount of money.

Mary reminded him that the shipping company he was working for was an old and dependable company; it would be risky to give up his job with them to look for another that was uncertain. And what would happen when the Americans had finished building their bases and began to lay off the men working for them now. He would be out of a job, and the shipping company would probably not want to rehire him. And his cabinet-making hardly brought in anything because of the few tools he had and lack of a proper workshop (his only convenience was a rough workbench under a mango tree).

Her manner in putting forward these arguments was as weak and irresolute as his own in debating his case. Had she held out longer and shown some spirit it is likely he would have decided to continue in his present job. But once again the too-yielding streak in her character settled the issue.

Jason resigned and went off to seek employment with the Americans.

The only job he was able to secure was that of a watchman, and to his dismay he discovered that it brought him very little more than his old job had done. His acquaintances who made fabulous sums were chauffeurs, mechanics, electricians, carpenters and masons whose rates of pay were much higher than the rate allowed a watchman. Further, they earned overtime, whereas he, as a watchman, worked regular hours every night. Within a short while he became so disgruntled that he took to drinking and reckless living. He lost his job and contracted venereal disease. The last Mary heard of him was that he had gone to St Lucia on a sloop.

For over six months Mary had been employed at the office, and no one, except Mr Jagabir, ever found fault with her. Mr Jagabir was the assistant accountant and an East Indian, and Mary was contemptuous of all East Indians (cheap coolies, she called them), so Mr Jagabir's fault-finding did not count; it was what she would have expected of him, she assured herself.

She was half-alert for his arrival. She could sense the muscles of her face steeled to twist into a scowl the instant he appeared. It happened every morning, no matter if she were in a good mood or not.

When she heard footsteps on the stairs – her job was nearly two-thirds done – she had no doubt whatever as to who it could be. None of the other gentlemen, or none of the ladies, for that matter – would think of coming to work at such an early hour. But with Mr Jagabir it was different. He made it his duty to be here as soon as possible after the office opened. He had no cause to come before eight o'clock, which was the hour the staff (save the one who was opening) was required to be at the office. But Mr Jagabir liked to impress on his superiors that he was a hard-working clerk. And it was said, too – so Mr Lorry had told her one morning – that he was prying; he came early on purpose to read the correspondence in files that did not concern him.

She had not guessed wrong. It was he. A dark Indian, handsome and with thick, black hair brushed back from his forehead in a high, domed mass, and thick, black eyebrows that gave to his face more a troubled and thundery than a suspicious (as some people considered it) expression, he paused at the top of the stairs and sent his probing gaze round the office. He had pale brown eyes which, against his dark brown complexion, constituted his most noteworthy feature. Had they held a humorous instead of a distrustful twinkle they would have been very attractive eyes. Eyes that a woman of any race might have found fascinating.

His gaze flicked past Mary and eventually rested on Horace, a mere two or three feet from him. Seeing Horace here was no surprise to him, for he had overheard Mr Murrain telling the boy that he was to open the office in future. He made it his business to be well-informed concerning everything that went on in the office. His ears were perpetually on the alert, for the fear was always with him, that, despite his efficiency as a bookkeeper, he would one day be thrown out. He had been brought up to feel that an East Indian's place was in the Field – the cane-fields of a sugar estate, cocoa or citrus plots; shovelling and weeding. An office was meant for white people and good-class coloured people. He considered his officiousness justified; it was his defence against possible attack and the ejection that might result from such an attack.

Horace, who had merely glanced up on his approach, continued to read. He too, did not like Mr Jagabir. From the first day he had come to work at the office Mr Jagabir had begun to nag at him. Horace considered him a mean, quarrelsome man.

"You might say morning, Xavier," said Mr Jagabir.

Horace, prepared for this, looked up. "Who? Me? I thought it was your place to say morning. You come in and find me here." There was no respect in his voice as would have been the case with another member of the staff.

Mr Jagabir hesitated, unsure of himself, then said: "I'm your superior."

"If you were the king it was your place to tell me morning when you come in and find me here."

Mr Jagabir did not argue. He suddenly knew that he had erred. The boy was probably right. The person who arrived ought to greet first. The rules of correct behaviour were not all familiar to him, and on occasions such as this he preferred to withdraw rather than press the point, much as it hurt his vanity. Frowning heavily, he passed through the barrier-gate and went to his desk which was the one in the extreme north-western corner; it was separated from Mr Murrain's, which was to the right of it near a window, by about five yards. On his way, he gave Mary a swift, sideways glance. Horace's rebuke still moved like a pebble in his chest, and he was very much aware that he was being guilty of a second breach of good manners in refraining from saying good morning to Mary. A feeling of frustration and resentment tightened his inside, and he told himself that he had every right to ignore Mary. She was an insolent woman. She hated him – as all the rest of them hated him. Because he was an Indian, because he was the son of indentured coolies, they all looked upon him as dirt.

Arrived at his desk, he glanced keenly around and under it to discover the slightest sign of dust or debris on the floor. But the floor had been swept with Mary's usual care and thoroughness, and he could find nothing to take the woman to task for. He was about to sit down when he noticed the nib.

It lay on the R–Z ledger which rested on his blotter and which he had been looking through yesterday afternoon just before leaving the office. It was a Waverley nib – a used Waverley nib.

"Mary!"

"Yes, Jagabir?"

His lips parted to say: "*Mr* Jagabir, please," but the words would not shape themselves into sound. He had pulled her up so often about this without avail that he had come to realize how hopeless it was trying to make her see that he was deserving of the title. With a twinge of despair, the knowledge had sunk into him that, despite his position in the office, he was still a coolie – still her social equal. He would have to endure her impertinence. To report her to the Manager might seem like insisting too much on his rights; it might jeopardize his position in the office.

"Come here, please!"

"What you want?"

"I'm calling you."

Reluctantly, Mary approached. She was scowling.

"You put dis nib on my desk?"

"What nib?'

"Dis nib." He held it up for her to see.

"Ah ain' know what you talking about. Ah ain' put no nib on you' desk."

"How it get here, then? Who put it here if not you?"

"Look, Ah ain' in no mood to quarrel dis morning, see! Ah tell you, Ah ain' put no nib 'pon you' desk."

"It wasn't here yesterday af'noon when I left here, so how it get on dis ledger now? You pick it up from the floor when you was sweeping just now and put it here – dat's what happen. Well, don't let it happen again, or Ah will have to report you to Mr Murrain. You can't dump rubbish on my desk as you feel. You got to have some respect for me."

Mary sucked her teeth and walked away.

Mr Jagabir threw the nib into the wastepaper basket…

Twenty-one hours ago the nib had been fixed in a penholder wielded by Sidney Whitmer, an overseer seated in his room in the Junior Overseers' Quarters on the Tucurapo cocoa and citrus estate, which was situated in the north-eastern section of Trinidad and owned by the company known as Tucurapo Cocoa & Citrus Producers Ltd (Essential Products Ltd was a subsidiary company of Tucurapo Cocoa & Citrus Producers Ltd).

Sidney, twenty-three and English, had come to Trinidad in 1945, immediately after his discharge from the Army in which he had served since 1942. His uncle, Mr Rostock Lenfield, one of the principals of the London office of the Tucurapo company, had arranged his appointment as overseer.

Following the example of British-owned sugar estates in the West Indies, Tucurapo Cocoa & Citrus Producers (which was British owned) had always adhered to the policy of employing white men only as overseers, and white men, preferably, straight from England or Scotland. The black and East Indian labourers, it was felt, would respect an English or Scots overseer more readily than they would one who was coloured or one who was a creole white and spoke with a creole accent. Further, it was a good thing for the Old Country, for it provided employment for young men who were not too bright or who, for divers reasons, were *persona non grata* types at home.

Sidney Whitmer – who differed somewhat from the usual type sent out – was writing a letter to his mother in Bristol.

Among other things, he told her: "I'm absolutely fed up with Trinidad. The life on this estate is cramping my spirit. At first, the sensation of feeling like a king was novel and pretty good. In England I was a nobody, but the instant I arrived here my white skin alone was sufficient to give me entrée into the best circles – at least, what passes for the best circles here. As I mentioned some letters ago, I'd hardly stepped ashore when I found myself being admitted to functions at the exclusive Country Club just outside Port of Spain – a club that considers you an aristocrat, and therefore eligible as a member, simply on the strength of your pink skin and your English accent. I've met chaps there who, in England, would be sniffed at by a Hoxton charwoman. Now I've got to hate this club and find no more pleasure in going there, because I've come to see it for what it really is – a cheap, tawdry institution infested with pretentious, shallow local whites, many of them not even pure white but trading on the accident of a fair complexion and the fact that they happen to be moneyed.

"The whole social set-up here depresses me. I've met several coloured chaps whom, from the point of view of intelligence and culture, I found superior to the people who flaunt themselves around the place as white and deem themselves the 'leaders of the smart set' – yet if I dare become too familiar with these chaps I'm threatened by the whites (both real and pseudo) with ostracism. Only yesterday I had a coloured (olive-skinned) chap up here to tea. He's a painter and I've bought two of his pictures; really good work. After he'd left the Deputy Manager called me and gave me what he called a 'friendly talking to'. He says that that sort of thing – meaning my entertaining coloured chaps in my quarters – 'doesn't pay out here'.

"I'm seriously thinking of resigning, but before doing anything rash I'm going to take a trip to town this afternoon to have a chat with Everard Murrain. He's the chap I told you of who came out here, soon after the Dunkirk mess, to take up the post of assistant manager of Essential Products. He's supposed to be the Chief Accountant, too, but he's told me frankly he doesn't know a damn thing about accountancy. The Indian chap under him, Baggabir or Jaggabir, is the real accountant and does practically all the work Murrain should be doing. Murrain himself has a few beastly ideas about the position of the white man in the tropics – especially the Englishman – but he's personally one of the best, and has been very friendly towards me. So I'm going to talk things over with him before deciding finally what I'll do…"

So Sidney Whitmer had come to Port of Spain to see Mr Murrain. He arrived by one of the firm's jitneys at a quarter past four when most of the staff, including Mr Jagabir, had already gone home. It was while he sat at Mr Jagabir's desk waiting for Mr Murrain to end his interview with Mr Brasher, the Chief engineer from the factory at Turcurapo, who had also come to town, that Sidney happened to slip his hand idly into a coat pocket and discovered the nib.

He felt around in the pocket for the holder. The nib had dropped out of the holder; it had always fitted loosely. He had been doing, he told himself, all sorts of dotty things today as a result of his depressed spirits, so it was no surprise that he had dropped the pen into his pocket this morning after writing that letter to the mater.

He began to tap the nib against the ledger on the desk – the R-Z ledger – and was still doing this when Mr Brasher suddenly bade Mr Murrain goodbye and Mr Murrain smiled and signalled Sidney to come across.

Sidney dropped the Nib on the ledger and hurried over...

Mr Jagabir had no doubt whatever that it was Mary who had put the nib on the ledger. His desk, of course, was of no importance in her eyes, he reflected bitterly.

"Xavier!"

"Yes!" (Not even a "sir".)

"Come here."

Horace came.

"Take this. Go and post it right away."

Horace took the letter.

"I wanted it post since yesterday af'noon. I sure I must have tell you to do it."

"No, you never told me."

"All right, don't stop to argue. Go on!"

The letter consisted of a corrected account, and could have waited for the regular batch of mails Horace took to the post office at the end of the day's work, but Mr Jagabir felt the urge to indulge in a display of authority. It assuaged his battered vanity somewhat to watch Horace retreating down the stairs to carry out one of his commands.

He was further soothed to note that Mary was going into the lunch-room to put away her broom preparatory to departing. He experienced that thrill which never failed to go through him when he realized that he was about to be left alone in the office. In less than a minute he would be free to roam from desk to desk.

Mr Jagabir smiled as he regarded the paper. But like a patch of blue sky vanishing just as it has given promise of fine weather, the smile faded and a look of gloom and regret overspread his features.

If only, he thought, he had been able to go to high school after he had left primary school. Tiny nerves twitched under his eyes.

Now, at thirty-eight, he would have known all about Shakespeare and the other great poets. At primary school he had merely heard about them. Once he had been made to recite Tennyson's *Charge of the Light Brigade*. He could still remember bits of it. And *Young Lochinvar*. But Shakespeare. He had never done anything by Shakespeare. Had he gone to high school he would have been able now to understand long words in the newspapers and in books without having to go to the dictionary. He would have been able to speak correctly and fluently like Mrs Hinckson and Miss Henery – like Mr Reynolds and Mr Lorry and all the others. He gave his head a jerk of resignation and reread what was written on the paper.

"A quotation from Shakespeare addressed to my beloved:

But upon the fairest boughs,
Or at every sentence end,
Will I Nanette write,
Teaching all that read to know
The quintessence of every sprite
Heaven would in little show.
Therefore Heaven Nature charged
That one body should be fill'd
With all graces wide-enlarged:
Nature presently distill'd
Helen's cheek, but not her heart,
Cleopatra's majesty,
Atalanta's better part,
Sad Lucretia's modesty.

Thus Nanette of many parts
By heavenly synod was devised;
Of many faces, eyes and hearts
To have the touches dearest prized.
Heaven would that she these gifts should have,
And I to live and die her slave."

Of course, it must be from some male admirer of hers, though it was strange that it should be in block letters and not in ordinary handwriting.

He frowned and rubbed his forefinger along the back of his ear, trying to think of some reason. This paper held no interest for him. Mrs Hinckson's admirers, known or unknown, could have not the slightest effect on his own affairs. But he always deemed it a matter of principle that nothing should go unsolved. To admit that he was completely baffled – no matter if it were the most trifling issue involved – made him feel that he was losing his shrewdness, that a decline had set in. But after a while, he was compelled to shake his head. With a sigh – which, to him, seemed a tiny crack in the structure of his security – he replaced the paper in the tray.

He riffled through the letters that lay beneath, pausing now and then to read a sentence or two. But there was nothing of importance, so far as he could see. The usual routine letters and minutes from the principals in London. Nothing about prices or transfers or new projects... Wait! What did this letter say? ... "Concerning your request in respect of the proposed new labels for the lime juice products..." No, nothing to trouble over. He knew all about that already. He had overheard Mr Waley discussing it with Mr Murrain last week. Prices and transfers and new projects were what worried him most. A bad slump in prices might indicate a cut in staff – and that could easily mean disaster for him. The transfer of Mr Waley or Mr Murrain back to London or to the Tucurapo office meant a new man in the town office here – and he might be the kind of man who disliked East Indians. New projects could involve drastic changes in all departments.

The trays marked *Incoming* and *Outgoing* yielded nothing either, and he passed on to Miss Bisnauth's desk, but did not bother to look through the trays here, for Miss Bisnauth's work consisted chiefly in making copies of minutes for filing. What reposed in her trays this morning would have been in Mrs Hinckson's yesterday morning. He gave the desk a cursory survey, however, to satisfy his sense of routine.

Having already inspected the other desks before coming to Mrs Hinckson's, he wandered over by the barrier and paused to frown across at Horace's desk, which he did not consider worthy of his careful attention. All the same, he always thought it just as well to give it a skimming glance over. He saw the open book and grunted. He did not need to take a closer look at it, for he had discovered the title more than a fortnight ago. It was some book by Charles Dickens. Something about two cities.

Gloom and regret possessed him again. He thought of Horace and his youth and unmarried state. The boy was educating himself. He was reading good books and learning shorthand and typing. He would get on in the world. You could see it in his eyes. One day he would be well off. He might get into the City Council or the Legislative Council and be in a position to pull strings. But look at me, thought Mr Jagabir, heading for forty and with a wife and four children and another child on the way, and an old mother to support, and never knowing when the white people might decide I'm of no use to them any more in this office.

There did occur moments when he realized that this fear of being dispensed with or demoted was an irrational one. Mr Murrain knew hardly anything about accountancy and never exerted himself to become familiar with the books. Without Mr Jagabir he would be lost – and Mr Murrain knew it, as did Mr Waley the Manager. Still, felt Mr Jagabir, he was an East Indian, and that made all the difference. He was a coolie; he had worked in the fields for four years after leaving primary school; he had been cursed at and threatened and humiliated by white overseers – once nearly kicked: only his agility had prevented the muddy boot landing in the seat of his pants.

The fourteen years he had spent working his way up as a bookkeeper in the Tucurapo office had not been easy, either; he had had to suffer in silence many an insult, many an unjust scolding, many a threat of dismissal. Never for a day had his white superiors forgotten to make him know his place. Even when, four years ago, the assistant accountant in the office here, a good-class coloured gentleman, had died and Mr Waley had sent for Jagabir, it had been impressed upon him that it was only "a temporary measure as an emergency has arisen"; if he did well he might be made permanent on the office staff in town.

After a mere two months he had done so well that it was decided he should remain; in fact, Mr Murrain had sent in an overwhelmingly favourable report, and Mr Waley had congratulated him personally.

Yet, those early impressions could not be eradicated, and fear died hard.

A scene from the past arose... His mother pleading with the Deputy Manager... "Me son, 'e good at figures, boss. 'E schoolmaster say he's a bright boy. Me want beg you please – *please*, boss – give 'e a try in de office. He can write good, good. Perfect! Just give 'e a try in de office..."

And the Deputy Manager smiling and looking lofty and amused.

Beside his mother, Jagabir fidgeting and hanging his head – a barefooted boy of sixteen in dirty khaki pants and a soiled, torn cotton shirt.

"He's got to work a few years in the fields. It's the only work we have for him now. No openings in the office at present. You can let him go on practising to write and do his arithmetic. Perhaps some day..."

The some day had come when he was twenty —

He heard the slam of a car's door.

That would be Mr Murrain.

Mr Jagabir hurried to his desk. He settled down and opened the ledger, pretending to be deeply engrossed in the columns of figures. He did not take off his coat as the other men did, for without his coat he would have felt that he had lost his dignity and what little respectability he had.

Mr Murrain came in with long, unhurried strides; his gait was a trifle nervous and indecisive. He glanced at Mr Jagabir and smiled and said good morning in a voice that was neither curt nor familiar. He was a tall man – well over six feet – but had round shoulders and practically no buttocks. His clothes sagged around his slim frame in long folds. He weighed about eleven stone. His hair was pale yellow, with glints of red, and lay flat and sparse over a head that was long and bony. Of Mr Murrain's head Mr Lorry had once remarked to Miss Bisnauth: "When he was being born the midwife must have pulled him out by the chin." His chin was an extremely mobile one; it was never at rest; he had a habit of shifting his lower jaw from side to side as though it were loose in its sockets and needed perpetual adjusting. He was doing this now as he took off his coat and hung it on the peg on the wall near the safe – the safe in which the petty cash, cheque-books and salary records were kept.

Settling down at his desk in the swivel-chair was always a ceremony. First, he had to take up the cushion and beat it briefly to make sure there were no lumps in it. Then having sunk down upon it, he would jerk his body experimentally to see how his rear fitted into the newly distributed contents of the cushion. It might mean rising again to give the cushion another beating, or a few pats here and there. Then perhaps the swivel-chair would creak in a way that grated on his nerves, so that would require remedying. The oil-can in the lowest drawer of his desk on the right would be needed.

This morning it was not necessary to use the oil-can but twice he had to rise to reshape the cushion. The first time he confined himself to beating it, but the second time he thought it fit to pat it gently with little massaging touches.

Settled at last, he stretched his neck – a neck long in proportion to the length of his head and body – and made a slight adjustment to his tie. He rolled up his shirt-sleeves to a little above the elbow.

"The newspapers not yet here, Jagabir?"

"Oh." It was a sound of dismay rather than an ejaculation. Mr Jagabir rose with a loud scraping of his chair and craned his head towards Horace's desk.

"No, not yet, sir. No, I don't see dem, sir." His voice was tinged with solicitousness and faint annoyance on Mr Murrain's behalf.

"All right, don't bother. Suppose they'll arrive before long."

"The newsboy ought to throw dem in by now downstairs, sir. I could go down and see, if you want, sir."

"No, no. Don't trouble." Mr Murrain smiled.

"It's Xavier who open de office this morning, sir. 'E say you tell him to open the office in future." Mr Jagabir spoke as though he had known nothing about it before. His tone and manner indicated expectancy of confirmation.

Mr Murrain nodded, frowning. He suspected that Mr Jagabir was dissembling and it irritated him. "Yes, yes. Mr Lorry can't find it convenient to come at seven. By the way, where is he – Xavier?"

"I send him to post a letter, sir. De account what Burke's Grocery sent back yesterday saying it wasn't correct."

"Ah. I take it you corrected it?"

"Yes, sir. It was Miss Henery's fault. I always talking to her and warning her to be more careful when she typing out de accounts."

Mr Murrain made no comment. Miss Henery, he knew, was perfectly efficient. And, in any case, it did not interest him who had been at fault. He drew towards him a price-list of confectioneries which the London office sent out periodically. Confectioneries manufactured by firms in which the principals of the Tucurapo company held interests. Firms which depended almost solely upon the Tucurapo company for their cocoa and citrus supplies. Essential Products were the distributing agents in Trinidad for many of these firms. Mr Murrain was not in the slightest interested in the manufacturers' quotations – he considered this the business of Mr Waley, the Manager, or Mr Reynolds, the salesman – but the price-list served the purpose of disguising the fact that he was idle.

Except for dictating a very occasional letter to Miss Henery, signing cheques and consulting with Mr Jagabir or Mr Reynolds on some matter concerning the accounts – some matter which Mr Jagabir or Mr Reynolds would already have attended to with their customary efficiency, hence which needed hardly any attention from the Chief Accountant – Mr Murrain had virtually no work to do (though upon him rested the responsibility of the whole accounting department). But realizing that it would be bad policy to appear idle, he had had recourse to invent various subterfuges. The price-list was one, Mr Reynolds's sales-record another (sometimes he went through it page by page, hardly seeing, much less noting, the contents), and there were the ledgers which he pretended to examine when they were not in use by Mr Jagabir.

Mr Murrain was thirty-four and a man of slightly-below-average vitality. Many times it troubled him that he did so little work yet drew such a big salary – three hundred and sixty dollars a month – when his hard-working junior, Jagabir, received only a hundred and twenty. But, on the whole, idleness did not bother him; not having an excess of energy, he never suffered from boredom.

Often, by a feat of reasoning, which deep down he knew to be specious, he justified his idleness to himself. As one of the heads of the office, he argued, the assistant manager as well as the Chief Accountant (and a white man, at that, among coloured peoples of the tropics), he had every right to be idle. The company had put him here, in reality, to superintend these people – not simply to work along with them. They were a subject people, and he was an Englishman in a colony dominated by the British Crown.

Sometimes this attitude struck him as both contemptible and absurd – especially, for instance, when Mr Jagabir presented him with a trial balance concise and explicit in every detail, correct to the last cent. Again, too, when Mr Waley or the Tucurapo office needed information from the accounts department and he realized that it was Mr Jagabir to whom he had to turn for it – and it was always supplied without hesitation or fumbling – Mr Murrain experienced a discomfiture which, in its intensity, frightened him. It was a psychopathic discomfiture, he felt; it brought back remnants of that impotent, distracted feeling which had been with him for so many weeks after his Dunkirk adventures. A special kind of shudder – the trapped-in-the-skin shudder, he had dubbed it to himself – would go through him.

He looked up from the price-list. Horace had just come in. Besides the newspapers, he had a batch of letters.

"De newsboy throw dem in when I was out, sir," he said, holding out the newspapers – the *Trinidad Guardian* and the *Port of Spain Gazette*. (Like most West Indian creoles of fair but not good education, Horace sometimes pronounced his dental aspirates, sometimes did not; sometimes said "I", sometimes "Ah".)

"No letters for me?"

"Nothing, sir. I look through dem."

Horace crossed to Mrs Hinckson's desk and deposited the batch of letters in the letter-tray marked *Incoming*. His body tensed. Automatically his eyes had strayed into the *File* tray.

The paper with his quotation was not as he had left it. He had folded it across once and placed the phial with the vitamin tablets upon it. Now it lay spread open, with the writing upward, and the phial barely touched the bottom right-hand corner.

At his desk, Mr Jagabir was covertly watching Horace. He was curious to know what the boy could be staring at so concentratedly on the desk. Could it be that there was some unusual letter among the batch he had brought from the post office? Or was it simply that he was examining the stamps on one of the envelopes? Yes, it must be that. Horace collected stamps.

Mr Jagabir, however, continued to regard the boy. He saw his lips part, saw them snap shut and tighten. His face looked upset – greyish under the chocolate complexion. No, something was wrong here.

Then Horace turned and glanced at Mr Jagabir, and the boy's face, Mr Jagabir noted, expressed hatred and anger. His head seemed to tremble slightly. He suddenly went towards the barrier.

Horace was thinking: the nasty dog. It must have been him. I'm sure it must have been him. He was searching through the letter-trays when I went out. Just like a coolie. He wouldn't have been a coolie if he hadn't done something underhand like that. Rage tore through him. He could hear his breath lisping.

To Mr Jagabir's eyes came a glint of understanding. He saw everything. It was Xavier who had written that quotation and put it in the *File* tray. Now he understood why it was written in block letters and not in ordinary handwriting. So Xavier was in love with Mrs Hinckson! Well. If that wasn't a joke! A stupid little black boy like that. How Mrs Hinckson would laugh if she knew!

Not by the twitching of a muscle did Mr Jagabir betray what was going through his mind. His face, to Horace who was staring at it now, had its customary frown of concentration, and, to all appearances, Mr Jagabir was deeply engrossed in matters relating to accountancy. Horace felt relieved. Anyway, he assured himself, there had been no means of Mr Jagabir knowing who wrote it. Thank goodness he had decided to do it in block letters.

Mr Murrain was getting ready to read the newspapers. He had turned down Mr Jagabir's offer to go downstairs for them purely for the sake of appearances. It would not have done for him to have seemed too eager to read the newspapers when (if only theoretically) he had work to do, and it would not have looked well for Mr Jagabir, as assistant accountant, to have been seen performing a task which, properly, was the office-boy's.

In reality, Mr Murrain had been itching to cast aside the price-list in favour of the newspapers. Reading the newspapers in the morning at his desk seemed befitting for an office head – and it was an occupation he genuinely enjoyed.

A copy of the *Trinidad Guardian* was delivered every morning at his home in the Maraval district, a picturesque valley district much favoured by the élite, just outside the city limits of Port of Spain, but he never had time to read it. He made a point of leaving home at seven-twenty in order to reach the office by seven-thirty, and this meant getting out of bed at six-forty-five. Making his toilet and taking breakfast occupied every minute of the thirty-five at his disposal, and he was not the kind of man who could skim through a newspaper between gulps of coffee; he liked to do his reading at ease.

His early arrival at the office dated from only seven months ago. It resulted from a ruling by Mr Holmes of the Tucurapo office who, as Manager of the Tucurapo estate in Trinidad, was the superior of both Mr Waley and Mr Murrain. Mr Holmes, in an informal conference on one of his rare visits to the town office, had expressed the opinion that he considered it "not good policy" that both office heads should arrive at half past eight. "One of you should be here at least half an hour before the regular staff arrives. I know they're a pretty dependable lot, but as a matter of policy someone at the top ought to be here well in advance."

After he had left, Mr Waley, in a spirit of chivalry, had decided that he would come at seven-thirty. But Mr Murrain had shaken his head and said that his conscience could not allow it.

"I do little enough work in the place as it is. The least I can do is to come out early."

Between himself and Mr Waley, reasoned Mr Murrain, there was no need for hypocrisy. They were Englishmen together in a backward colony of the Empire.

Mr Murrain selected the *Trinidad Guardian*, putting aside the *Port of Spain Gazette*. He never read the *Gazette*; he had a prejudice against it because it was supported by Roman Catholic interests. He never went to church and would in no way have been affected had there been no churches at all in Trinidad, but he had been christened and confirmed in the Anglican church – like his parents before him – and had been brought up to feel that the Roman Catholic church represented something sinister. He did not hate Catholics, for he lacked the energy to hate anything or anyone; he was simply suspicious and wary of everything connected with the Pope.

The column entitled "Talk of Trinidad" always held his attention more than any other. In this column a writer who signed himself (or herself) "The Humming Bird" recorded the movements and doings of people who mattered. These included highly placed civil servants; the heads of big commercial firms and of sugar estates and oil companies; air force, naval and army officers, English and Americans; consuls; Government-nominated members of the Legislative Council; whites and people who passed for white.

Mr Murrain saw with satisfaction that he and Mrs Murrain had been listed as having attended "the cocktail party held at the home of Mr and Mrs Rolf de Bergere" – the Guardian type suffers from a lack of accents; "communique" must suffice for "communiqué" and so forth – "to welcome home Flight-lieutenant Eugene (Binny) de Bergere who arrived in Trinidad from England Monday last after being demobbed from the R.A.F. with which he served since June 1942. After the party, the hosts with their guests went to dance at the Trinidad Country Club…"

The sight of his name in print always thrilled Mr Murrain. It was because as a boy he had had ambitions of becoming an author. At twelve he had written verse of the idealistic and sentimental variety and filled exercise books with lengthy descriptions of flowers and mosses collected over the Surrey countryside (outdoor games and athletics had never attracted him). But his father, a country doctor with a wide and lucrative practice and a man who considered writing "an occupation that ought to be followed by the very rich or the very poor – the very poor are accustomed to starving; the very rich won't have to starve", had not encouraged him.

Fingering his little red waxed moustache one day, he had said: "Thousands – possibly, hundreds of thousands – of self-fancied geniuses have tried their hand and flopped at this sort of thing, Everard. I may not be the first father to advise his son against it as a career, but that doesn't make what I say any less the truth."

And he had slapped the blue-covered exercise book down on his desk with a crack of finality, adding: "You have no talent, boy." His massive frame began to quiver with mirth, for he was a man with no small sense of humour.

If there was one thing Doctor Murrain lacked it was the traditional pomposity of the country medico; his wisdom and irony derived from a core of solid character. He was the one man Everard Murrain had ever genuinely respected. His housemaster at the grammar school in north London had come close, as had later on Mr Minshall, a good friend of his father's and the managing director of the Tucurapo company in London, who had secured Everard a place in the firm as a clerk after his interrupted studies at Cambridge (for the doctor's sudden death had disclosed that he had not been as well off as most people had imagined; his generosity, it came to light, had exceeded his wisdom), but even Mr Hamersham and Mr Minshall had failed to achieve, in Everard's fancy, the stature of his father. And the old buzzard had advised him wisely. In the years which had followed he had come to discover that he had no talent, that he would be a good reader but never an artist with words.

His enjoyment of the newspaper waned abruptly; it happened like this every morning.

For Miss Henery had arrived.

He glanced at the wall clock situated over the office-boy's desk against a jalousie kept permanently closed. Eight minutes to eight.

This meant that Miss Henery's bus had been on time this morning. She lived in the Diego Martin valley, five miles out of town, and the time of her arrival at the office depended upon the vagaries of the buses that plied between Diego Martin and Port of Spain. When the seven-thirty bus was late you could expect to see her any time between eight and eight-fifteen; when it was on time, between a quarter to and eight.

Mr Murrain heard her greet Horace – a pleasant, polite "'Morning, Xavier!" – and then listened to her footsteps clipping and clopping towards her desk. Her desk stood at a point equidistant from the windows and the lunch-room wall, and also from his own desk and from Jagabir's. Once during idle reflection he had thought: It's an equilateral triangle, Jagabir and I forming the points at the base and she the point at the top.

Just before she put down her handbag she gave Mr Murrain a casual glance, smiled slightly and said: "Good morning, Mr Murrain."

"Good morning, Miss Henery."

"Good morning, Mr Jagabir."

"'Morning, Miss Henery." Mr Jagabir fidgeted and added: "I have a whole batch of accounts here for you to do when you get a chance."

"All right. Give me a minute to settle down, please!"

In an aggrieved tone, Mr Jagabir said that he had not intended her to do them this minute. "Ah say *when* you get a chance."

She ignored him.

The mobility of Mr Murrain's chin increased. This always happened when he caught the first whiff of Miss Henery's perfume. The urge to say something to her became imperative. He rustled the newspaper.

"Miss Henery, did you – did you notice my fountain-pen on the desk here yesterday afternoon? I somehow seem to have misplaced it."

"Your fountain-pen? Didn't I see you signing that cheque for the Pelham Works with it around three o'clock time?"

"Cheque for the – oh! Yes, of course!"0

He began to open and shut drawers.

Miss Henery observed that his head was bent so that the newspaper partly concealed his face; he still clutched the paper with one hand. She noted, too, that his complexion was pinker than it normally should have been.

A very slight smile came to her lips. She told herself that she knew exactly what the trouble was.

"Ah, here it is! I've found it."

"Very good, Mr Murrain."

She never addressed him as "sir". Nor did Mrs Hinckson. Miss Bisnauth and Miss Yen Tip and Miss Labelle would have said "sir", but with the example set by Mrs Hinckson and Miss Henery, they automatically felt that it would have been an indignity for them, too, to indulge in this form of address.

Miss Henery – like Mrs Hinckson – belonged to the coloured middle-class, and was very conscious of her background of gentility and her social superiority over the negro, East Indian and Chinese elements which counted, in her estimation, as low-class. The whites debarred her from their society, but – like everyone in her class – she considered herself the equal of the whites in breeding and general culture. Her pride forbade her addressing a white man as "sir".

Miss Henery was something of a problem for Mr Murrain. She had come to work with the firm a little over a year ago, her predecessor having resigned to get married. From the first day of her advent Mr Murrain had found himself unaccountably attracted to her. At least, he had tried to assure himself there was no way of accounting for it even while the secret, honest parts of him told him there was no mystery. He refused to admit it, so to speak, in open conference with his ego, but he knew that Miss Henery stimulated him sexually.

She was no more than five feet three, and short women had never appealed to him. As a younger man, in his moments of sexual fantasy, he had always rejected short women; he had felt he would be awkward with them in bed because of his height. Yet Miss Henery attracted him.

Perhaps it was the way she moved her hips in walking. Watching her recede, he sometimes imagined himself as possessing the ears of an insect: he thought he could hear the lisp of stockinette panties against the smoothness of her buttocks. Or perhaps it was because her breasts, though small, sagged slightly and gave through the dress, the indication of large areolae. Or it might be her brief, muffled laugh. When she laughed her eyebrows became elevated and her chin jerked forward and her shoulders seemed to shrug inward forming swift hollows under her collarbones.

It might be any of these things, but Mr Murrain did not care to analyse his reactions too meticulously. Now and then he considered it absurd, even demeaning, that he should be experiencing any attraction for her at all. He tried to despise himself. Miss Henery was an olive-skinned girl with kinky, negroid hair artificially straightened; her features were more European than negroid, it was true, and she was pretty – but the fact remained that he was a white man: an Englishman.

He tried to convince himself that he was above race and class prejudice, but the feeling of aloofness remained. The final conclusion would always be that he was distinctly on a higher level (a level of what he never troubled to define; his intellect balked at such an abstraction).

She was a spirited, haughty young woman, and had so often outraged his sense of authority and feeling of Caucasian superiority that he had grown to be unsure how he felt about her. At times he was positive he disliked her; at other times it required a great deal of restraint to prevent himself asking her to lunch with him, or to go for a drive with him one evening.

Folding up the newspaper, he remembered that there was this question of her annual fortnight's leave that was still hanging fire. She wanted to take her leave this month instead of in July or August, the customary time. Some cousin of hers going to Barbados, and who had invited her to accompany her.

He had told her that he would have to discuss the matter with Mr Waley, as he was not sure whether she could be spared at this particular time. He was well aware that Miss Bisnauth could do her work while she was away and that it was quite unnecessary to consult Mr Waley, but it was not in his nature to commit himself to any decision on the spot.

Further, he preferred to keep her waiting; it would teach her not to be so confoundedly haughty and independent.

He stretched his neck and drew the price-list towards him.

For Horace, the critical moment had come.

Mrs Hinckson was on her way up.

He had heard her enter downstairs, because his ears had been on the alert. The traffic in Marine Square was rumbling and trumpeting at that newly heightened pitch always characteristic of eight o'clock, but even this had not prevented him from catching the tip-tap of her steps on the threshold. It could have been Miss Bisnauth or Miss Yen Tip, but, somehow, he had known that it was Mrs Hinckson. His soul, he explained it to himself, had been attuned to divine her approach.

He happened to be right. The voice he could hear on the stairs now was hers – and the laughter. The male voice belonged to Mr Lopez, the junior accountant. She generally came in along with Mr Lopez, who lived in the street next to hers and caught the same bus.

Horace sat at his desk, his head bent over *A Tale of Two Cities.* He read, but no meaning registered on his brain. The blood seemed to whir in his head, and he could hear a thin singing in his ears, as though a ghostly mosquito had invaded his eardrums – a singing interrupted by the voice of Mr Jagabir, nasal and East Indian.

Horace rose in a hurry. "Yes, Mr Jagabir! You calling me?"

Mr Jagabir was jerking his forefinger impatiently towards the switchboard in the south-eastern corner of the office.

"You don't hear de telephone buzzing, boy? You getting deaf?"

Horace pushed back the chair and hurried through the barrier, slamming the gate behind him. He paused and twirled nervously, tensed by an impulse to leave the gate open for Mrs Hinckson to pass in after him. He saw her almost at the top of the stairs now. He hesitated, irresolute, then went on quickly towards the switchboard, hopelessly confused.

It was his duty to answer the switchboard if anyone happened to put through a call before Miss Laballe, the operator, arrived, or when she was, for any reason, absent.

59

He was so upset that he said "Hello!" twice into the receiver before realizing that someone had, for the second time, asked for Mr Murrain.

"Mr Murrain?"

"Yes, yes. Mr Murrain, I said. I want to speak to him. It's Mrs Murrain."

"Oh. Yes, madam, he's here. Just a minute."

He switched the call over to Mr Murrain's desk, put down the apparatus and turned off to see Miss Laballe coming towards the switchboard.

She was looking in the direction of Miss Henery and smiling and calling out something in the special lowered voice everyone used when calling out to anyone else across the office. She was half Portuguese and half French creole, and her profile appeared to him a sallow blur.

He moved past her, hardly aware of his feet touching the floor, for he was experiencing an uneasy, apprehensive buoyancy. This fell far short of how he had rehearsed things. He felt a bitterness against Fate. First, Mr Jagabir officiously interfering with the note, then now this telephone call to take him from his desk at the very instant when he should have been seated at it so as to watch Mrs Hinckson enter…

…"Morning, Xavier!"

He looked up with a smile. "Oh, good morning, Mrs Hinckson!"

She went past him, leaving the usual trail of perfume – perfume that seemed to melt into his being in mysterious wisps.

He pretended to go on reading, but all the while kept his eyes on her as she approached her desk. He saw her sit down, jerk back her head slightly in the way she had, as though to adjust her loose-hanging dark hair that dangled about her shoulders in large, faintly glossy waves – genuine white-people hair; not kinky hair straightened with a hot comb like Miss Henery's.

He saw her pat her kerchief gently against her throat as she gave her desk the first cursory survey. Then her brows knitted. She had noticed the paper with the quotation. She reached out to the tray and took it up…

That was how it *ought* to have happened. That was how he had visualized it a dozen times in bed last night. Depression settled upon him, followed almost immediately by a surge of defiance. He suddenly saw this morning's events as illustrative of what might happen to him in the future. He breathed deeply, and told himself that nothing would thwart him. He would smash his way through and beat Destiny. Beat God Himself and Jesus and the Virgin Mary if they tried to hinder him from getting what be wanted out of life.

Sinking down at his desk, he felt the reaction set in. He had blasphemed. How shocked his mother would have been if she could have heard him! He felt contrition. His hand groped into his shirt and grasped the medal attached to the thin brass chain which hung around his neck. It was a medal embossed with the portrait of Our Lady. He clutched it hard, but did not say a prayer to beg forgiveness; he felt that his remorse would be divined and understood Above and he would be forgiven. In any case, he meant to go to Confession on Friday.

He heard a smothered laugh – Mrs Hinckson's laugh. He found himself staring at her.

But though she sat at her desk, it was not the paper with the quotation she was holding and laughing at; it was at something Miss Henery had said to her. Miss Henery stood beside her murmuring. He wished he had been close enough to hear what they were discussing – though that would be eavesdropping; he felt a swift pang of self-reproach.

"...soon as I landed in the office," Miss Henery was telling Mrs Hinckson, and Mrs Hinckson laughed again – another smothered laugh, for no one (save Mr Reynolds, the salesman, and his was a special case) ever indulged in loud laughter in the office; it would have been considered bad form.

"Before long he's going to follow you into the lunch-room."

"Or the Ladies' Room," said Miss Henery.

"You're right. I won't be surprised."

Mr Waley was coming through the barrier-gate.

"'Morning, Miss Henery! 'Morning, Mrs Hinckson!"

He paused, brisk and vital, gave Mrs Hinckson a brief, amused smile. "You notice how early I am this morning. You know what that means?"

Mrs Hinckson smiled back: "I know. I'm coming in right away."

After he had moved on: "I have a whole morning of dictation before me, my dear. The London mail has been piling up for the past week or more."

"Our friend over there should take a leaf out of Mr Waley's book. If he had more work to do he wouldn't have time to be watching me on the sly." She indulged in an obscene analogy, and Mrs Hinckson pinkened.

"Kathleen, you're the limit!"

"Isn't it the truth? Next time he rigs up any thin excuse like a fountain-pen to talk to me about, I won't hesitate to tell him just what I think is really the matter with him."

"I can hear you telling him."

Mrs Hinckson took the morning's mail from the *Incoming* tray, secured her notebook and pencil, and rose.

As Horace watched her vanish beyond the frosted glass door of Mr Waley's sanctum a groan moved within him. Another setback. Another variance from the picture as he had dreamt it.

Anxiously he regarded Miss Henery to see whether she would discover the paper in the *File* tray. But she moved off and went back to her own desk.

He began to wonder whether he should not find some excuse to stroll over to Mrs Hinckson's desk and smuggle away the paper and so put an end to the whole business. But Mr Jagabir would be sure to spot him. Mr Jagabir would be curious, and would probably call out and ask him what he was doing there, what paper it was he had taken up. Nothing escaped his prying eyes. And in any case, why should his original scheme be allowed to fizzle out in this tame way? That would be failure. No. Let it remain where it was until she eventually found it. Let it stand as a kind of test. If he lost heart and cancelled the scheme, in future he would cancel greater and more important schemes.

He put aside *A Tale of Two Cities*. He saw on his blotter the blue-pencilled words and faces he had inscribed in moments of dreaming.

Chief Accountant – that was what his mother hoped he would be one day.

assistant accountant… Chief Clerk… Manager… He had laughed to himself when he had written that. No matter if he were the most brilliant business genius the world had ever produced, he could not hope to be Manager of this office... An office manager with a black skin!

assistant manager...

Why was it certain posts demanded initial capitals when you wrote them, and others small letters? He had seen it in circulars and letters. *Chief Clerk* but not *Assistant Accountant...*

English people were too queer in their ways —

He started, and scolded himself for indulging in aimless thoughts. He took from a drawer the Pitman's testbook on shorthand and the exercise book in which he wrote the exercises set by his teacher. At five-fifteen this afternoon he had to take in two exercises, and they must be neatly and correctly done, for he wanted to keep up the reputation he had won for good work at the commercial school he attended.

It was a private school run by a coloured lady at her home, and the fees were within his means. He reckoned it as one of his minor triumphs that Mrs Brandon had accepted him as a pupil. All the other pupils were fair or olive coloured young ladies and young gentlemen; good-family people. It was only because he had heard that Mrs Brandon was a broad-minded person willing to help ambitious young people, irrespective of their class or colour, that he had had the courage to approach her. Even so, he had sensed the hesitation in her manner. But she had been very nice. She had questioned him about his job and his plans, and had seemed interested in him. He knew that he had impressed her, but had still felt a great relief when, at length, she nodded slowly and said: "Very well, Xavier, you can come. From the first of next month." She had spoken in a kind, friendly voice and without any patronage.

Within a minute he had switched his mind completely over to the study of the lesson, though all the while he kept on the alert for a call. He had so trained himself that he could be forever vigilant for a call or a signal from any member of the staff even when deeply engrossed in his own occupations. He was determined not to be caught napping as Mr Jagabir had caught him a little while ago.

When a moment later he heard the assistant accountant's chair scrape he glanced up, but Mr Jagabir was only moving across to Miss Henery with a sheaf of papers.

"Dese are the accounts Ah was telling you about, Miss Henery," Mr Jagabir said to Miss Henery.

Miss Henery jabbed her thumb towards the letter-trays. "Put them there. I'll see to them in a little."

As always when she had to deal with him, her manner was stiff. It was not that she hated East Indians; one or two of her very good acquaintances were East Indian. Miss Bisnauth was an East Indian, and Miss Bisnauth and she got on very well; she liked Miss Bisnauth. But this man Jagabir made her sick in every way. His dissembling, his slyness and prying habits, his sycophancy, his ingratiating, yet at the same time nagging and accusatory, voice – all, combined to create friction with her fearless, volatile temperament, and to breed within her a deep contempt and disgust for him.

Her upbringing, too, did not help matters. In her social sphere, a child was from an early age made to feel that the East Indians were inferior, contemptible people. They were dirty coolies, you learnt, who had come from India by the shipload to work on the sugar estates; they were a low filthy people who wore *dhotis* and smelly rags and who walked about barefooted; they ate nothing but rice and curried salt-fish and lived in stinking tenement barracks, hoarded their pennies in mattresses.

It was only of recent years that East Indians had begun to get rich and become somebodies. Her grandparents, Miss Henery had learnt through the remarks of adults, were ladies and gentlemen living in respectable surroundings – educated, well-bred people – when the East Indians had still, in every sense, been coolies labouring in the cane-fields.

Mr Jagabir placed the accounts in one of the trays but did not move off.

Out of the corner of her eye Miss Henery noticed that he was smiling.

"Miss, you see de paper with de love verse? Mrs Hinckson show you?"

"What's that?"

Mr Jagabir knew that Mrs Hinckson had not noticed the paper.

He had watched her every movement and action from the moment she had come in. But he considered this the best way of introducing the subject to Miss Henery. Ignoring the brittleness of her manner – he was inured to it – he said: "Somebody put a paper wid a love verse write on it in one of her letter-trays. When I come to work a lil' while ago I happen to stop by her desk to fill me pen, and Ah notice dis paper. It's somebody in dis office who put it dere, I know. A poem by Shakespeare."

Miss Henery's curiosity so overcame her contempt that she relaxed a trifle and returned: "No, I'm afraid I haven't seen it. How do you know it was somebody in the office who put it there? Why couldn't it have come by post?"

He shook his head and smiled mysteriously. "No, miss, it didn't come by post. I happen to know it didn't come by post."

Miss Henery made no comment.

"It's somebody who you would never suspeck. De person *fancy* nobody see dem, but *I* see dem when they put it there."

She was about to tell him bluntly to stop hedging and reveal who it was, but at this point Miss Bisnauth came in and called: "Hallo, Kathleen!" on her way to her desk.

"Hallo, Edna! How're things?"

"Not too bad, child!"

While these greetings were being exchanged Mr Jagabir took the opportunity to glide back to his desk. In any event, he would not have made any further revelations. He was satisfied that he had set to work the leaven of intrigue. Nothing delighted him more than intrigue. To be instrumental in a plot aimed at disgracing or ridiculing anyone was one of the compensations of a fear-ridden life...

Horace turned his head at the quick footsteps. Without doing so he would have known it was Miss Yen Tip. She always ran up the stairs – as though her bubbly, vivacious nature could not tolerate leisurely movement.

She gave him a swift smile and an "Ay, Xavier!" as she skipped past him so that he had to start and half-shout: "'Morning, miss!" to be sure she heard him. His cheeks went warm; it was as if her vitality, like a thin, pleasant flame, had flicked them.

She went straight to Miss Henery's desk, and Miss Henery saw that her slanting Chinese eyes were narrowed in accompaniment to the smile which revealed her white, even, but slightly projecting, teeth.

"I have some lovely news for you, Kathleen!"

"Olga, you're always with lovely news."

"No, man, but dis is really lovely!"

"What's happened?"

In a breathless murmur Miss Yen Tip told her: "Our friend. He was there last night."

"At the De Luxe?"

"Yes. He went wid Cynthia and her mother."

"You don't say! Her mother went along, too!"

"Child, I nearly scream out!"

Miss Henery laughed – and Mr Murrain flicked over three leaves of the price-list in rapid succession. He called to Mr Jagabir to bring him the A-D ledger. Called in a hurried stammer.

After a few more exchanges, Miss Yen Tip said: "Girl, lemme go and get some letters fixed up before Mr Benson come in and scold me." (Mr Benson was the Chief Clerk, and came in at eight-thirty; Miss Yen Tip was his stenotypist.)

"I'll give you some more details," said Miss Yen Tip, "later on before de morning out. Ronny and I were sitting right in front of dem, and I heard her mother say somet'ing dat made me nearly die wid laughing."

And she was off to her desk, short, slim, chic, full of little gay chortles.

Mr Jagabir gave her a disapproving glance.

Miss Henery smiled reflectively as she flicked the flannelette duster over her desk preparatory to settling down to the day's work.

The "our friend" Miss Yen Tip had referred to as having seen at the De Luxe cinema was Herbert McGlenny, the young man who, for a long time, had been trying to persuade Miss Henery to marry him.

She was not in love with him. She liked him. Now and then she considered giving him an answer in the affirmative, for he was in every way eligible as a husband. His father's commission agency was making thousands, and his father had taken him into the business as a partner. His earnestness and persistence, too, sometimes moved her – and he was a handsome fellow whom several girls were assiduously bent on capturing. He came of good class, had a light olive complexion and hair with large waves ("good" hair, Miss Henery thought of it as; as a member of the West Indian coloured middle-class, she conceived of human hair in terms of "good" and "bad" – sometimes "good" and "hard"; "good" hair is hair that is European in appearance: "bad" or "hard" hair is hair of the kinky, negroid type).

Herbert's family was one of the best in Trinidad. His father's father had been a well-known barrister who had gained renown despite the disadvantages of a dark complexion and kinky hair (it was whispered that he was a pure black man). Herbert's mother was a Harrould; her brother was the late Doctor Harrould, and old Mr Harrould, her father, had been Mayor of Port of Spain on two or three occasions in the past.

Miss Henery murmured a "Damn!" as an eraser went flying off the desk. It described grasshopper motions on the floor and came to rest not far from the iron safe against the wall.

Two chairs scraped simultaneously – Mr Lopez' (Mr Lopez' desk was just behind hers) and Mr Murrain's, the swivel-screw squeaking as well.

Mr Murrain rose and leant outwards to recover the eraser, but Mr Lopez proved too athletic for him. Mr Lopez behaved as though he were fielding a ball on the cricket ground; he took one swift crabwise stride, an arm flashed out – and the eraser was in his grasp.

Mr Murrain pinkened and laughed softly. "I hope you'll be as fast when you play against Barbados next week."

"He's no good in the field, sir," grinned Mr Lorry, who had just arrived in time to witness the incident. "He can only handle a bat."

"That won't do in cricket," said Mr Murrain, wagging his head. "You've got to be an all-rounder."

He took the opportunity of this opening to ask Mr Lopez how the Colony Eleven was shaping at practice. Next week a cricket tournament between Trinidad and Barbados commenced at the Queen's Park Oval, and Mr Lopez was one of Trinidad's best bats.

Cricket was one of Mr Murrain's weaknesses. He had never handled a bat nor bowled a ball, but he was an enthusiastic spectator, and had even allowed himself to be elected a committee member of one of the leading clubs.

Miss Henery, accustomed to these cricketing conferences in her vicinity, proceeded, unperturbed, to fix the first account form into her machine. But as she worked her thoughts kept straying back to Herbert McGlenny.

Herbert had an attractive personality, and she felt that, in time, she could coax herself into falling in love with him. At present, it would be out of the question, for she was too infatuated with her cousin's husband, Gerard Beaton.

Actually, the affair had started shortly after Miss Henery left Bishop's High School upon obtaining her Cambridge School Certificate. Confined to glances, smiles and conversational innuendoes when she and Gerard happened to be alone, the affair had not really emerged as a tangible fact until late one afternoon about three months ago. She and Gerard had met accidentally in the Rock Garden; they had sat on a grassy embankment to talk; darkness fell – and suddenly there was an explosion of feelings and an impassioned revelation. Though they had not gone beyond kissing and fondling, they had both realized that if they continued to see each other a consummation was sooner or later inevitable.

Gerard Beaton was a civil servant, efficient and zealous to the point of splitting hairs; he was an active Presbyterian. But despite these limiting factors, he had shaped for himself a fairly liberal outlook; he did not exclaim in horror at fornication; listened to and retailed smutty jokes; saw nothing wrong in getting drunk on festive occasions. He felt, however, that such things as duty, loyalty and honour were not to be treated lightly.

Kathleen Henery was approximately of the same philosophy, but sex obsessed her so much that sometimes she wondered whether it were possible⁻ for her ever to have a set code of morals. Her parents were Anglo-Catholics who went to church every Sunday and whose codes were rigid. They had trained her up to believe that fornication and adultery were grave sins which could only result in catastrophic social repercussions (though not necessarily in hell-fire in the Hereafter; they were too educated to stress this).

Her cousin Rachel was one of her best chums; their friendship dated from primary school days. The thought of beguiling Rachel's husband into a sex affair and causing Rachel much unhappiness disturbed Miss Henery. She would feel wretched if her friendship with Gerard took such a turn.

Divorce was not to be thought of; Gerard looked upon marriage as a "sacrament", and she herself would have considered the idea highly distasteful. So she had had to rule out the possibility of their ever getting married. And she knew that, above everything, she wanted to get married.

Herbert wanted to marry her – very badly – but she knew that if he found out that she had been sexually intimate with Gerard he would not want to, because Herbert, in spite of his charm and apparent worldliness, was an unsophisticated, old-fashioned young man. And, naturally, reasoned Miss Henery, she would have to be honest with him and tell him everything before they came to the point of marriage.

She took from the machine the first completed account. Removing the two carbons – for she had done it in triplicate – she saw her face, slightly distorted, reflected in the paper-release lever which was of highly polished nickel plating. She stared at it in idle contemplation, telling herself that she had no reason to be ashamed of her looks. A short, straight nose with narrow nostrils – nothing negroid about it. A mouth small and well shaped, the lips full but not thick. Her shoulders had an inclination to be round, but the shoulder-pads of her dress prevented this defect from being too apparent.

It was not so easy, however, to disguise her not-too-straight spine which gave her a slight stoop, and in order to correct this she had fallen into the habit of throwing out her chest when sitting, and being careful never to slouch when standing. Her figure was far from ideal – her breasts, apart from being too small, had sagged too early – but she made the best of it by not wearing brassieres and by favouring thin dress materials.

Men found her round, fearless stare her most exciting feature. The expression of her eyes did not belie her nature; she was brave, she was spiritually adventurous; she revelled in any situation that carried with it the element of moral danger or the other sort of danger which involves social disaster. This was why she could continue her secret affair with Gerard at the risk of discovery and in the face of her scruples. It was why, too, she could accept Rachel's invitation to accompany the family to Barbados on holiday. She could visualize the many occasions when it would be convenient to whisper and exchange glances, to let Gerard kiss and fondle her. The consummation might become a *fait accompli*. A dangerous thing to picture in cold blood – dangerous and lovely – but she intended to go through with this holiday. She could face it, come whatever might.

She frowned and turned her head suddenly so that out of the corner of her eye she could see Mr Murrain. She had just remembered that he had not yet given her an answer about her leave. She must tackle him about it this very morning.

She pushed out her chest and got ready another account for the machine. She winced and uttered a lisping sound as she caught her knee a crack against the right front leg of the desk...

It was an old-fashioned desk made of crabwood – the only one in the office of its kind. It had been purchased at an auction sale four years ago when a desk had been urgently needed in the office. In respect to its right front leg...

One night, in July 1936, Wilson O'Brien, a negro cabinet-maker, was at work when he heard a sound at the door of his workshop and glanced round to see his assistant enter. "Wha' keep you back so late, Aubrey?"

Aubrey Mowbray, his assistant, did not reply. He seemed in a surly mood, and O'Brien guessed what the trouble must be. Aubrey had been gambling and had lost. Gambling and women – especially women – were Aubrey's weaknesses.

"Wid dis kind o' life you leading, boy, you can't prosper."

Aubrey said nothing. He was a short negro of about twenty-two.

"Your mother plead wid me and beg me to give you dis job. Ah sorry for you and tek you on and dis is de way you carrying on."

Without a word, Aubrey prepared to resume work. Before

going home for dinner he had half completed the right front leg for the new desk (at that time it could have been right or left; only when the desk was being assembled this leg had happened to be placed on the right).

Taking up the unfinished leg from the workbench, Aubrey turned it over contemplatively in his hands, and O'Brien heard him grunt.

Aubrey set the lathe going and was soon busy. He worked, O'Brien thought, with a steadiness unusual for him.

It was a chilly night. A thunderstorm had raged shortly after three that day, and now at half-past ten at night the air was dense with the water vapour that billowed down from the heavy-wooded hills – the hills that describe a semicircle around Port of Spain.

A cool drift of air came in at the window over the tool-cupboard on O'Brien's right, and O'Brien decided that he had better close the window. He did not take cold easily, but suddenly the feeling possessed him that the chilly air might not be good for him; he felt uneasy about it for no particular reason.

He had pulled in the two wooden leaves of the window and slammed the bolt into place and was returning to his workbench when he noticed that Aubrey had left the workshop. His lathe was still going, and O'Brien assumed that he must have gone outside to urinate. A pity, he told himself, the boy could not steady up. His mother was such a good woman – and his father, before he died last year, was a highly respected man in the district; one of the best carpenter-masons in the city. Aubrey's father had been made churchwarden two years ago, and he had belonged to two lodges.

Fully five minutes must have elapsed without any sign of Aubrey. The lathe was still going, and annoyed that the current should be wasted in this way, O'Brien shouted: "Aubrey! You not coming in to work? You gone out and left de lathe on! I got to pay for de current, you know!"

There was no reply from Aubrey.

O'Brien walked over to the door. He looked out on the pavement and about the street, then moved round to the side of the small building where he was certain he would find Aubrey.

71

But the narrow alleyway was empty. The street light illuminated it sufficiently for him to be sure no one was there. Even the street was deserted. It was a little back street, and seldom saw much traffic by day, much less by night.

Puzzled, O'Brien returned to the workshop. He paused by Aubrey's workbench, automatically switching off the lathe. He saw the desk-leg Aubrey had been at work on – saw that it was completed. It was a good job, and O'Brien felt a little mollified.

He turned at a sound from the door.

It was Victorine – Aubrey's sister, a girl of about fourteen. She said, in a tearful voice, that her mother had sent her with a message. Aubrey was dead.

"Aubrey dead? Wha' you telling me, child?"

"Yes, Mr O'Brien, he tek sick after dinner and 'e dead." O'Brien laughed and told her that her mother must be joking to send him a message like this.

"Aubrey was here not five minutes ago. Look at de time. Twenty-five to eleven. And he walk out of here at half past ten and left de lathe on. He just finish turning dis desk-leg."

"He didn't go nowhere after dinner, Mr O'Brien. He was eating dinner and he say he got a pain in his stomach, and he fall sick and die off."

O'Brien told her she was talking nonsense. He was a matter-of-fact man of forty-eight and entirely lacking in superstition. "Look, child," he told Victorine, "spirits and *obeah* and *voodoo* don't come my way. Nor I don't know none o' my friends who believe in such things. I'm sure you' mother don't hold wid such foolishness, either. She's a sensible woman. Only de people in America and England know about de *obeah* and *voodoo* we West Indians is suppose to practise. Nobody can fool me Aubrey wasn't in dis shop working —"

A tall, slim negro entered. "Wilson, you hear about Aubrey?"

Henry Chalmers, a mechanic, was a good friend of O'Brien's. He lived next door to the Mowbrays. He told O'Brien that shortly after nine o'clock Mrs Mowbray, Aubrey's mother, had called over to tell them that Aubrey had collapsed while eating his dinner and was dead. The doctor said it was prussic acid.

A week later, O'Brien was called as a witness at the inquest, but in his evidence he stated that the last time he had seen Aubrey was just before Aubrey had left the workshop at eight o'clock to go home for dinner.

O'Brien felt that only trouble could result for the Mowbray household if he told the facts as he knew them to be, and Mrs Mowbray was too old a friend upon whom to bring unhappiness. For some reason known to the family, they were trying to make out that Aubrey had died at shortly after nine, and the Chalmers, their neighbours, were conspiring to back up this story. Very well. Let it go at that... Yet it did strike him as queer that the boy could have died at his home not five minutes after leaving the workshop at half past ten. It would have taken him at least eight minutes to get home, and Victorine and Chalmers would have required another eight minutes to arrive at the workshop with the message of his death.

There was a big mystery here, thought O'Brien. He was convinced it could be explained on a physical basis, but he preferred not to make inquiries. He was not a curious man, and he had a dread of the court-house.

Often nowadays he wondered whether he had done right in using the finished desk-leg he had found on Aubrey's work-bench. Perhaps he should have put it away in the odds-and-ends cupboard and made another to replace it.

On occasion, he asked himself idly where that desk could be now...

Horace, on this occasion, was not in a position to curse Destiny again, for it happened that he was not present to witness the incident – which in his way of seeing it – would have constituted Destiny's latest act of perverseness.

At around a quarter to nine (a few minutes after Mr Benson, the Chief Clerk, arrived) Mr Lorry told him to go to the Control Board for a batch of export licences covering certain shipments of Tucurapo Grapefruit Juice and Tucurapo Marmalade due to leave for St Kitts and Nevis and Antigua in a day or two. It was during his absence that Miss Bisnauth, having cleared her own letter-trays of the residue of yesterday's work, crossed to Mrs Hinckson's desk to collect the contents of the *File* tray and so discovered the paper with the quotation.

Miss Bisnauth began to read it with a slight frown, her deep brown eyes gradually assuming an amused look, her full-lipped, rather wide mouth stretching in a smile so that dimples appeared in her cheeks. She laughed, and her whole slim body vibrated, the blood intensifying the touch of rouge on her olive-brown cheeks. It was a tinkling laugh but restrained and entirely lacking in maliciousness, and produced in her an effect as though she were emitting rays of good nature, vital and saturating – a good nature the warmth and naïvety of which gave the impression of surrounding her personality with an aura of insulation proof against the invasion of evil. For this particular instant she had a transfigured, spiritual air.

She knew without doubt that Xavier had done this. Mrs Hinckson had mentioned once or twice that she had noticed something in the boy's manner which made her feel that he was attracted to her.

Softness and pity came into her eyes.

The passage was familiar. It was from *As You Like It,* only, of course, he had substituted "Nanette" for "Rosalind". She had done *As You Like It* for her Cambridge School Certificate Examination when she was at Bishop's High School, and this was one of the passages she had had to memorize.

Watching her from under the shelter of his curved hand which rested against his temple, Mr Jagabir smiled. He had the inclination to stroll across and give her a hint as to whom he suspected of being responsible for this farcical piece of paper, but, after a moment's thought, decided against this course.

She would only snub him. She was an East Indian like himself, but she was educated and moved with well-to-do Indians – Indians educated like herself – and even with good-class coloured people. Her father was a wealthy provision merchant in Henry Street, and she did not need to work in this office; she could stay at home and live in idleness like a lady if she wanted; she regarded him with as much contempt as the others did: to her, too, thought Mr Jagabir, he was only a dirty coolie.

He went on with his work, inside him the old slow burning of envy and impotence.

Miss Bisnauth replaced the slip of paper in the now empty tray, and was on her way back to her desk when footsteps and sobs came from the stairs.

It was Mary, the sweeper.

Miss Yen Tip exclaimed, "Eh-eh!" and sniggered shrilly. Miss Bisnauth hesitated, then changed direction and went towards the barrier-gate.

The attention of the whole office became centred on Mary Barker.

"What's wrong, Mary?" The concern and sympathy on Miss Bisnauth's face and in her voice were so sincere that they were communicated to Mary at once.

The woman looked at her, trying to control her sobs. Her mien was tortured and burdened, as though life, for her, had reached its final depth, its ultimate degree of blackness.

"Trouble follow me steps dis morning, Miss Bisnauth. Everywhere Ah turn trouble."

"Is it your son again?"

"Dat's one set o' trouble, miss. Ah wake up out me sleep dis morning to hear Richard get arrest last night for disorderly behaviour —"

"Arrested!"

"Yes, miss. De police got 'e lock up. Oh, God! Troubles never

75

come singly, no! Before Ah leff home dis morning for de office Ah roll up a five-dollar note and put it in a ole envelope and Ah put de envelope right in me skirt pocket here, miss. But when Ah reach home lil' while ago and Ah searching for de note Ah can't find it miss – can't find it nowhere."

Miss Bisnauth kept looking at her, the sheaf of papers from Mrs Hinckson's *File* tray held against her breast, her eyes unblinking with a reflection of the woman's misery.

"Ah come all de way back here, miss, to look see if Ah could find it. Ah say to meself perhaps Ah drop it somewhere." Mary bowed her head and groaned.

"But if you dropped it in the street you won't be able to find it now."

"Ah know, miss. Ah know. But Ah had to mek a search. Ah so worried Ah ain' eat nutting for de morning. Oh, Jesus!"

"But why did you bring out so much money this morning, Mary?"

"Miss, when Ah hear Ah got to appear in court Ah so upset Ah say to meself: 'Look, you better tek out somet'ing from you' savings in case you got to pay a fine for Richard', so Ah stoop down and pull out me trunk from under de bed and Ah tek out dis five-dollar note. All Ah had save up was seven dollars, and it tek me five hard months to put away even dat lil' bit."

Miss Bisnauth began to look round slowly. "You're sure you couldn't have dropped it in the office here when you were sweeping?"

"Ah don't t'ink so, miss, but Ah come back here to tek a look-round. If Ah drop it in de office here Ah woulda sure to notice it when Ah was sweeping. Me eyes been on de floor all de time."

Mr Benson called out and asked Miss Bisnauth what was the trouble. He was frowning with some disapproval, for he detested emotional displays in the office – especially from people like Mary. Himself three-parts Negro – he had close-cut kinky hair and unmistakably negroid features – and of lower middle-class stock, he disliked negroes. His sallow-olive complexion and his position as Chief Clerk were circumstances he found it impossible to forget.

Miss Bisnauth explained, and Mr Benson clicked his tongue

and said: "All right. Well, let her make a search and get it over. She can't be disturbing the office like this."

"Come, Mary, I'll help you to look around."

Mr Jagabir rose, a look of simulated concern on his face. "What money is dis you drop?" he said, giving Mary a shifty glance.

Mary, forgetful of her contempt for him, told him, and he joined the search. They glanced under desks and chairs. Then Mr Jagabir frowned: "Ent you is keep de broom in de lunch-room?"

Mary said yes.

Mr Jagabir went into the lunch-room which occupied ten feet by ten of the north-western section of the over-all office space. It corresponded to the Manager's sanctum in the north-eastern section which, however, was larger. Between these two apartments were situated the Men's Room – immediately adjoining Mr Waley's sanctum – and the Ladies' Room, the western wall of which separated it from the lunch-room.

Mr Jagabir reappeared from the lunch-room. He held out a crumpled, dirty-looking Manila envelope. "Just what Ah tell you! I found it on de lunch-room floor – not far from de broom, besides."

"Oh, God! T'ank you, Mr Jagabir! T'ank you kindly!"

Mr Jagabir felt weight and confidence in his steps as he returned to his desk. His head whirled slightly with a growing warmth. He felt the elation of a martyr who sees his sufferings beginning to show justification. He sat down at his desk certain that the whole staff was watching him and experiencing remorse. He could still hear Mary's voice emotional with gratitude as the woman made her way towards the stairs.

"I'm so glad you've got it back, Mary," Miss Bisnauth was saying. "I hope Richard will get off and you won't have to pay it in a fine."

"'Ow, miss! Ah trust so. Ah praying every minute, every minute."

She uttered a long sigh as she began to descend the stairs.

Horace met her on the pavement outside Roalk's Hardware. He had just leant up the office bicycle and locked it when he saw her. When she had told him why she had come back he grunted and said: "You got to be careful. I never keep paper money loose in my pocket. Always put it in a purse or a wallet. If de purse or wallet fall out you must hear it give a flop on de ground."

He uttered the words with a note of wisdom and self-importance, his manner implying that he was too alert and competent a human being to fall a victim to such misfortunes.

Mary, too relieved and too humbled by her experience, thanked him for his advice and said that he was quite right. She moved on with a heavy sigh.

Horace had already handed the blue licence forms, approved and stamped and perforated by the Controller of Imports and Exports, to Mr Lorry and was on his way back to the barrier-gate when he noticed that the *File* tray on Mrs Hinckson's desk was empty save for his love message. He felt a contraction in the top of his head. What had happened now? Who had emptied the tray?

He remembered. It was Miss Bisnauth's duty to clear the *File* tray on Mrs Hinckson's desk. Miss Bisnauth made copies of the minutes from the London office for filing.

He glanced at her, and at the same instant her gaze met his. She lowered her eyes at once, but he noticed that a slight smile came to her lips.

He took a swift breath, the tight feeling in his head increasing.

He returned to his desk, sat down and stared at the half-finished shorthand exercise. Surely it couldn't be that she had guessed! No, that was out of the question. Yet, that smile...

He began to curse himself. He had made a mess of things. He should have known better than to have put it into one of the trays. He ought to have inserted it into one of her desk-drawers. She locked her drawers every afternoon before going home and at noon before going off to lunch.

It came upon him that he was not as clever as he had fancied. The future crumbled in his imagination. He would turn out to be a failure, after all. Another black man – a bank messenger, at the best – struggling along on a meagre salary and saying "Yes, sir!" to the white people and the good-class coloured people. He felt a burning in his chest as though grains of sand were slowly trickling through his lungs. His face twitched, and he put his hand up to conceal it from anyone who might be looking.

But Miss Bisnauth had seen, and her eyes became soft with

pity. She stopped typing and turned her head very slowly, letting her gaze move along the floor. A poem was coming to life in her, its theme love and pity and humility. Her fancy welded the three into a single whole, and a crevice in the floor upon which her gaze became fixed took on the nature of a symbol... Love, pity, humility ... a dark crevice between two closely set floorboards...

> *"A potent flower of petals three:*
> *Love and humility and pity..."*

She stretched out and pulled towards her the blue-covered stenographer's notebook which she kept specially for the purpose of making jottings of poems. It rested always on the *Cassell's Simplified English Dictionary* near her letter-trays.

She wrote rapidly, then paused, biting her lower lip.

The next two lines came.

> *"Oh, I wish it were mine, this flower,*
> *Just to hold to myself for an hour..."*

She stopped writing, breathing fast, her eyes half-closed, the lids quivering slightly. She did not seem at all ridiculous, for her mien was too earnest, too intensely sincere; there was almost anguish in her sincerity.

She was telling herself that, at last, it seemed as though she was about to write a really deep and lovely poem. She conjured up a picture of Arthur Lamby... He read it and nodded. He looked up and said quietly that yes, this was all right. She had done it... And that she knew, would be praise, for though Arthur and she were in love with each other they never allowed their emotions to warp their detachment as critics of each other's creations. When Arthur wrote a short story he expected her to be coldly candid in her judgement of its literary worth, and when she wrote a poem she expected the same of him – and they each did their best to live up to this agreement.

The impulse to phone him at the newspaper office where he worked and tell him that she had just begun a new poem came upon her.

She half-rose, but sat down again, deciding that she would do it later in the morning. The chances were that he had not got to the office yet. As a feature writer, he did not have to be out until nine-thirty, though some mornings he did arrive at nine when he had something special or urgent to do.

Neglectful of her office work, she tried to continue the poem, but nothing more would come. With a feeling which her fancy visualized as a crooked metal bar writhing in a dark room, she realized that her poetic imagination had become a blank; a shutter seemed to face her where there should have been an opening that emitted waves of creative plasm... She began to grow suffocated and constricted with panic.

The Nightmare Moment was upon her.

It happened to her anywhere and at any time. Now at twenty it was no less vivid or terrifying than at fourteen when she was at school.

Positive colour departed from her surroundings; everything took on a sepia hue. Her lungs – she could see them as two phosphorescent bellows in a grey-black twilight – pumped the air in and out of her body in a laboured and deliberate rhythm. Her pectoral muscles tightened so that she could feel her breasts, which were still round and girlish, harden into mounds of lead. Her throat felt dry and hot as though at any second it would burst into flames, and she could feel the blood creeping like icy ants up through her arms and down through her legs...

Then it passed.

Arthur said it was a neurosis – the result of her naturally vivid imagination coupled with repressions she had suffered in her home, especially during early childhood when she had had as nurse an old relative of her mother's who was deformed and who had often frightened her by making grimaces at her and loud panting sounds. Whenever Betsy Ramdeen thought that Edna ought to be restrained from doing something she would call in her husky voice: "No, you can't go out dere now!" or "Stop dat noise, Edna!" And if Edna disobeyed, Betsy would make the grimace and the panting sounds as a punishment.

Miss Bisnauth began to type again, but all the while she could see Arthur's face. His grey-green eyes set in his light-brown face. His domed forehead that seemed to become more domed every day, because he was inclined to baldness and his close-cut kinky hair was receding. His straight nose and firm mouth and chin. In features he had taken more of the European than of the Negro or Chinese.

For Miss Bisnauth, Arthur was the best man in existence; the different bloods of which he was composed meant nothing to her. Once he had told her: "But do you realize I have English, French, German, Chinese and Negro blood in me? I'm a regular U.N. Council."

"Then we must have thousands of U.N. Councils in the West Indies," she had laughed.

Her parents thought well of him. Her father admitted that he ought to get far in the newspaper business; her father conceived of every occupation as a business – the provision business – the hardware business – even the law business and the poetry business; they were all the same to him.

But though her parents thought well of Arthur they could not be persuaded to see him as their son-in-law. They were thoroughly Christian and western in outlook, like their parents before them – Hinduism had ceased with their grandparents, the sugar estate coolies – but they were still clannish; it was as though this trait had continued subconsciously in them from the seed of their forebears, so that whenever there came a decision that involved a mixing of racial strains it rose to the surface. They had told her that an East Indian should marry an East Indian. They just felt so; they could offer no explanation of the matter.

Several of their friends were coloured, and were invited to the home on such occasions as a birthday party or a Christmas or Easter party. The Bisnauths spoke not a word of Hindustani; they belonged to the India Club, but the India Club is run on western lines; its members wear European clothes and dance to English and American dance music, play tennis and bridge, drink rum and whisky at a bar no different from the bar in any other club…

Yet, they objected to Arthur as a son-in-law because he was not an East Indian.

But for this one problem, felt Miss Bisnauth, life for her would have been a pure, clear song. She had a comfortable home and parents who were easygoing and generous. Her father made thousands in the wholesale provision business, but he was not close; he spent freely on his children's education and on the comforts of the home. Her brother, Rufus, who was two years older than she, was in Montreal at McGill studying medicine, and she herself could have gone to England or Canada to further her studies in music; she simply had to say so tomorrow and it would be an accomplished fact. It was her own choice that she had decided to work in an office; she had told her parents that she preferred writing poetry to playing the piano. She liked music – would always like it – but the linking together of words fascinated her far more.

Her object in working in an office was so that she could meet people and study them and get to feel sympathetic with their different outlooks – understand them – for she had read in a magazine article that only in this way could one ever hope to become a great poet. A natural intuition, imagination and the gift of self-expression were, of course, prerequisites, but, said the article, you must first know human beings before you could successfully interpret life through your poetic fancy.

Miss Bisnauth, though with modesty and humility, felt that she possessed a natural intuition, imagination and the gift of self-expression, and her parents did not try to discourage her in her literary efforts. Her father had given her a portable typewriter on her last birthday, though he had joked about it afterwards. Her mother, last Christmas, had given her T. S. Eliot's *Four Quartets*.

They were good parents, and towards them she felt a deep love and reverence. Her mother had a kind heart, and often helped friends who were not so well off – coloured as well as East Indian. During the war she had done volunteer work at the Harbour Canteen and at the hospital for injured survivors from torpedoed ships. Many nights she would come home from the hospital and weep when she related the sufferings of some of the men.

Miss Bisnauth was sure that it was from her mother she had got her soft nature and her intense pity for all living creatures – though she did give her father some credit, too. In spite of his shrewdness, even slickness, as a business man, he had a strong humane streak. There were two families now, both coloured, that he could foreclose on for mortgages – and they were not even his friends – but he had said that he could not make the poor people miserable; he would wait and give them a chance to settle up in their own time. For over two years he had been waiting, and only one family seemed likely ever to pay off their debt. Yet, he took no action against the other…

> *"What cool, distilled fragrance would it breathe*
> *Into my baffled being…"*

It was coming again…
No…

> *"Into my poor baffled thoughts which seethe…"*

She started.
Miss Laballe was calling her.
"Hallo! What's it? Phone for me?"
"Yes. Mr Reynolds's desk."
Miss Bisnauth hurried across. She was tall – five feet eight – but not very supple. Her gait was tripping and stiff, lacked freedom and grace.

The switchboard stood only about six feet from her desk whereas Mr Reynolds's desk was fully twenty feet away, midway between the doors of the Men's and Ladies' Rooms. Miss Laballe could easily have let her speak from the switchboard. But it was an unwritten law (laid down by Miss Laballe) that if one of the desk-phones was not in use and a call came through for a member of the staff whose desk did not have a phone, the call must be switched over to the unoccupied instrument.

This was Miss Laballe's way of showing courtesy. Speaking at the switchboard you would not have been able to prevent Miss Laballe overhearing what you said, unless she rose and left the switchboard temporarily, which she could not very well do without seeming to fail in her duty as operator. But at the desk-phones you could speak with a sense of privacy – even if you suspected that this sense was merely one of make-believe. For, in actuality, as everyone knew, Miss Laballe's courtesy was adapted to expediency. If someone stood beside her at the switchboard and spoke it meant that she could not listen-in to the speaker at the other end without betraying this fact to the person present (her finger would be seen manipulating the switch), but when the speaker used a desk-phone she could listen-in to what was said at both ends without anyone being, in fact, or in effect, the wiser.

Mr Reynolds was not yet in the office, because, as a salesman, he had the privilege of keeping irregular hours; the nature of his work dictated this. It might happen sometimes that for a whole day he would have to be about town, or in the country in his car or in one of the firm's delivery vans, engaged in securing orders for Tucurapo Marmalade or Tucurapo Grapefruit Juice or the many English biscuits, confectioneries and general food products handled by Essential Products Ltd on a commission basis.

It was Arthur Lamby.

"I'm sure this is telepathy," said Miss Bisnauth. "I was *just* wondering if I should give you a ring."

"Maybe," said Arthur. He was sceptical about telepathy. "You're at the office already?"

"Yes. Just got down. Something I should have broached last night and clean forgot."

"Nothing too private, I hope," said Miss Bisnauth quickly, but tried to make her tone casual and bantering, for she would have been desolated had she felt afterwards that she had said something which in content or tone of voice had proved hurtful to Miss Laballe. It was Miss Bisnauth's secret watchword: Never hurt anyone if you can help it. It was human, she felt, that Miss Laballe should want to listen-in. Feminine and human.

"I never have anything private to discuss over the phone," Arthur chuckled. "It's about that chap I was telling you about – Mortimer Barnett. The fellow who writes short stories and novellas and a poem now and then."

"Oh! The telescopic objectivity fellow. He believes we should pay far more attention than we do to inanimate objects, isn't that it? In a story we shouldn't devote our attention only to human characters but we ought to tell the stories behind dumb objects like chairs and beds and doors and so on."

"Same fellow. Well, he wants to bring out a collection of long and short stuff in booklet form – but you know the usual procedure in the West Indies. He's got to stand the printer's bill himself, so he's trying to get a few pages of advertisements to help cover the cost. I suggested he should come round to your office and try to get an ad. from you people. You do a fair amount of advertising."

"Oh, yes, I'm sure he ought to get a page from us."

"Well, when do you think it will be convenient today for him to drop in and see your manager? That's what I really rang to find out."

"Mr Waley is going to be very busy today. He's trying to get off the London mail – it's been piling up. And at any minute he might get a call and have to leave off to go and keep some appointment. But he could see Mr Murrain, the Chief Accountant – he's supposed to be assistant manager, too. Mr Murrain would give him an ad. – if he's in the mood. And I've told you how interested Mr Murrain is in books. Nothing would please him better than to have a long chat with Barnett."

"Good. Well, shall I tell him to drop in this morning?"

"Yes. He can see Mr Murrain at any time he likes." She sniggered – then regretted it. She was about to say, "He does no work at all," but decided that this would have been an uncharitable thing to voice. Instead, she said: "Mr Murrain is never as busy as Mr Waley!"

"Right. I'll tell him to come in, then."

"What is he like? Shortish, you said —"

"Yes, shortish and well-built. Square shoulders. About my light-olive in complexion. But he's got better head-grass than mine."

"I like yours just as it is." She would have added "darling" but for Miss Laballe.

He laughed. "Reserve all compliments for this evening."

"Oh, have you found out? Will you be off this evening?"

"It's beginning to look so. Anyway, I'll give you another ring about three and let you know for certain."

After she had told him about the new poem and they had exchanged a few commonplaces of a personal nature (all, however, censored of tenderness and endearments because of Miss Laballe), she returned to her desk to find that Horace stood there waiting for her, an expression of tense anxiety on his face.

Horace had decided on a desperate ruse.

"Miss Bisnauth, something I wanted to ask you."

"Yes, Xavier?"

She smiled at him as she took her seat, trying not to betray that she was conscious of her tenseness but knowing that she was not succeeding.

"Miss, this morning when I turned out to work I was passing Mrs Hinckson's desk, and I happen to see a paper wid a verse. I stop to read it – and I sure Ah know it. I see it somewhere before in de Shakespeare book I have at home, but I can't remember what play it come from. I was wondering – I say maybe you might remember."

He was changing from one foot to the other and grinding the palm of his hand into the corner of the desk.

"I know you know plenty about books and poetry, miss, dat's why I asking you."

Miss Bisnauth felt the blood coming gradually to her face. Hers was a nature which could not, at a moment's notice, adapt itself to a situation that called for a display of hypocrisy. She had imagination and therefore resourcefulness, but her resourcefulness was of the delayed kind; it could not cope with an instantaneous emergency.

She ran her fingers across the keyboard of her typewriter, making a soft, rippling tinkle-click. A biting of her lip and twitching of her brows were involved in the hesitation which preceded her too-quickly-blurted: "Yes, I did read it myself. You mean that paper in the *File* tray – it's from *As You Like It.*"

"Oh! It's from *As You Like It?* Oh, t'ank you, miss." Horace's hands were icy. "I was wondering. I like Shakespeare, you know, miss – and – and I feel I musta read dat passage in de book I got at home. Sorry to trouble you, miss."

"It's no trouble at all, Xavier."

"Every time I see a piece of poetry anywhere I always try to find out who de author —"

"Wait! Mr Jagabir is calling you. I think someone…"

He stumbled round. "Yes ! Yes, Mr Jagabir?"

Mr Jagabir was signalling him towards the barrier. "You getting deaf *and* blind, boy! You can't see a gentleman come and waiting dere to be attended to? I calling and calling you – and yet you can't neither see de gentleman standing dere or hear me calling you!"

The gentleman, who was coloured – he was sallow-complexioned and had dark, close-cut, bristly hair (more good than bad) – smiled and told Horace that he wished to see Mr. Waley. He had taken off his pince-nez and was polishing them, his manner assured and easy.

"I'm from Chelton's Amalgamated Groceries," he added in a noncommittal tone.

"Your name, sir?"

"Prentice."

As Horace hurried across and tapped on the frosted glass door of Mr Waley's sanctum it was as though he could feel a cold draught spiralling through him – up from his feet to the top of his head. It seemed to possess a quality of eternity; it would never stop; it would go on in spiral after spiral like this even after he had died.

He snapped his mind back to sanity. The situation had reached a crisis. Miss Bisnauth knew. He had noted her reactions too closely to be mistaken. How she had discovered was beyond him – but she knew, and his ruse had not fooled her. She would tell Mrs Hinckson the instant Mrs Hinckson came out into the main office.

This was disaster. He could not face Mrs Hinckson if Miss Bisnauth told her. The absurdity of his position would be too much for him. He a black boy – a cook's son; she a good-class coloured lady, the daughter of Mr Charles Barnfield, K.C. – the retired barrister-at-law who had served as Mayor of Port of Spain in his day, and also on the Legislative Council as an elected member and, for two terms, as a Government-nominated member. A sallowish man with bristly hair like the hair of this coloured gentleman come to see Mr Waley. Horace had seen him several times walking on the pitch-walk promenade around the Savannah, escorted by his widowed sister, Mrs Lafargue, for, of course, he was blind nowadays... His father and grandfathers and uncles before him had been big people, too. Racehorse owners, cocoa-planters, doctors, high Government officials.

Horace's mother had told him tales about the proud coloured families of Trinidad. She could remember, she had said, the days of her girlhood when carriages instead of cars moved on the streets; she had described the homes of the big coloured families and the grand functions they used to hold… the carriages-and-four… the very wealthy, top-rank families had these big carriages drawn by four horses, and it was a sight to see them going to the races, the ladies with large feathers in their hats and decked up in the latest fashions…

And here today he a black woman's son, a nobody with not a drop of white blood in him, was saying that he was in love with a daughter of the Barnfields. He had written out a passage from Shakespeare on a piece of paper addressed to her – "my beloved"!…

No, it would be too much for his pride. He was only black but he had pride. He would prefer to die on the spot than continue to face her knowing that she was secretly laughing at him. He would have to throw up his job this very morning.

When Mr Waley said "Come in!" in his clipped but good-humoured voice (when he was extremely harrowed it could be clipped and irritable) Horace pushed in the door. He felt the draught inside him congeal into a pillar of ice as he announced: "Mr Prentice from Chelton's Amalgamated to see you, sir."

Mr Waley took a deep breath and looked across at Mrs Hinckson, who had just finished taking down his last sentence.

Horace saw her as in a haze. The scene might have been a mirage. It would melt in a moment, but the deep burning in him would continue for ever.

Mr Waley pulled his face as long as it would go in a droll way he had. "The first interruption. When did you predict it would come, Mrs Hinckson? Ten o'clock, you said?"

"Ten-fifteen." She smiled. She glanced at her wristwatch. "Twenty past nine. I'm nearly an hour out."

"Anyway, it's important. Must see him. It's about the ships' stores. He did mention yesterday he'd drop round."

As she prepared to rise: "No, you can remain. Nothing confidential. Xavier, show Mr Prentice in."

Mr Jagabir shook his head deprecatingly as he returned from the barrier after having hastened across to tell Mr Prentice to have a seat. He stopped by Miss Henery's desk and murmured: "You see dat, miss! Dat boy couldn't even have de courtesy to offer de gentleman a seat. And it's Mr Prentice, one of de directors of Chelton's Amalgamated! Man own t'ousands of dollars in property and got his name in every company in dis city – and look at de way Xavier treat him. Dat boy got too much on his mind what he shouldn't got."

With a furtive glance towards Mrs Hinckson's desk, he added: "You remember de paper Ah was telling you of, miss? De paper wid de love verse in Mrs Hinckson's letter-tray? It's Xavier write it and put it dere."

"What?"

Miss Henery, who had ignored him up to now, turned her head sharply.

"Yes, miss. It's he who do it."

"Xavier wrote it and put it there? How do you know that?"

He smiled. "I know, miss. He fancy nobody see him, but I watch him good when he put it dere dis morning. I always come in early in de morning – and plenty things I see in dis office what people fancy I don't see."

Miss Henery gave a dry, significant laugh, but Mr Jagabir, pretending not to notice the purport in it, glanced round at Horace who was returning to tell Mr Prentice that Mr Waley would see him.

"Lil' half-penny black boy like dat to mek out he in love wid a big-family lady like Mrs Hinckson. He properly rude."

Miss Henery made no comment. Mr Jagabir's news did not impress her very much. She had serious doubts as to its authenticity. He was such a liar and dissembler that everything he told you had to be treated with reserve until it could be endorsed or denied by someone more reliable.

She went on with her work, ignoring him, and Mr Jagabir

began to feel foolish standing there by her. To justify his presence and save his face he said: "By de way, miss, I wanted to mention it. You made a lil' mistake wid de account for Burke's Grocery last week. They sent it back and Ah had to correct it and post it back to dem."

"What mistake was that?"

"You type down nine hundred and forty-three dollars instead of seven hundred and forty-three."

"I'm sure that's not my fault. It's probably yours." She pulled out a drawer and brought out a batch of accounts done in handwriting in the rough by Mr Jagabir. She flicked through them and then paused, and put her finger on a total at the bottom of a page.

"Look. There you are. Just as I thought. What do you call that? A seven or a nine?"

"Dat's a seven, miss."

Miss Henery uttered a sigh of exasperation. "Mr Jagabir, I'm getting tired of this thing. You're always making your sevens like nines – and vice versa. You expect me to be for ever trying to decipher your figures?"

"But, miss, Ah tell you you must always ask me if you in doubt about any figure I write down."

"Oh, so you think I'm going to call you every time I want to discover whether you've written a nine for a seven or a seven for a nine? Well, I'll be calling you every two minutes of the day, at that rate. I'll never get any work done at all."

Fear rose in Mr Jagabir. He saw Mr Murrain reporting it to Mr Waley that his handwriting was illegible, and, as a result, the typist could not make out the figures he wrote. It was causing much inconvenience and annoyance. Several firms were beginning to complain. Mr Waley reported the matter to Mr Holmes, the Manager of the Tucurapo estate, and Mr Holmes came to town for a conference... This coolie, Jagabir, was no good, after all. He was growing grossly inefficient. They would have to get rid of him... Well, in view of his past services, perhaps, it would be better to send him back to the estate to some field job instead of dismissing him right off.

"It's all right, miss. I didn't mean no harm." He began to

massage his wrist, his brows creased. "I'll try and see if I can make me figures a lil' plainer in future."

As he made a tentative move to return to his desk: "Oh, and Ah just remember! About your two weeks' leave dis month" – he bent towards her, his voice a throaty whisper – "Ah would advise you to go now and ask Mr Murrain to fix it up. He seem as if he in a good mood."

After he had glided back to his desk she smiled, thinking what an officious coolie he was. How had he come to know that she was asking for two weeks' leave this month? There seemed nothing in the office that could be hidden from him.

Anyway, it was a good thing he had mentioned it, because it just occurred to her that he might be right. This very moment seemed the opportune one to bring it up again with Mr Murrain. The cricket conversation he had with Mr Lorry and Mr Lopez had left him in an exceptionally cheerful humour. He was smoking one of his Gold Flakes, and as a rule he smoked Anchor, the local brand.

It was Mr Jagabir who had informed the office that Mr Murrain smoked Anchor in the office and Gold Flakes at cocktail parties and at home; how he had discovered this no one knew, but observation had seemed to confirm it to a certain extent. Mr Murrain brought to work a tin of Gold Flakes, but it was only when something pleased him that he took the tin from a drawer to smoke one of its contents; at all other times he selected an Anchor from the open case which always rested on his desk near the inkwell.

The dress she was wearing, too, thought Miss Henery, boosted her figure considerably – more so than did any of her other work dresses – and that factor ought to prove helpful. For all she knew, it was that which had made him so self-conscious and jittery when she had come in; the material was thin, and the areolae of her breasts were vaguely, tantalizingly visible. No wonder he had had to go asking her about his fountain-pen when he knew very well he had not misplaced it.

Suddenly, however, she felt impatient. Why should she have to go using her wiles on him and taking advantage of his mood to get her leave? She was entitled to two weeks every year, wasn't she? And she had already broached the subject with him. It was his place now to give her an answer. Perhaps he was purposely keeping her waiting. These white people were so mean and nasty sometimes – especially the English. She recalled the case of Mr Reynolds. About two years ago Mr Reynolds was getting ten cents commission on every case of grapefruit juice; he pushed the sales up to such a peak that he was soon earning an income almost equal to Mr Murrain's salary. Mr Murrain kept sniffing and raising his brows, eventually called Mr Waley's attention to the fact; no one in the main office knew exactly what he said to Mr Waley, but Mr Waley abruptly announced to Mr Reynolds that the company could not see its way to let him have a commission of more than four cents per case in future.

She fidgeted.

A dirty lot of people. And who was Murrain at all! For all she knew, she had much better class than he. Most of these English people who came out to the colonies were of the dregs. But the instant they arrived they turned gods. Who knew if Murrain had not been dragged up in some London slum? His white skin was all that made him somebody in Trinidad. Her parents and grandparents were ladies and gentlemen...

A feeling of pettiness swept her. Her attitude suddenly struck her as small, mean. Could it be a sense of inferiority that made her think such things? A subconscious envy?

She drummed with her fingers for an instant on the side of the machine, her brows knitted. Then she straightened up, pushed out her chest, a look of decision on her face. There was a letter in her tray for his signature – one of the rare ones he dictated; a letter of three-and-a-half lines.

She went over to his desk and placed the letter on the A-D ledger which, shortly before the cricket conference, he had been pretending to look through but which he had now put aside in favour of the price-list again.

"This is the letter for Grantley's, Mr Murrain. And I've just remembered something. Have you asked Mr Waley yet about my two weeks' leave?"

The office was not always accurate in its assessment of Mr Murrain's moods, for the office (save for Mr Waley) did not yet fully understand his English temperament. Mr Murrain might appear in a good mood, and this outward aspect might well be a reflection of the inner. But there were occasions when he was depressed or irritated yet concealed these feelings under such a convincing display of affability and good humour that the spectator was completely deceived.

Middle-class West Indians brought up in the Victorian and Edwardian schools of restraint and genteel hypocrisy (Miss Henery was one of these, and her parents were more Victorian than Edwardian) can also successfully disguise their real emotions under a mask of good cheer. But even the technique of such West Indians could not equal that of Mr Murrain, whose English county background had forged invisible steel strands and ball-bearings for the easy manipulation of his facial expression and the functioning of his vocal cords to produce laughter and cheerful tonal effects of speech under adverse conditions.

Even the cigarette test the office had not fully grasped. First, it was untrue that he smoked Gold Flakes only at cocktail parties and when at home. The fact was that he had sentimental idiosyncrasies. For more than ten years Gold Flakes had been his favourite brand, and in Trinidad, where they were now scarce because of postwar conditions, he reserved them for special moments; their flavour evoked nostalgic memories of the Old Country. These special moments covered occasions when he happened to be in an extremely optimistic or sunny mood. But what the office had failed to discover was that when irritated he also resorted to Gold Flakes, for at such times he felt that an Anchor was inadequate; the Anchor was a Trinidadian cigarette; only an Old Country cigarette could soothe him.

Despite his appearance now of being in the best of moods, and despite his show of bonhomie during the cricket chat with Mr Lorry and Mr Lopez, he was in an exceptionally savage mood – a mood for which his wife was responsible.

He had hardly been in the office twenty minutes when Mrs Murrain had phoned to tell him that he had forgotten to sign the savings-bank withdrawal slip which he had made out for thirty-two dollars.

"Oh, I dare say it must have slipped me," he had replied, but he knew – and he knew that she knew – that it had been no lapse of memory.

His savings-bank account at Barclays Bank he regarded as his one rock of stability in a sick and uncertain world. In moments of depression it gave him courage to go on, for one day he hoped that it would be big enough to enable him to go back to England and retire for the rest of his life in a cottage in some quiet part of Surrey, where he would devote his time exclusively to reading and the study of plant and insect life; he had a vague hope that one day in this peaceful future he would write and publish a book on some botanical or entomological subject: perhaps even a novel.

For the present, his life consisted of building up, month by month, this savings account, and at the same time defending it against the depredations of his wife.

Cocktail parties took money. Mrs Murrain, who was very socially ambitious, insisted on their holding a cocktail party at least twice a month. Normally his salary could stand this, and without affecting his savings; but at the end of last month they had bought a new refrigerator on the hire-purchase basis and the down payment had been heavy. So heavy that he had advised strongly against any cocktail parties this month.

Caroline, though reluctantly, had agreed that he was right, but last night on their way home from the Country Club she had insisted that something would have to be done about a party for Eugene de Bergere. Eugene was leaving next week for San Fernando, in the south of the island, where he was going into a job with one of the oil companies, and everybody who mattered in Port of Spain was throwing a cocktail party in his honour (after all, he had served the Old Country nobly)... "Nonsense, my dear! They're not throwing parties in his honour. It's only a pretext for showing off and having a spree."

But long before morning Caroline had wheedled him into agreeing to withdraw thirty-two dollars from his savings account – which amount was what had come to be considered the "dire minimum" on which a cocktail party could be arranged, but his acquiescence had been characterized by heavy frowns.

This morning he had resorted to an old ruse. He had made out the withdrawal slip but omitted his signature, then rushed out of the house before any questions could be asked or the discovery made that the slip was not negotiable. It was a dirty trick, and he had felt guilty all the way to work, but he had settled it with his conscience by assuring himself that Caroline was irresponsible and must be tricked as one would trick a child – for its good.

The effectiveness of this ruse lay in that Caroline was very sensitive to rebuffs, and when she saw that he had omitted his signature she would know (from past experience) that the omission was deliberate; this would get her into a huff and she would never again mention a word concerning the party. It would mean a day or two of coldness, but Mr Murrain felt that the protection of his savings account must at times involve some inconvenience and unpleasantness.

This time the ruse had failed. Caroline had refused to get into a huff. Without the slightest trace of aggrievement – in a sweet, innocent voice – she had called him up to say that he had forgotten to sign the slip and that she would drop in at the office around half past ten for him to do it. She had to do some shopping, she said, so it would be no trouble at all for her.

Absorbed in bitter reflections, his head bent as he toyed with a leaf of the price-list, Mr Murrain had failed to hear Miss Henery's steps approaching his desk. Her voice came as such a shock that the mechanism of his hypocrisy suffered a jar. He started and scowled. But in a fifth of a second a smile had taken the place of the scowl. He asked her what she had said – and she repeated it.

"Oh, yes, yes! Your leave. The truth is I haven't had an opportunity to discuss the matter with Mr Waley."

He pushed away his cigarette-case, pulled it towards him, shifted in his chair.

Miss Henery, fully aware that there was no necessity for him to see Mr Waley, nodded. Her poise remained perfect. "And may I ask when you think you'll be able to find the opportunity?"

As a rule, Mr Murrain was impervious to delicate sarcasm, but in his present mood his sensitivity was unusually acute. His mobile chin joined in the general pattern of his fidgetings. A slight smile passed across his face. It was an acid smile, for Miss Henery suddenly awakened in him a deep resentment. Resentment and frustration. This girl attracted him, but his chances of possessing her seemed so blankly remote that even to contemplate it brought on a trembling of distraction.

He lost his balance for the moment. He thought: a mere olive-skinned native (he employed the word in its racially discriminative – not in its indigenous sense) arousing an urge like this in me – and not content with that, actually having the impertinence to address sarcastic remarks to me!

"Miss Henery, I don't think there is any necessity to be quite so importunate. Please remember it's only a favour the firm grants you in allowing you two weeks' leave."

Miss Henery's reaction was as though, somewhere inside her, an ignition-pin had struck a cordite charge. The blood exploded into her face. "A favour! Really! You must know very little about the law of this island, Mr Murrain. I can assure you it's no favour. I'm entitled to two weeks' leave every year – legally entitled to it."

Mr Murrain realized that she was right. He had spoken without thought and out of sheer agitation. His error, instead of humbling him, infuriated him. Very white, he said: "But, Miss Henery – really, sometimes I wonder if you forget that to your ancestors such a luxury as leave was entirely unheard of."

"Which of my ancestors? Some were white. Could you be referring by any chance to the English ones who were made slaves from childhood in the factories of your nineteenth-century industrial England?"

If a dog attacks you in the street you automatically aim a kick at it which may or may not land home; if it does the dog runs off yelping, and your immediate feeling is one of satisfaction. But gradually this satisfaction turns into remorse and compassion; it was only a dumb creature, after all.

This was how Miss Henery felt as she settled down at her desk. She could sense the eyes of the office on her. Neither she nor Mr Murrain had raised their voices, and what they had said had probably gone unheard (except by Mr Jagabir whose hearing, from long practice, had grown preternaturally acute), but the rest of the staff must have known from their attitudes and the inflection of their voices that battle was in progress.

She knew that if she glanced up and caught Miss Yen Tip's eyes Miss Yen Tip would smile and wink in congratulation of her victory (the office never had any doubt as to who would emerge the victor in a verbal conflict between Miss Henery and Mr Murrain). But she did not want congratulation.

Mr Murrain sat very still, his face pale. His chin moved from side to side as he regarded his left forearm. He was experiencing the trapped-in-the-skin shudders. Outwardly they were not visible; he knew that, because even Caroline, who was familiar with most of his oddities, could never tell when he was suffering an attack.

His fingers felt icy – and the scar on his forearm tingled.

It was on the scar that his gaze was fixed. It stood out palely against the pink of his skin, running diagonally across just above his wrist where the arm began to thicken. As a rule, it was pink, so that his skin appeared white in contrast – but now it tingled and was pale.

It was about three inches long, and in width varied considerably, for it was ragged all along its length – like the map of an island with a much indented sea-coast...

"... and for God's sake, Murrain, keep these fellows here. Understand? Don't let them stray off on their own. We all want to get across, but we won't do it if we're going to scatter in odd groups searching for bits of flotsam. Hey, you there! Pull yourself together! No sleeping. Murrain, that's another thing. See they don't sleep."

"Yes, sir. I'll do my best."

"I won't be gone a minute. If you see anything of Major Towne tell him to switch his lot over that way – by Harrow's outfit. God! Look at that! There's a fellow potting at them with his rifle. Guts, some of these chaps, by heck!"

There was a rent in the Colonel's tunic from the shoulder to the side so that you could see the shape of his scapula. The soiled khaki flapped away so that a triangle of grey shirt showed underneath; it was the grey shirt that outlined his scapula so clearly.

Everard Murrain watched him plod up the embankment, noting the motion of the scapula. He was a man of medium height, Colonel Dollard, slim and muscular, with a high nose that had always reminded Everard of the actor Aubrey Smith.

The men had nicknamed his ragged, yellow moustache 'Dolly's Hair'.

Before he had got to the top of the embankment Everard saw him stiffen. Then he was rolling down, causing a minor avalanche of sand in his wake. You saw a red patch of sand – then the avalanche blotted it out.

The platoon let out a "Jesus!" and a "Christ!" and a few obscenities, but one or two of the men simply whimpered and averted their faces. One fellow buried his face in a boot. He had had to take off the boot because of an injury to his foot.

Most of them lay on their backs staring up at the sky where the crackle and buzzing went on unabated. They were seeing the sky but not noticing it. They had stopped cursing the sky. Only two things they thought of now – the shipping in the Channel and sleep.

The Channel was visible; a mere two or three hundred yards off the waves lapped. But so much was going on, and going on all at once, in the Channel that you feared to make guesses about anything. You were afraid to hope.

Every now and then somebody stopped and gave you orders about staying in this or that spot.

Or waiting…

Not too much hurry there, you!…

Not too much crowding together. . .

Stop there! Where the ruddy hell are *you* off to? Think the whole blasted Navy is at your service?…

And obscenities…

Sometimes you heard the Navy was in as bad a mess. But you didn't bother. Thoughts wouldn't come as they should. Sleep warped everything that entered your mind. Sleep wrestled with you like that picture you remembered seeing as a youngster… Hercules wrestling with Death for the soul of Alcestis.

It mustn't win, of course, because you were a subaltern and had to set an example to the men.

If you told them not to sleep you had to keep awake to show them your mettle, by gad!

You laughed at yourself for your old-fashioned chivalry. Hell! "Come! Lift him, Wayne. Grimmet. Give us a hand here!"

Nobody moved.

You spoke in a sharper tone this time.

Wayne and Grimmet came – tottering with sleep…

"It ain't no use, sir," Grimmet told you a minute later. "'E's dead."

"Who's dead?"

"Dolly's dead."

It went round like a dirge in a big cave. A big cave going darker and darker because it was sleep closing over you… Shake yourself!

A whine from Earne. Welshman. Short with sandy hair and grey-green eyes. Had a way of mumbling whenever he was on the point of getting to his feet. As though the action – rather than the effort – of standing was the one bane of his life. He was never lazy on the march or when he was in a fatigue party. A good worker. But he grumbled every time he had to stand up.

Now he was whining, a hand pressed to his stomach, the sand under him getting red.

The earth shook with a dull clump!

The old routine. Flop flat.

Everard had just risen when he heard somebody say: "Murry's hit!"

Out of the corner of his eye he caught a glimpse of something red – but that would be the Colonel's spittle and blood which had made a streak from the pip on his shoulder down to the upper part of his sleeve.

Grimmet called: "Your arm, sir! Look!"

Everard looked down and saw that his left forearm was soaked with blood. His own blood.

He felt no pain at all.

When Mr Waley had told Mrs Hinckson that she could remain Horace had felt an immense relief. It postponed the issue and allowed him an interval in which to think out a plan of action. If she had left the Manager's sanctum and returned to the main office she would, almost for a certainty, have discovered the paper in her *File* tray. At this very instant she would have been reading it. She would have begun inquiries, and Miss Bisnauth would have told her what she suspected.

But how had Miss Bisnauth come to suspect him of being the author?

She must have read it, of course, in clearing the tray. That must have happened when he was at the control board. But the block letters should have concealed the identity of the author. Yet when he had glanced at her she had met his gaze and smiled in a definitely knowing way.

And to confirm it, when he had tried that ruse, she had betrayed all the signs of being aware that he was dissembling, that it was really he who had written the love verse and was trying to cover it up. Could it be that she had made a blind guess and hit on him?

He wondered.

Maybe she would not tell Mrs Hinckson, though...

Miss Bisnauth was a nice young lady. He could approach her far more easily than he could any of the other ladies – or gentlemen, for that matter. Why, he could not explain. Could it be, he asked himself, because she was a coolie?

He fidgeted. He should be doing his shorthand exercise. He had no right to be letting himself think all these thoughts. They would get him nowhere. Time was going.

He willed himself to forget his problems. He succeeded and resumed work on the unfinished exercise. Even the sound of Miss Henery's voice, subdued but sharp-pitched and evidently rebuking somebody for something, only caused him to glance up briefly. Within a few minutes he had completed the exercise and started on the next.

But when Miss Bisnauth rose and went over to Mrs Hinckson's desk he stiffened. The chilly draught began to spiral up inside him.

Miss Bisnauth, however, merely put something in the *Outgoing* tray and went back to her desk.

Mr Benson was calling him.

Without annoyance or irritation he rose. His sense of duty overcame all other considerations. He must never let anything stand in the way of his work. It would be a terrible disappointment to his mother if he proved a failure. He had a vision of his mother, grey-haired and wrinkled, sitting among an audience of two thousand in the Princes Building, a smile of reverence on her face. His Worship the Mayor, Mr H. Xavier, was speaking on an important occasion... Yes, he would be Mayor one day. Colour and class were no barriers to political success in Trinidad. The present Mayor of Port of Spain was a negro – and last year another negro had been Mayor.

The Chief Clerk handed him two long, fat official envelopes and told him to take them to the Chief Accountant of the Royal Bank of Canada and wait for an answer.

The door of the Manager's sanctum opened and Mrs Hinckson entered the main office.

Mr Waley's interview with Mr Prentice was lasting longer than had been anticipated, and Mrs Hinckson had decided to occupy herself in getting a few short letters typed – letters which she had taken down in shorthand the day before but had not yet had a chance to transcribe.

Unaware that Horace, standing at his desk fumbling with the two official envelopes Mr Benson had given to him to take to the bank, was watching her covertly and with anxiety, she settled herself before her typewriter and propped her notebook up beside the machine. Her movements were ordered and deliberate, easy and leisurely.

Pulling out a drawer to her right, she selected her stationery. She jerked her head back slightly to adjust the mass of dark, shifty hair that dangled as far as her shoulders (she did not believe in elaborate hair modes). She patted her cheeks slowly and lingeringly. It was subconsciously to reassure herself of freedom from wrinkles. She had a smooth skin and a pale olive complexion upon which her twenty-nine years had left no blemishes; the one or two tiny freckles, if anything, enhanced her looks. A lover had once called them "dusty beauty spots". Her nose was straight, and of the exact length and width to go with her wide face and rather high cheekbones, and with her deep-set grey-brown eyes.

She began to type with precision and rapidity, but had hardly done two lines when she found it necessary to pause and glance up.

"Want me, Mr Jagabir?"

Mr Jagabir's smile was tentative, diffident. With Miss Henery his nervousness was inspired by fear alone, but with Mrs Hinckson it sprang from awe and veneration as well.

"Ah come to trouble you, miss. You can spare me some o' your blue ink?"

"Certainly. Go ahead."

She stretched out and opened the carton containing the bottle of ink which stood near the *Outgoing* tray. She detested him no less than any of the others did – but she never showed it openly.

"You seem fond of blue ink, Mr Jagabir."

"Yes, miss. I always prefer blue ink to blue-black. De bottle on my desk gone dry and I didn' remember to get Xavier to buy another one." (The bottle on his desk was two-thirds full.)

She was examining her notes.

"When Ah come in dis morning I fill me pen, but it not drawing too good. It didn' take in enough, it seem."

"Oh, I see."

"Ah fill it at de desk here from your ink. I know you wouldn't mind."

"Not at all. It's quite all right."

She knew that all this was only a performance, that he had another object besides filling his pen, but she resumed her typing as though she accepted it as perfectly natural that he should come to her for blue ink. Within a moment the object would become clear; she had no need to worry.

Horace, still standing at his desk – he kept rummaging aimlessly in his desk drawer – watched them. The pulsing of his heart had become a single powerful action that commenced at the crown of his head and ended at his toes. He felt himself wanting to sway forward and backward to its rhythm.

"Mr Waley busy dis morning, na, miss?" said Mr Jagabir.

He was corking the bottle.

"Miss, you see de paper?"

The vaguest wince betrayed her irritation. She shook her head, smiling automatically. "No, I'm afraid I haven't yet. Haven't had a chance. Any interesting news?"

"Oh! No, miss, Ah didn't mean de newspaper. Ah was referring to dat paper in de tray dere. I happen to notice it dis morning when Ah was filling me pen. It look like if somebody write you a love verse."

"A what?"

She stopped typing to glance at the tray he indicated. "A verse from Shakespeare, miss."

She frowned and took the paper from the tray.

Horace left in a hurry…

The blood gradually crept into her face as she read. Her lips twisted to one side in a smile of uncertainty. Then she put the paper in the tray again without comment.

Mr Jagabir, who had discovered that his pen needed some adjustments, lingered, seemingly engrossed in these adjustments.

"Miss, you would never guess who write dat and put it dere," he remarked.

Without a smile now, her tone bland but of a blandness that chilled Mr Jagabir, who was familiar with it, she said: "Have you got all the ink you want now, Mr Jagabir?"

"Oh, yes, yes, miss! T'ank you!"

He hurried off, mumbling: "Dis pen giving me a lot of trouble."

Mrs Hinckson went on typing, but she was biting her lower lip now.

Mr Jagabir did not have to tell her who had written the love verse. She had known at once that it was Horace. It flattered her, amused her, called forth some pity – then depressed her.

She had not failed to notice the change in the boy's manner towards her during the past three or four weeks. A diffidence and self-consciousness had come into his attitude when in her presence; he was shy of meeting her gaze, and stammered when he addressed her. All the signs of infatuation had been plain for her to note. She knew, too, that he was fond of reading Shakespeare, for she had more than once seen the battered *Complete Works* lying open on his desk.

Same old story, she told herself. The intellectual ones, the artistic ones – they always fell for her. Her husband had been one.

She had admired Ralph and had been fond of him, but she had never loved him. An electrical engineer employed by the Trinidad Electricity Board from the time he left school at nineteen to his death at thirty-four, he had spent most of his spare time with books and boy scouts. Ralph had never been an enthusiastic sexual partner. He had believed in rigid control. His rule was "twice a week and no more. That's Martin Luther's rule, my dear – and personally I think it's a splendid rule."

She had not made a fuss – nor attempted to go after other men for complete satisfaction; she had accepted his and Martin Luther's ruling. But the yearning for a man who was a man had always remained in her. She lacked the libido of a nymphomaniac, but she had a strong sensual streak, and she would have liked a man who could have made love to her with a wild and unrestrained recklessness.

A lover had told her that she gave off personal rather than animal magnetism; he was a student of Yoga. Often she thought he must be right, for she had met the kind of men who appealed strongly to her – but they had never responded. They would be friendly towards her in a brotherly fashion – even be shyish and infatuated in a worshipful way – but would never try to make a pass at her. It was as though they feared to desecrate an unseen barrier.

It was always the artists and intellectuals with whom she had to be satisfied. Since her husband's death nearly two years ago – he had died of tetanus resulting from a cut toe, after a hike with his troop – she had had lovers, and each, in turn, had wanted to marry her. But she had turned them down, for she had realized that it would be a repetition of her first marriage; the details would have differed, but the general pattern would have been the same. For they had all been intellectuals. Dull ones.

Were there no intellectuals and artists who could at the same time be masculine men? Unthinking, hot-blooded lovers?

Horace. The office-boy. Apart from his age, his social position and the fact that he was black made him an impossible candidate. But he was a human being – a male human being. He represented another Instance. He was the intellectual type. The serious, plodding, ambitious kind who studied at night and who had "noble" ideals. She admired and respected such men because, ironically, she herself was an intellectual. She liked books, she liked to discuss philosophy and politics and all serious subjects. She liked to think that her life was governed by her reason rather than by her emotions.

Yet she could not fall in love with men fashioned this way. She took up the paper again and re-read the verse, trying to think what play Horace could have taken it from. "Nanette" obviously had been substituted for the actual name in the play.

She returned the paper to the tray.

It was a long time since she had read any Shakespeare. Not since schooldays, and she had left school ten years ago.

She had learnt shorthand and typewriting during the early days of her married life. It was a means of relieving her boredom. And the thought had struck her that she might find office work congenial. Contacts with other people in the course of commercial affairs might help to counteract the heavy stagnancy of spirit which had fast been settling upon her as a result of Ralph's ordered, unimaginative existence, and the burden of being a wife to him.

Six months after Dudley was born she secured her position as chief stenographer with Essential Products – a job which, eventually, evolved into a secretaryship to the Manager as well. Dudley was left during the day to the care of his Aunt Mildred – Mrs Renwick – a younger sister of her father's.

Securing her job with Essential Products had been a matter of great ease, because the Barnfields were reckoned as among the ten best families in Trinidad, and their influence in all circles, social and business and professional, was extensive.

Some of them mixed with the whites socially, and were accepted into the Country Club. They were not only upper middle-class, but Upper Class.

Doctor Hilary Barnfield was consulting medico to several insurance companies as well as to the executive and overseer staffs of the Tucurapo company.

Mr James Barnfield, O.B.E., was a chairman on several boards of directors and a retired solicitor whose practice had encompassed a wide clientele among the elite; he owned three racehorses, and was a popular turfite.

Mr Justice Edwy Barnfield had once acted as Chief Justice for Trinidad, and had been associated with a number of *causes célèbres*.

These were her uncles.

Her own father was King's Counsel whose name was known throughout the British West Indies not only for his forensic successes but for the part he had played in Trinidadian – and, often, in British West Indian – politics. He had been a delegate on more than one commission to the Crown Office. Even the fact that he was blind now did not detract from his old world charm. He was still a highly respected figure of the community, and his name still carried considerable weight. He was no less adept at pulling strings than he had been seven years ago when his sight began to fail.

No, there had been no trouble at all in securing this job. She had not had to apply. Her father had simply got in touch with one of his friends, and within a week everything had been settled.

She heard male laughter.

Mr Waley and Mr Prentice.

Mr Prentice, though coloured, was accepted in the white upper class; he and Mr Waley treated each other as equals. Like her father and her uncles and aunts, Mr Prentice came of a good coloured family; not as distinguished, it was true, but a family of means for the past two generations, at least; the Prentices were the merchant rather than the professional type.

"Mrs Hinckson, I'm afraid you're going to swear at me again. I've got to run out with Mr Prentice. Going down to the wharf to inspect some cases. I don't think I'll be very long, though."

"Very well, Mr Waley."

Mr Prentice smiled at her and murmured: "Righto, Nanette!"

"Righto, Ted!"

Nothing unusual in Mr Waley's going out. She had half

anticipated it. No doubt, he would come in in an hour's time and settle down to dictation, only to discover that he had to run out again to keep another appointment.

Miss Bisnauth came and placed a batch of minutes in the *Incoming* tray. She smiled: "He's run out on you again, eh, Nanette?"

"Yes, my dear."

They discussed details relating to the minutes for a short while.

Miss Bisnauth had that slightly detached air which meant that her mind was more on a poem than on her office work. Mrs Hinckson thought her a sweet creature – so fresh and unspoilt – and admired her for her creative talents. Nearly every Sunday she published a poem in the newspaper. Mrs Hinckson could not bring herself to be impatient with her for being less attentive to her office work when the muse was in operation. She smiled and said: "I can see your mind is not here. You're writing another poem?"

"How did you guess?"

"I can always tell from the look on your face."

"Yes, I just got an idea for a new one."

"Don't forget to let me see it when you've finished it."

"Oh, you can be sure I won't."

A moment later Miss Bisnauth returned to her desk.

She had made no reference to Horace's love verse. It was not that she had not thought of doing so, but she was sensitive about it. True, Mrs Hinckson had remarked now and then on the boy's infatuation, but still, felt Miss Bisnauth, it would be officiousness on her part to allude to the love verse. Had Mrs Hinckson broached the subject Miss Bisnauth would readily have discussed it.

Mrs Hinckson was on the point of resuming her typing when her eyes fell on the brown phial in the *File* tray.

She stretched out and took it up.

She had seen it in the tray since settling down to work, but it had not impressed itself on her attention until now. Her mind must have consigned it to the limbo of unnoticed objects. She was well accustomed to seeing some bottle or carton on her desk – a sample of this or that confectionery or this or that jam or biscuit.

107

Vitamin B tablets.

This could only be Mr Lorry's doing. Yesterday she had remarked to him that she was overworking and inclined to suffer from nervous exhaustion, and he had suggested that she should take Vitamin B tablets. He said he knew of a good brand at the drugstore near where he lived.

It would not be the first time he had done this sort of thing. He was one of her admirers – one whom she was uncertain whether to encourage or discourage. Unlike Horace, he had no lofty ideals; his one aim was to go to bed with her.

On every possible occasion he complimented her on her charms or invited her to dine with him or to go for a drive with him; his elder brother's car was at his disposal every evening. He left casual gifts for her on her desk – a packet of Craven A cigarettes, a novel, a tin of butter when the butter shortage was acute.

He never delivered these gifts in person. She always found them on her desk, and when she challenged him he would shrug and pretend to be unaware of what she was talking, though with that solemn twinkle which made her know (for he intended her to know) that he was the donor.

He represented an instance of inconsistency. In his case, the rule of sex attraction – as she had conceived it as applying to herself – did not function. Twenty-two and light-brown, with wavy hair (definitely good), he was the masculine type. Yet he repelled rather than attracted her. Further, if she were to judge from past experience – and her Rule had been built up on past experience – no masculine man ought to have responded to her charms.

Yet, Mr Lorry was attracted to her.

It confused her when she tried to think it out, so she had decided that it must be another illustration that nothing on earth could follow a set pattern. You formed a rule about some process or phenomenon – then nature produced a glaring exception which refuted all the seemingly fool-proof conclusions you had carefully worked out and arrived at.

Something new occurred to her. The phial and the paper had been together in the tray. Now, surely… But Pat Lorry was not the bookish kind. It was true he was well educated – he was an old boy of Queen's Royal College – but literature was not his love. Though wait! It was he who opened the office every morning (she was not aware that Mr Murrain had assigned the opening of the office to Horace from this morning). It would have been a simple matter for him to have put this paper and the phial in her tray when he came in, if it was he who had...

She glanced round and called: "Mr Lorry! Just a minute!" He came over, sauntering in his easy, leisurely way, his muscular five-foot-nine body animated with an athletic grace so that though his movements were not rapid his muscles seemed to throb and ripple alertly over his large, strong bones.

He was certainly an exciting man, and many times she had thought seriously of letting him have his way with her. But a remote intuition always warned her that afterwards she would be disgusted; she would despise herself.

He gave a slight bow of mock courtesy.

"At your service, madam!"

She held up the phial.

"I take it you must know something about this."

He examined it with the air of a druggist.

"Vitamin B, eh? Splendid thing for nervous exhaustion. This is what I was recommending to you yesterday. Glad you followed my advice."

"How much did they cost? I insist on paying for them."

"But why such a tone? You're behaving as if I'm preventing you from paying your bills."

"What's the price, please?"

"That's a delicate question. I can answer it in several ways."

She stared at him – then lowered her gaze and bit her lip.

She could feel the maleness of him engulfing her. There was a breathlessness in her.

"Look here, let's stop hedging," she said in a quick stammer. "There's something – another matter I wanted to ask you about. I take it you read Shakespeare?"

He assumed a perplexed expression. "Who is that now? You don't mean the Stratford-on-Avon fellow?"

"The very one."

"I believe I have a book of his plays at home."

She handed him the paper from the *File* tray.

"Read this."

He read it. "Not so bad at all." He scratched his head. "I think I know this passage. It's from *As You Like It.*"

She pretended to be interested in her notes.

He placed the paper beside her notebook. "It should have been Rosalind, but I agree with whoever it was altered the name to Nanette."

"For your age, you're a little naïve sometimes."

"I've always been an innocent boy. It's only since I came to work here that you've corrupted me."

"You probably mean it the other way about. Did you write this thing?"

"Me? I'm not a poet. Thanks for the compliment, all the same."

"Stop quibbling and come out with it."

"Well, now you mention it, I feel I must have copied out something like this last night before going to bed. I was thinking about you all last night."

"Don't you think you're too grown-up for this sort of thing? There it was; I could have sworn it was Xavier."

"Oh, Xavier is in love with you, too?"

"All right, Pat. Go back and do your work."

"I can't do it properly until I know something first."

"What's that?"

"You'll dine with me tonight at the Kimling?"

"No."

"All right. Won't try to force you. But you're only postponing the issue. Look at this lovely, lovely hair!"

He went off sighing ecstatically.

Horace was in a ferment. He knew now, for a certainty, that Mrs Hinckson had seen the love verse. He called himself a coward. Why couldn't he have remained to see what her reactions would be? Why did he have to dash away the instant she had stretched out and taken up the paper?

Returned from the bank, he leant up the bicycle and locked it, but when he turned and saw the office stairs rising beyond the doorway he could not go up at once. He felt an old fear menacing him. A fear that derived from an incident in his boyhood.

One Saturday morning, his mother told him to go and search about the grounds of the de Germain residence for a hen which, she said, had fallen into the habit of laying all over the place; it refused to go into the coops.

Horace went off, glad to be free to roam between the trunks of the tall mahogany and *poui* trees and the clumps of hibiscus and crotons. His mother did not know – she would have disapproved strongly – but he had brought his sling-shot in case he should spot any birds.

It was a lovely morning, and the air was filled with the musky scent of tree-blossoms and dry leaves. On the ground the shadows lay shifty and dappled, and the hills, in the distance, looked smoky-blue in the sunshine.

On the outskirts of the ground, he peered through the slats of the wooden fence and saw two olive-complexioned boys at play on the adjoining premises. They were the sons of a well-to-do, good-class coloured gentleman who lived in the big house he could see between the trees some way off. They were boys of his own age and knew him by sight, as he knew them, but never spoke to him or asked him over to play, for, of course, he was black – and a cook's son.

He was surprised when one of them called: "Hey, boy! Lend me your sling-shot. A bird up in the tree here!"

A pebble already in his sling-shot, set for action, Horace hesitated. He would have liked to take a shot at the bird himself. He called back: "Where de bird? Show me, lemme shoot it!"

"You can't get it from there! Lend me your sling-shot. Pass it through the fence, quick!"

Horace thought he detected a note of insincerity in the boy's tone, but he was so pleased and mesmerized at being spoken to by this good-class coloured young blood that he went to the fence and surrendered his sling-shot.

The boy retreated from the fence. With a giggle, he and his brother climbed into the fork of a low flamboyant tree that grew not too far from the fence.

As Horace hesitated, watching them, he noticed that they were making no preparation to shoot the bird. They were staring at him and grimacing and giggling.

He called to them: "Where de bird you say you want to shoot?"

For answer, the one with the sling-shot took aim, and a palm-seed whizzed past Horace's head. It rebounded from the *poui* tree just behind him, and he saw it settle near his foot. A dry hard palm-seed.

He realized that the boys' pants pockets were bulging with palm-seeds. They must have been collecting them under the tall, fan-leafed palm not far from the flamboyant tree.

Horace called: "What you doing? You nearly hit me!"

The boys shouted jeering taunts… "Hi, Black Sam!"… "Tar face!"

Another palm-seed came at Horace.

Fear and anger possessed the cook's son.

"Dat's what you tek me sling-shot to do? To shoot 'pon me? Gimme back! You hear me? Gimme back!"

He began to dance about and gesticulate.

One of the seeds hit him a small stinging blow on the side of his neck. His anger melted. Only fear remained.

He could not call to his mother for help. She would flog him for having brought out his sling-shot to "kill the poor innocent birds", as she called them. If he ran off he would lose his faithful sling-shot which he had laboured over to make more than six months ago; it had taken him two weeks to find the fork alone – he had cut it from a guava tree.

He could not cry out or move. He simply stood staring at the two olive-skinned boys while palm-seeds whizzed about him.

One of the seeds hit him on the cheek. A sharp current of pain rushed through him. He shrieked. He fled towards the de Germain kitchen, the grinning faces of the boys hovering before him as he ran.

For two or three years after he had always experienced a shrinking, trembling fear at the sight of an olive complexion. An olive face had made him want to turn and run.

He envisaged Mrs Hinckson's face now as he ascended the office stairs, and the old fear gripped him. He broke out in a cold sweat, trembled. He felt as if the moment he entered the office and met her gaze he would recoil in expectation of receiving a fusillade of palm-seeds.

"I'm a fool," he muttered.

But the feeling was still with him as he settled down at the desk.

Nearly a minute must have elapsed before he could bring himself to glance up to take the first survey of the scene.

She was at her desk, typing in her usual rapid, concentrated manner.

Miss Bisnauth, too, was busy, though every now and then she paused to glance towards the windows, her face strained-looking. She must be writing a poem; her face always looked that way when she was writing a poem.

Mr Murrain was moving his chin from side to side and turning the leaves of a ledger before him, though his gaze was fixed dreamily on some point well above his desk. Was it Miss Henery he was looking at?

There was the old deep frown on Mr Jagabir's face; he seemed to be making entries in a journal from a batch of accounts.

Mr Benson was speaking on the telephone, and Miss Yen Tip sat beside his desk with her notebook and pencil, waiting. Without glancing at Miss Laballe, he knew she was reading a story in *Woman's Home Companion*; he could hear the rustle of the leaves as she adjusted the book to suit her comfort. She was always with some American magazine.

Mr Lopez was biting his thumb and frowning at the ledger before him. He stretched out suddenly and snatched up a black notebook in the swift, abrupt way that was characteristic of him.

Mr Lorry...

Mr Lorry had his chin cupped in his hand, his elbow resting on his desk. He was staring at Mrs Hinckson with an expression of lecherous speculation. Horace had seen him doing this before; it infuriated the boy.

Facing Mr Waley's door, you saw Mrs Hinckson's desk about four feet to the right, and Mr Lorry's about six feet to the left. Mr Lorry's was nearer to the wall than Mrs Hinckson's, so he could watch her without her being aware.

I can kill him.

The fury in him gradually became infiltrated with bitterness. Mr Lorry was of her class. He was coloured – olive complexioned. A shade or two darker than she, but that didn't matter. She would not consider it presumptuous of Mr Lorry to look at her in that way. But me...

He cursed himself for being in love with her. He wished he could rip the feeling out of him. What was there in love that it had to make him helpless like this? He turned and stared out at the morning. A brown and yellow bird perched on the limb of a tree in Marine Square flapped its wings and cried "Kisk-kiskadee!" A shrill, aggressive cry. Aggressive with the spirit of independence. It was like a mocking laugh directed at him.

His hand tightened on the back of the chair... I'd give up everything now, not care about my ambitions or anything at all, if only I could just find myself changed into a kiskadee.

So passionately did he wish this that he felt afraid. A strong wish was as good as a prayer, he had read. He shuddered. Suppose he had really become changed into a kiskadee. It was wrong of him to tempt the Virgin Mary. Suppose she had interceded with God and God had taken him at his word.

He stumbled to his feet.

"Yes, Miss Laballe!"

"Take over for a moment, please!"

"All right, miss."

She made her way towards the Ladies' Room, and he had hardly taken her place at the switchboard when he heard Mrs Hinckson's steps approaching Miss Bisnauth's desk.

She stopped at the file-cabinet which stood beside Miss Bisnauth's desk, for Miss Bisnauth did most of the filing in the office.

Horace, no more than six feet off, tried hard to give his attention exclusively to the switch-keys. He could hear Mrs Hinckson clearly as she said to Miss Bisnauth: "I'm looking for that minute from Mr Minshall – Alectra Jellies and the Leverhill Biscuit Company. You filed it yesterday, didn't you?"

"Yes. HM-HO. Number Sixteen."

A pause.

Horace vowed not to eavesdrop, but eavesdropped. "Oh, yes, I've found it."

"I haven't filed the duplicate in GW-TO yet. I'm waiting for Mr Waley's reply so I can make one thing of it."

"Yes, that's right. By tomorrow morning you should have it – if we don't have any more serious interruptions between whenever he comes in and four this afternoon."

"He's still out with Mr Prentice, eh?"

"Yes, he hasn't come back yet." She took a casual glance at the typewriter. "How's the new poem getting on?"

"I've finished the first draft – but it needs plenty of polishing up and working over."

"Did you see mine, by the way?"

"Yours?"

"I mean the Shakespeare one addressed to me – in the *File* tray."

Miss Bisnauth laughed, automatically glancing at Horace's back.

Horace felt as though the door of a refrigerator had just opened behind him. The board clicked softly, and he disconnected Mr Benson with fingers that seemed to contain sticks of ice instead of bones.

"Yes, I did notice it," said Miss Bisnauth, fidgeting. "When I was clearing the tray. I couldn't help seeing it."

"Oh, it's nothing private. Who else but Pat Lorry? He can behave like a real schoolboy sometimes."

"Mr Lorry? But…"

"Yes, he did it, my dear. Didn't you see the Vitamin B tablets in the way, too? He left them there for me along with this Shakespeare verse. I tackled him about it and he admitted it."

"Well! I could have sworn…" She went no further. She

glanced at Horace again, hoping the boy would not catch on. She would hate to make him uncomfortable.

Mrs Hinckson caught on. She smiled and said: "Yes, I did think so myself, at first. In fact, I was certain – until I challenged Pat about it."

"I never would have guessed Mr Lorry did it. He doesn't seem the sort, you know."

"Same here. Oh, men are puzzling creatures, Edna. I've long ago given up trying to understand them."

On her way back to her desk, she met Mr Lorry's gaze. It was no chance encounter; she felt she had to look at him.

He stared back without constraint or inhibition.

She became burningly conscious of the motion of her hips, of the slight jolting of her breasts. She felt angry – and yet...

And yet she wants me like hell, Mr Lorry told himself. Woman won't realize I've got her down on my current Agenda.

To himself – and to his intimate male friends – he classified women under a referential heading known as his Agenda. For instance: "See that craft going there? I've got her down on my future Agenda." With a soft sniff: "She's a back number on my Agenda." Repudiatingly: "That scrawny young mare? She could never hope to feature on my Agenda."

Since his school-days Mr Lorry had discovered that he was attractive to women. At Queen's Royal College he had not shone particularly in either the cricket or the soccer eleven, but girl spectators had always singled him out for high compliments and neglected the real stars of the match.

No girl had ever refused him a date; it might merely be to go cycling round the Savannah of an afternoon or to meet him at a cinema show (not necessarily to be taken by him; this was a rare honour he conferred), but no girl would think of failing him.

Light brown tending to olive, wavy-haired, he was not particularly handsome. He had a high-bridged nose, the lower part of which was too bulbous to enhance his looks. His cheekbones were low like his mother's. His mother was fair-skinned-coloured with dead-straight hair; she was a mixture of negro, East Indian and white. His mouth, too, was his mother's – it was full and sensual but not thick-lipped like a negro's; it was a European mouth, cupid-bow in shape, and only the lower lip gave it its full, sensual look. His grey-green eyes, it was said by the older folk, came from his paternal great-grandfather, a Scotsman, James Roy Lorry, the founder of the big Frederick Street firm of haberdashers, Lorry & Nicholson's.

He was not in love with Mrs Hinckson. So far, he had not succeeded in falling in love with any woman. But Mrs Hinckson intrigued him because of her unwillingness to respond to his beckonings; she was attracted to him, he knew, but it was just that she would not respond. Thinking up ways and strategies to get a woman into bed with him was something he was unaccustomed to doing; she was the first woman he had found necessary to tempt and flatter with gifts. As a rule, no woman required more than a word and a stare from him. Young or old, they all went under without a struggle.

It would not disturb him very much if Mrs Hinckson never yielded. He had the sporting spirit. He regarded her as he regarded, in football, the opposing team's goal; he longed to slam the ball into it, but if he failed – well, it was the luck of the game. What mattered was the fray and pursuit rather than the victory.

As inside-right of the Poui Sporting Club's soccer eleven, he was, through both his performance on the field and his personality, admittedly one of the most popular men in Trinidadian sporting circles. He played in first-class cricket, too, but had not yet, like Mr Lopez, reached Colony standard.

He was so popular that even the Raiders' Club sometimes invited him to their social functions – and quite often to play billiards in their club-room – and this was considered no mean honour, for the members of the Raiders' Club were white – or people who though not white had every appearance of being so. A pink or sallow-pinkish complexion and straight hair were the only qualifications one needed to become a member of the Raiders' Club. It could be known that your grandfather was a coal-black negro – the Raiders would not mind, so long as you yourself could show a fair complexion and not too rippled a head.

The Poui Club, to which Mr Lorry belonged, was run on similar lines. It was exclusively for members within a certain range of shades, beginning from sallow and ending at very light brown and taking into consideration, at the same time, quality of hair (anything from passable good – small waves but not outright kinky – to straight hair would satisfy the committee). A pure-blooded Negro stood no chance of admittance into the Poui Club.

There was the Belmonters' Club for pure-blooded Negroes of no class, and the Woodstock Club for pure-blooded Negroes of the socially-rising, lawyer-doctor-civil-servant class.

On the field, everybody forgot race and class differences, and white and near-white and olive and black mingled in the atmosphere of camaraderie engendered by the game. On the field, all that mattered was good play.

Among all these clubs, however, Mr Lorry threaded his way, an enchanted fairy prince immune to the discomforts of race and class prejudice. Bridge this afternoon at the Woodstock, billiards tomorrow at the Raiders', a knock at the nets on Saturday with the Belmonters. He had acquaintances in every stratum of society (acquaintances, however, who could not all visit him at his home, for his parents would not have tolerated black people in the house; his father was a civil servant, his mother a cousin of the Tellos, one of the best coloured families).

He had made conquests in every circle and clique. Black girls whom he met through the Belmonters or the Woodstock fellows became enamoured of him; light brown and pale olive girls in his own set; white girls of the Raider sort; even Chinese and East Indian and Spanish girls.

But sometimes – like now – he had moments of depression. Depression bred not of failure or the thought of failure, but depression that sprang from satiety.

At last, he assured himself, he saw definite signs of Mrs Hinckson yielding. His experienced eye had not failed to note her reactions during the conversation concerning the vitamin tablets. He could visualize her for the next day or two turning him down as usual when he asked her to dine with him or go out for a drive. Then – it might be the day after tomorrow – she would nod and murmur: "Very well." At night in the car she would be passionate; she would breathe hard and say in a strangled whisper: "Oh, God! I love you! I love you, Pat!" as though it were something she was astounded to discover – something she had never dreamt she could feel for him. In the days after that she would get more and more importunate; she would want him oftener and oftener – and he would begin gradually to push her aside: softly, imperceptibly, so as not to hurt her too much...

Yes, it was depressing.

Would there never be a woman who would give him back a look that was genuinely aloof and indifferent, genuinely superior to his charms? He knew that if he could meet such a woman he would fall in love with her; for the first time in his life he would be enslaved.

Sex had lost its glamour for him. He half-envied the fellows who had to struggle to win their women. A conquest for them meant a big event in their lives – something exciting. But for him...

He watched Miss Laballe go past, noted the motion of her hips as a matter of routine.

Not for his Agenda – definitely. The puny, small-boned type. He saw Horace returning to his desk beyond the barrier. The boy flashed him a look... What have I done to you, son? Wonder if it's really he who wrote that verse.

He shrugged and went on with his work, forgetting Horace, unaware that Horace was cursing him.

Horace felt a soreness as though tiny, rough-edged pebbles were moving in his chest.

I bring a verse for her, and he takes the credit. Trying to gain her favour at my expense...

For the first time that he could remember, he doubted the existence of God and the Virgin Mary. How could God and the Virgin Mary be in Heaven and let an injustice like this occur?

But the next instant fear and remorse shot through him. He must not think such blasphemous thoughts. It was Fate, that was all. Destiny. Destiny had played him another dirty trick. He mustn't blame God.

He began to toy with a pencil. Defiance rose in him. He would win out yet. He would never let Destiny have the last word. He would have to think out some way now to let her know it was not Mr Lorry who had put that paper in her *File* tray – and he would have to let her know this without her suspecting that it was himself.

He recalled the conversation he had overheard… "I could have sworn," Miss Bisnauth had said, and then had broken off. Then Mrs Hinckson had said: "Yes, I did think so myself, at first. In fact, I was certain – until I challenged Pat about it."

This puzzled him somewhat. What could Miss Bisnauth have sworn? Could it be that she was about to say: "I could have sworn it was Xavier"? Perhaps. Or perhaps not. He mustn't jump to conclusions. Anyway, whatever Miss Bisnauth had been about to say, whatever she had thought before, she, too, must feel now that it was Mr Lorry who had put the love verse in Mrs Hinckson's tray.

He did not know that Miss Bisnauth was watching his face. She was studying his expression idly and feeling perplexed and disillusioned.

Her poem had been inspired by the compassion she had felt for him – her awareness of the hopeless infatuation which had driven him to copy out this love verse and put it on Mrs Hinckson's desk. But now that Mrs Hinckson had revealed that it was Mr Lorry who was responsible and not Xavier, Miss Bisnauth felt that her compassion had been wasted, that her poem had been falsely inspired. She was experiencing a sense of let-down.

The poem was complete – in rough draft – but it needed a lot of going over and vitalizing. Had it not been for this *dénouement* she would have been at work on it now. But all urge had left her.

Mr Lorry's reputation with women was well known to her. She always tried not to think uncharitable thoughts about him, for she believed that no human being was really bad. And apart from this, she liked his eyes; his eyes were grey-green like Arthur Lamby's – though, of course, Arthur's, in expression, were far more *spirituel*. And he did make her feel sort of quivery and excited when he happened to say anything to her: he had charm, she must admit.

All the same, she could not help feeling that the love verse incident had now acquired a tarnished character. Mr Lorry had left this paper in order to further his campaign of seducing Mrs Hinckson. His motive was an unworthy and reprehensible one.

He was lusting; he was not in love. Looked at in this light, the incident was ugly, not beautiful.

She felt cheated.

Of what use was it to try to do anything more about the poem? What lofty fire could come out of her now while she carried the knowledge of this... of this hoax?

No, that was defeatist. Arthur would scold her. Arthur believed that men would triumph eventually over their hypocrisies and the ills their hypocrisies bred. He could be cynical when he wanted, but at heart he had faith in humanity. Take, for instance, that fairy-tale he wrote a month or two ago. It always gave her courage to think of it. She had a copy of the manuscript at home, and it had left so deep an impression on her that she could almost recite it word for word... It was called *The Jen*...

A little girl called Mooney lived in a big house near the Canje Creek. The water in the Canje Creek is black, and along the banks the bush is dense; you never knew what might be wriggling in the water besides fishes, and sometimes strange cries that frightened Mooney came from the bush.

One day rain fell so heavily that Mooney could not go for a walk with her nurse Beatrice, so she had to remain at home and let Beatrice tell her stories. Beatrice told her of the Jen.

"Is it an animal, Beatrice?"

"No, it's not an animal."

"Then, what is it?"

"It's a Thing."

"What sort of Thing?" asked Mooney, very curious now.

"A bad Thing," Beatrice answered.

"You mean it has teeth and can bite?"

"It's worse than that."

"Has it long claws, then, and can scratch and tear people's eyes out?"

"If that were all it wouldn't be so bad," Beatrice told her, looking very grave.

"You mean it can spout fire from its mouth like the dragon you told me about yesterday?"

"Worse than that. Even a dragon can't be as bad as a Jen."

"Does it live in the bush out there?"

"Yes – and sometimes in the water."

"Is it there now – this minute – hiding in the bush?"

"This very minute it's there hiding in the bush – or in the water."

Mooney looked out at the bush and the water. She was afraid – but not very, for she was sure her father and mother and Beatrice could keep off the worst bad Thing that lived.

"Has the Jen a head, Beatrice?"

"Don't let's talk any more about it," said Beatrice.

"Why?"

"It makes me sick to talk about it."

"Why? Are you afraid it might come and trouble you?"

"Me and everybody."

"Couldn't you and Daddy and Mother kill it if it came to trouble you?"

Beatrice sighed and shook her head. "Nobody can kill a Jen. Once a Jen is born and grows up, nothing and nobody can kill it."

"Then you mean it might soon kill everybody?"

"That's exactly what I mean."

"What sort of a sound does a Jen make?"

"Whooo-ooo! Whooo-oom! But don't let's talk about it. It's too dreadful a Thing."

For many days Mooney remembered what Beatrice had told her about the Jen. One noon when she was in bed where Beatrice had put her to sleep after lunch, Mooney heard a sound that she was sure must be the sound of the Jen. It went Whooo-ooo! Whooo-ooom just as Beatrice had said. It came from outside the house where the sun was shining, for today the sky was blue with small white clouds.

Mooney hid her face in the pillow, very frightened.

The sound came nearer the house, and soon it was right outside the window of Mooney's room. Her mother was downstairs in the kitchen with Beatrice, and her father had gone back to work, so Mooney was alone upstairs.

Mooney thought that the Jen might decide to pass her window and go back to the bush – or the water – as today was such a fine day. Surely Jens did not kill people on days when the sun was shining and the sky looked blue and white and the bush had such a lovely green-and-yellow colour.

But Mooney thought she must be wrong, because the Jen came in at the window and went Whooo-ooo Whooo-ooom! all round the room.

Mooney began to cry.

"Whooo-ooo! WHOOO-OOOM!" went the Jen just behind her bed.

But Mooney was really a brave girl. It was only because the Jen had come in so suddenly that she cried. Still keeping her eyes hidden in the pillow, she shifted her head so that her mouth was free and called to the Jen: "Take the chair by the window, Mr Jen. It's much cooler there."

But the Jen would not sit down or keep still at all. It kept on saying "Whooo-ooo! Whooo-ooom!" all the time as though to make Mooney know what a very dreadful Thing it was.

Trembling but still brave, Mooney said: "I am Mooney, Mr Jen. I'm five years old."

The Jen became silent, and Mooney told herself that perhaps the poor Thing only wanted to be friendly.

"Are you really a Jen, Mr Jen?"

"I am," said the Jen. "How do you do, Mooncy? Whooo! Phew! How hot!"

"I'm very happy to meet you, Mr Jen," said Mooney, still keeping her eyes in the pillow. "Very, very."

"You won't be after you get to know me well."

"Are you really so very bad as Beatrice says you are?"

"Much worse."

"You mean you're worse than a dragon?"

"Much, much worse."

"Have you a head, Mr Jen?"

"No, but I have a chain."

"What sort of chain?"

"A chain that's always in action."

"You mean you beat people with it?"

"Whooo-ooo! How hot!"

"There's an electric fan over the dressing-table, but the current is not on. It won't be on until six this evening."

"Just as well. I don't like currents."

Mooney giggled. "Do you like raisins?"

"I prefer reasons – because I am one myself. For many things."

"I really can't understand a word you're saying, Mr Jen."

"I don't intend you to. That's part of my badness."

"How bad are you? Have you horns on your shoulders?"

"If horns were all I had I should be good."

"Oh, I know what you must be like! You have tentacles like an octopus – long, slimy, coiling arms that reach out and squeeze people to death. Daddy has told me about an octopus."

"Beside me, an octopus would seem as harmless as a rabbit."

Mooney shivered to think what sort of creature it could be in the room with her which was worse than an octopus, but she kept on being brave.

"Please tell me what you're like, then, Mr Jen. I'm very curious to know."

"Not frightened, too?"

"A little, but not too much."

"Well, I'm dreadful very, very, very dreadful."

"Yes, but *how* dreadful? Tell me of something as dreadful as you."

"There is nothing as dreadful. Though – hum!"

"Though what, Mr Jen? Were you going to say something?"

"I did have a friend who was as dreadful – in his day."

"Isn't he dreadful any more?"

"Not since I came along."

"Did he kill lots of people?"

"He didn't have a chance to."

"Why?"

The Jen gave a long whooo-ing sigh. "You ask too many questions, child."

"But I want to know."

"Well, if you must know, people were too scared of his dreadfulness. They bought millions of masks to hide their faces from him."

"That was why he never hurt them – because he scared them too much with his dreadfulness?"

"You're an intelligent child. It's time for me to go."

"You won't try to kill me before you go, I hope."

The Jen began to weep.

"Oh, I'm so sorry! What's making you cry, Mr Jen?"

"I'm lonely. A great, lonely, dreadful Jen."

"Too great and lonely and dreadfully dreadful for anyone to let you hurt them? Is that what you mean?"

"That's exactly what I mean. Whooo-hooo-hooo! I must be off! Whooo!"

"But —"

But when Mooney removed the pillow from her eyes the Jen had gone already. She looked out of the window and saw that the sun was still shining. Little white clouds were still in the sky – and the sky was blue.

Yes, it was most heartening to remember Arthur's tale and to go over it in her mind. Arthur had genius, she was convinced. He would get far – but he must escape from that newspaper office. It was cramping his soul, killing his creative urge.

She turned her head sharply.

There were exclamations all over the office.

PART TWO

OTHER PERSONS · RECAPITULATION

Miss Bisnauth recognized it to be a ridiculous habit for which her musical education coupled with her imaginative temperament must be responsible: often on hearing some ordinary sound – a raised voice in the street or the blare of a car's horn – she would dramatize it to herself with a mentally ejaculated conventional musical term.

"To hell with the bloody British Empire!"

"Shut up, Sidney. We're at the office!"

"What if we are! I don't care two ruddy —!"

Sforzando! was how Miss Bisnauth dramatized the obscenity to herself.

Mr Jagabir's face was expressive of disaster. Sudden and irrational – but disaster. The day had come, at last. They were going to send him back to the estate to work in the fields.

Normally, Mr Benson would have scolded Miss Yen Tip for not attending to him ("...you don't attend to me, that's why you're always making so many mistakes..."), but instead, he, too, had turned his head.

Mrs Hinckson, rigid with restraint, bit her lower lip but Miss Henery's mouth gaped slightly, her hand gripping the top of the typewriter.

Afterwards, Miss Bisnauth described Miss Laballe. "You looked like Lot's wife. I was waiting for you to turn into a pillar of salt," she laughed.

Mr Lopez was not at his desk; he had gone into the Men's Room only a moment before.

The widened stare of Mr Lorry was followed immediately by a slow smile. A smile of comprehension.

Horace was afraid to move, though he had risen. The instant be had heard the steps and voices on the stairs he had sensed trouble and had felt it his duty to intervene and remonstrate.

But when he had seen that it was two white gentlemen a subconscious fear had restrained him. He could not rebuke white people and good-class coloured people. This was something only a member of the main office staff could handle.

Mr Murrain was already through the barrier-gate. "Whitmer! I'm surprised at you!"

"You would be, Murrain. Exploiting snob!"

"You can't come in here —"

"Ignored your advice yesterday afternoon. Handed in my resignation thish morning to that old bashtard – Mr Holmjh."

"Quiet, Sidney!"

The red-haired young man in a grey tropical suit was trying to wheel Sidney Whitmer back towards the stairs, but without success. Sidney staggered against the barrier, and the barrier vibrated. Mr Murrain grasped his arm.

"Leggo, Murrain!"

"Quiet!"

"Stinking snobs! You Britishersh! Leggo my arm!"

"The Men's Room, Herrick. Get him in. Come."

"Take your hands off me!"

After a moment, he stopped resisting and let himself be led into the Men's Room.

"Mr Lopez! Would you mind bringing in a chair, please!"

Mr Lopez darted out – returned with a chair.

"Sit down, Sidney. Come on. Pull yourself together, man."

Mr Lopez murmured to Mr Murrain that Mr Lorry had some Alka-Seltzer in his desk-drawer. Mr Murrain nodded hastily, and Mr Lopez was gone like lightning.

Sidney sat glowering at the floor. "Had to come and tell you, Murry. 'Pologies!" He put out a hand as red and perspiring as his face.

"That's all right, Sidney. That's all right," said Mr Murrain, wincing.

"Resigning's all I could do. Couldn't stick it there any more. Wrote Mother telling her."

"I tried to stop him from coming here, sir," said Herrick in distress.

Mr Murrain nodded.

Sidney began to laugh.

"Now, Sidney! Now!" ...

"That's Mr Lenfield's nephew," Mr Jagabir was murmuring to Mrs Hinckson. "One of de principals in London. What Mr Lenfield going to say when he hear of dis?"

"Oh, is that Mr Whitmer?"

"Yes, miss. Dat's Mr Whitmer – Mr Sidney Whitmer. Mr Lenfield's nephew. It's Mr Lenfield who get him de job and send him to Trinidad from England. But I hear 'e don't get on well wid de other overseers. He mix wid too much coloured people – and de overseers don't like him for dat."

"I see."

Without a glance at Horace, without a word of greeting to anyone, Mrs Murrain walked into the office and headed for her husband's desk. She must have been half-way across when it seemed to occur to her that Mr Murrain was missing. She paused and glanced around irresolutely. Her gaze rested, after a moment, on Miss Henery.

"Where's Mr Murrain?"

Miss Henery went on typing as though deaf. Deaf and blind.

Mrs Murrain, tallish, thin, pretty in an English, narrow-faced way, not very well dressed, repeated the question – this time sharply.

Miss Henery typed on. Her mouth tightened, her eyes grew steely.

"You!" Mrs Murrain pointed at Miss Henery. "I'm speaking to you. I'm asking where is Mr Murrain?"

Miss Henery stopped typing and looked up. "When you learn manners," she said, "I'll listen to what you're saying. Not before." She went on typing.

Mrs Murrain's eyes and complexion reacted perhaps less expressively than the stiffening of her body.

"Do you know who you're speaking to?"

"I'm perfectly aware *whom* I'm speaking to." (Cheap, thought Miss Henery, but I couldn't resist putting her right on her King's English.)

"You're impertinent!"

"You're disturbing me at my work!"

Mr Jagabir's hands were clasped together tight. His eyes were the eyes of a man hypnotized.

Miss Yen Tip was silently convulsed – a convulsion of delight and approval.

Mr Benson muttered, "Good. Good," with anguished approval. His eyes glittered. "The unmannerly white pig!"

"I shall report you for this!"

"You may do as you please!"

Mrs Murrain turned. Her gaze moved in jerks about the office. It settled on Mr Jagabir, still petrified beside Mrs Hinckson, hands together.

"Mr Jagabir!"

"Yes, miss! Yes, Mrs Murrain!"

Mr Jagabir moved towards her at a stumbling trot.

"Where is Mr Murrain?"

"He – de boss – he in de Men's Room, miss. Somebody come." He trembled perceptibly. "He – he engaged at de minute, miss."

"Engaged? Engaged with whom?"

"Ah can't say – I mean, miss – Ah t'ink it's Mr Whitmer from de estate."

Mrs Murrain frowned at him, puzzled and uncertain, then turned and went towards her husband's desk. She seated herself in the chair near the safe, fumbling in her handbag for a cigarette. She lit it and flicked the match towards the window, tilted her face and exhaled, crossed her legs…

"… and look how she's dressed," Miss Laballe was murmuring to Miss Bisnauth. "Those down-at-heel shoes – and not even cleaned. And that dress looks as if she just took it from the clothes-basket." …

"… that's what I can't stand, Murrain The blasted snobbery! The hypocrisy and the *nerve* of you English hounds. You come out to these colonies and squeeze the guts out of 'em – and then you *piss* on the natives! Insult to injury."

Sidney Whitmer's voice rang clearly through the office.

Mrs Murrain's head tilted in alarm. She fidgeted. Her discomfiture was very apparent, but only Miss Bisnauth pitied her. Poor thing, thought Miss Bisnauth. She is overbearing, I admit, but such people should be pitied rather than despised or ridiculed.

"I can shake Miss Henery's hand."

"Yes, shake her hand," Mr Benson muttered again half to himself, half to Miss Yen Tip. He hated negroes, but white people he hated twice as much.

Mrs Murrain had risen. She began to look around again in that irresolute way. Suddenly she moved towards Mr Benson.

"Mr Benson, I think you're Chief Clerk here. Can you tell me what is happening in this office this morning?"

Mr Benson stumbled to his feet. His breath hissed. His olive-sallow moon-face expressed pleasure, deep respect, concern in swift succession. "Well, the truth is, Mrs Murrain, I'm afraid I'm just as —"

The telephone on his desk rang. He took it up.

"Excuse me a moment."

He put down the instrument before it had reached his ear. "Oh, Miss Yen Tip, please answer this for me! Come, come! Hurry!"

He was in such a dither of confusion that he took out his handkerchief and wiped his face hurriedly.

"The truth is, Mrs Murrain, I've been so busy —"

"Is Mr Murrain really in the Men's Room?"

"Yes, yes. I believe so. Is there – have you a message for him, Mrs Murrain? Could I do anything for you?"

Mrs Murrain clicked her tongue faintly. "But I can't understand what's going on here. Whose voice is that in there?"

"I think it's Mr Whitmer. Could I go in – you wish me to call Mr Murrain for you, Mrs Murrain?"

"No, it's all right. Don't bother. I'll wait." She spoke curtly and turned away, returned to the chair near the safe. Her face was pale and tense.

Mr Benson sat down, dabbing at his forehead with his handkerchief. He began to take up things and put them down. His face looked confused and ashamed. He called irritably to Miss Yen Tip, who had taken advantage of Mrs Murrain's advent to cross over to Miss Henery with congratulations.

"What about that phone call? Didn't I tell you to answer — ?"

"It was Barker's, Mr Benson. They said they'd call back in a few minutes. I told them you couldn't speak to dem right away."

"Well, don't run off the moment I'm not looking. Take a letter." ...

"...I know! I know all about it! Everybody's ridiculing British imperialism nowadays! It's the vogue. But they're *right!*" ...and thudding noises...

"...Well, this is a *kommess!*" said Mr Lorry to Mr Lopez.

"We're making history this morning, boy!" grinned Mr Lopez...

"... Y'haven't got to tell me that! I *know* I'm an Englishman, Murry! But I'm ashamed! Yesh. *Damned* ashamed!'... and urgent mumblings...

"... she may be arrogant, but for all we know, it might be a sort of shyness that makes her behave so. I've read of cases like that. These English people seem stiff and reserved, but it's really diffidence, that's all – and inhibitions. They only appear impolite and unfriendly. I think we should be sorry for them instead of despising or ridiculing them."

Mrs Hinckson looked sceptical. "I'm afraid I can't quite see it that way, Edna," she murmured.

Miss Bisnauth nodded. "I understand how you feel. I suppose it's foolish of me to defend them, but, somehow, I can never bring myself to condemn anyone outright. I always feel that if we looked beneath the surface we'd be able to discover that it's not their own fault, really..."

They were bringing him out – supporting him between them. His head drooped on to his chest, and his knees kept bending abruptly. His eyes were open but unseeing.

"'Pologies, Murry," he mumbled.

Mrs Murrain rose, but her husband did not glance in her direction, his efforts too concentrated on the task in hand. His face was strained and red and twitched sensitively.

Sidney began to hiccup as they passed through the barrier.

Mrs Murrain, a hand fumbling at her bosom, gazed after them. She sank on to the chair, then rose again at once and began to move with an air of uncertainty towards the barrier-gate.

They put him into Mr Murrain's car, and Mr Murrain told Herrick to take him to the club and let him sleep it off. "The doorman will give you a hand in lifting him upstairs." (Mr Murrain was a member of the Capstan Club, which existed for white businessmen exclusively.)

People on the sidewalk and in Roalk's Hardware paused to stare, and Mr Murrain hurried back into the building, his face still red and twitching. He encountered his wife half-way up the stairs waiting for him. He halted and recoiled. It was as though in the midst of having a tooth extracted he had glanced aside to see a surgeon with scalpel ready to remove his tonsils.

"Caroline! Why, I had no idea —"

"You were in the Men's Room when I came. What's been happening, Everard? Who was that young man you took outside?"

"Young Whitmer. Lenfield's nephew."

"Mr Lenfield of the London Office?"

"Yes. I believe this has been my worst experience since Dunkirk."

"Why did he come here in such a condition?"

"Dropped in to tell me he had resigned his position as overseer at Tucurapo. He was here to see me yesterday afternoon. I've always taken some interest in him. Asked me what I thought of his resigning and I advised him not to be a fool."

"What did he want to resign for?"

"It appears he's been associating with too many of these coloured people – even inviting them up to his quarters – and the other men began to object. He's a rather sensitive sort of chap, I'm afraid. Makes a fuss over everything. Badly bitten by the socialistic bug, too."

"Which reminds me. That typist of yours was most impertinent to me when I came in." She related the incident, and he listened with tightening lips and brows that drew closer and closer together. Fury stirred in him again. Fury and impotence.

"It won't happen again."

"You should get rid of her."

He nodded. "I'll speak to Waley as soon as he comes in." He mumbled the words, afraid to trust himself to speak louder. Afraid that she might detect all that was seething in him... The large areolae...

"These coloured people seem to think a fearful lot of themselves."

"Are you coming upstairs?"

"No, I don't care to go back up there now."

"But – the bank slip. Don't you wish me to sign it?"

"No, I've changed my mind."

"Changed your mind?"

She nodded. He noticed the chilly gleam in her eyes and misconstrued it.

"But, my dear, you must understand it was purely a slip of memory —"

"That's almost a pun." She laughed. "No, I'm not annoyed with you because you – well, let's say because you forgot. It's something else I came to tell you about. I'm mad, Everard. Simply mad."

"What's the matter?"

She told him. Madge Crippen was passing and hailed out. Mrs Murrain was in the garden discussing with the East Indian gardener the young rose plants Mr Murrain had bought at the Fredbanks' sale the week before last. Mrs Murrain invited Madge in, and they got to chatting about last night's cocktail party.

"And guess what Madge told me! She said Kathy de Bergère actually called me a frump – and apart from that, she as good as hinted that we bummed an invitation to their party."

"What!"

Mrs Murrain was trembling slightly and very pale.

"She included Madge and her husband, too, and Madge said she spoke purposely so that Madge could overhear —"

"I noticed she seemed to have been having more drinks than was discreet."

"I noticed it, too. Everyone knows she's a booze fish. But you take it from me, she was jolly sober. She knew what she was saying. Madge said she kept laughing at us. She was speaking to Major Ruskin – that local army man who's got on because of his family name, though everybody knows he's got a big whop of the tarbrush —"

"I heard it whispered she's having an affair with him."

"Oh, that's common property. You haven't any need to whisper it. But listen to this. You know what she had the nerve to tell him? She said you could always tell what these English people who come to Trinidad were in their homeland. Their manners and dress give them away. She said I dress like a charwoman at Brighton on a Bank Holiday Monday."

Mr Murrain uttered a restrained laugh.

"It's no laughing matter, Everard. It's a direct insult. She *meant* me to know what she felt. She knew Madge was overhearing and would have told me."

Mr Murrain shrugged. The incident did not trouble him very much, for he had no social aspirations, but he had to feign interest and annoyance if only for the sake of appearing sympathetic.

"It's the last time I'll be seen in their home. And I don't see why we should be throwing away money to entertain such people only to have them slander us behind our backs. I'll never give another party in this island!"

"I can frankly sigh in relief at that," Mr Murrain said, smiling and patting her shoulder – but did not sigh, for he knew that within a fortnight they would have another party. He was used to hearing complaints like this from Caroline. Her wrath never lasted – nor her resolutions. Perhaps before the week was out she would tell him that Kathy de Bergère had apologized for her behaviour.

"These French creole people of Trinidad think themselves blue-blooded aristocrats, that's what it is! And a more degenerate lot don't exist —"

"No, my dear! Please! Don't get yourself worked up." He patted her shoulder again. "Ignore the whole thing. It's not worth a second thought. Always bear in mind, we won't be in Trinidad for ever —"

"Yes, but while we're here it can be very unpleasant to hear such slanderous things spoken —"

"I understand, I understand…"

It was an immense relief when she had gone. But as he returned to his desk Mr Murrain could feel that trapped-in-the-skin shudder creeping through him. He had no doubt that the eyes of the whole office were upon him.

He remembered Miss Henery's impertinence to Caroline, and a pain of intense hatred and fury tightened his chest. A mere tuppenny coloured girl – a native – giving Caroline the length of her tongue! No, it wouldn't do. She had overstepped the mark this time. She would have to go. His mind was made up.

Miss Henery was at Mrs Hinckson's desk. She was discussing the incident with Mrs Hinckson, who agreed with her that she had acted just as she should.

"These English people must be put in their places, child. They've got to remember that this island belongs to us who were born here – they're in the minority. Hardly one per cent."

"And look at the creature! That's what got my goat. I wouldn't be surprised if she was a barmaid in some low pub in the East End of London before she married Murrain. The woman can't even dress. And our black cook at home can give her lessons in walking."

"It's always the way, Kathleen. They come out here mere nobodies – they might have been street-sweepers or scavengers in England – but the moment they land here in the West Indies they feel their white skins give them the right to lord it over us. They don't realize that we may be coloured but we've known genteel conditions for generations past."

"They won't lord it over me, you can be sure. They can sack me if they want. I can get another job as easy as kissing hands. Stenographers are always in demand in Port of Spain."

"Mr Waley would know better than to sack you for that. He's English, but I must say he's a decent sort…"

After they had chatted for a while on the topic of race relations Miss Henery was about to return to her desk when her gaze alighted on the love verse in the tray.

"What's this? Poetry?"

She took it up and began to read.

"Guess who did it."

Miss Henery laughed. "Oh, wait! This is the thing Jagabir must have been telling me about. He said Xavier did it."

"Xavier?"

"Yes. He said he saw him putting it in the tray here this morning when he came in."

"Don't bother with Jagabir. You know what a liar he is. It was Pat Lorry who did it."

"No! Pat Lorry!"

Mrs Hinckson explained about the Vitamin B tablets.

Miss Henery returned the paper to the tray and laughed. "Well, I can understand the tablets – but this love verse thing doesn't smell like Pat at all."

"What are you all doing? Slandering me?"

Miss Henery pinkened at once. Mr Lorry always made her self-conscious and unsure of herself. She told him: "If you were eavesdropping, that's your fault. Nanette, let me go back and do my work before this Englishman accuses me of idling away the firm's time."

"He won't dare accuse you of that," said Mr Lorry. "He'd be too afraid you might quote the Shakespeare saying about people in glass houses."

"You're full of Shakespeare today?"

"Me? Why do you say so?" Then he caught on and grinned. "But wait! You really fancy it's me who perpetrated that thing in the tray there?"

"All right. I'm not staying to argue. I hear the coolie man calling me to give me some more accounts." She returned to her desk where Mr Jagabir was waiting with a batch of accounts.

"Are you trying to deny it now?" Mrs Hinckson asked Mr Lorry. There was that breathlessness in her again. She despised herself for feeling it.

"I don't remember ever admitting it. All I think I said was I wondered if it could have been me who copied it out last night – or words to that effect."

"Don't quibble."

"How do you mean? If you jumped to the conclusion that it was me, that's your fault." His thumb and forefinger pecked lightly at her shoulder. "Grain of hair." He examined it and sighed softly. "Think I'll put this under my pillow tonight so I can dream about you."

She could not speak. She pretended to examine her notes. But the blood that crept into her cheeks gave her away, and as Mr Lorry watched her cheeks he felt desolation settling upon him again. It might be much sooner than he had thought...

As he began to move off he said: "When I want to compliment you on your charms I don't need to go to Shakespeare. The Poet Lorry is good enough."

She still said nothing. She could hear her breath lisping in and out.

After she had calmed down somewhat, she looked across the office at Xavier. He was at his desk, but, for some reason, he had an air of rigidity and pensiveness.

It was really he, then, after all.

She experienced annoyance – annoyance with herself as well as with Xavier and Pat Lorry.

Sometimes she detested men... No, I never do – that's a lie. The world would be a barren planet for me without men. I'm in a bad mood...

Xavier looked at her. Their gazes met.

The boy looked away and began to fidget.

His face seemed almost distracted. He was a fool. But he couldn't help it. It was his age. He would look back one day soon and laugh at himself and his greenness. He would get on in the city, she had no doubt. The character in his face was too plain for anyone to miss. He seemed just the type who would eventually get elected to the City Council and would force his way up in business via politics.

Never the Country Club for him, though, no matter how big a shot he became. The very most he could hope for socially was an invitation to Government House on some occasion when it was politic to have his presence there. And even then he would be ill-at-ease and be made to understand that a great honour had been conferred on him. His money and his influence in politics would be his only mainstays at such a function. He would be smiled at and flattered, but he would know that it was not he himself who inspired this attention – not he, the human being,

Horace Xavier. Behind his back they would sigh and say what an awful nuisance it was having to make oneself pleasant to these parvenu niggers. And it would not only be white people who would say this. People with negro blood in them would say it, too. People like herself with pale olive skins and Good Hair. The Fair Coloured. The people like her father and her uncles and aunts and cousins. People of genteel background and good class.

Well, that was the way it was. What could she do about it? And when you came to think of it, there certainly was a vast difference between a pure-blooded negro and a person like herself. In America she would be called a negro outright. They never made distinctions in America between negro and coloured as in the West Indies. In Georgia or Louisiana coloured West Indians like Sir Lennox O'Reilly and the late Sir Edward Davson and Colonel Sir Ivan Davson would have been debarred from certain restaurants and hotels and railway coaches as any coal-black stevedore would have been.

But that was wrong. It was inaccurate to clump together all coloured peoples of pure and partial negro strains and dub them negro. Why should a person be described as a negro because he happened to have a great-grandfather or great-great-grandfather who was a pure-blooded negro? A person one-eighth negro and seven-eighths white – if you looked at the matter both equitably and logically – should have more right to call himself white than black. "Coloured" was the correct designation for such a person, for it indicated that while he was not white neither was he black.

It all seemed so pettifogging. Why did men have to be of different races? Why not one complexion and one quality of hair? One big nation? But even if it had been so – and there had been one religion – you could be certain they would have invented some other way of practising segregation and bigotry on a large scale. It might have been stature. People beneath five feet five not admitted into this club. Only six-footers allowed in this restaurant. In this railway coach. So human beings were made; there would have been no escape. It was the egotism of the species.

However, liberal as she always tried to be in her outlook, she knew she could never bring herself to marry or have intimate

141

relations with a Negro. The idea would be too repellent. The way she had been conditioned, of course. She and her middle-class coloured kind. She remembered her Uncle Jim holding forth one day to his son Albert, who was politically inclined and always taking up the cause of the negro workers… "My dear boy, I don't object to what you're doing. It's a good cause. But hear me now! You can write letters to the press on their behalf, you can fight for them if you like, you can deny yourself for them, you can shout yourself hoarse on a platform to champion their cause, but" – wagging his finger solemnly – "the day you identify yourself with a negro you're lost!"

She clicked her tongue, impatient with herself for letting her thoughts stray. This seldom happened to her at the office.

She began to type fiercely, listening to the tiny clipped sounds, letting them soothe her, quiet the hunger that still moved like a twisted rag behind her breasts…

… while Mr Lorry, at his desk, watched her…

It might be this very evening, thought Mr Lorry.

Miss Yen Tip came and placed a batch of blue and yellow forms before him. "You can have them now, he says."

"Tell him he's a quick worker. I've only been waiting two hours."

"You know how fussy he is. He could very well have let you have dem at least an hour ago."

"Never mind, girl. When the two of us get married next month you won't have him to bother your soul again."

She laughed and went off, but not before she had given him a quick, gleaming look.

Hot lil' Chinee bitch… Might consider her for my Agenda.

He took up the forms. They were Customs entry forms and shipping bills. He glanced through them with quick but expert eyes, then rose and headed for the barrier-gate.

He was going to the Customs but did not trouble to put on his coat. Nowadays, no young man bothered to wear a coat during the day in the city. Coats were for the evening – concerts, lectures, parties and dances, the cinema. In the evening one had to bow to the traditions of one's forebears and appear respectably clad.

His father and uncles, reflected Mr Lorry, would have preferred execution on the block rather than be seen without their coats in public. Six in the morning, noon, three in the afternoon; seventy-five in the shade or ninety-two – they would have been unable to make any concessions in the matter.

On his way down he encountered an East Indian who was on his way up.

"De Chief Clerk upstairs, sir?" He spoke in a low, confidential voice.

"Mr Benson? Yes."

A moment later, the man told Horace that he wanted to see Mr Benson.

"What you want him for?" asked Horace, frowning, for the man was ill-clad. He had two or three days' growth of beard, and in his eyes there was a diffidence, Horace could sense, that sprang from degeneration; it was not the diffidence of self-consciousness alone. The man kept flicking his gaze from the barrier-gate to the ceiling. He was anything between forty and fifty. Tieless and collarless, he wore a shabby khaki suit and a dirty headgear which had once been an American sailor's cap.

"Just tell 'im Ah want to see 'im."

"He's busy now. What's your name?"

The man looked uncertain, then mumbled: "Mungalsingh."

Horace, with a look of doubt, went off and informed Mr Benson.

The Chief Clerk turned and scowled at Mungalsingh.

"Who is he? I don't know him. What does he want with me?"

Already raw with self-disgust at his conduct when Mrs Murrain had approached him, humiliated because he had not been able to prevent himself behaving like a sycophant, Mr Benson was in an exceptionally bearish mood.

"Tell him to go, sir?"

"No, wait."

The politics of Mr Benson's life were such that he could not afford to let the humblest caller depart without first discovering his business. The sight of Mungalsingh did not alarm him, but he experienced a certain foreboding. He did not know the man, but he was familiar with the type.

As he strode towards the barrier-gate he tried to bear his

shortish, rather plump body with as much dignity as he could. He kept his face as stern as possible.

"What's it?" he snapped at Mungalsingh with the air and tone of very-much-superior to very-much-inferior. He hated coolies as much as he hated niggers.

"Ah could see you private a minute, sir?"

"What about? What about?"

"Sir, if you can come down on de stairs we can talk better."

The obvious thing was to tell the man that he was confoundedly impertinent. But Mr Benson did not always do the obvious thing.

He scowled at the man, but without a word passed through the barrier-gate and headed for the stairway, Mungalsingh following. Half-way down he paused, aware of the gross indignity of the whole procedure. But it was his rule that dignity must never stand in the way of his security. The struggles of his youth had taught him this, and now at forty-two the conviction was strong in him that it was the obsession with dignity which was responsible for the downfall of many a gentleman. Mr Benson was always engaged in some underhand scheme – a bub-all, as Trinidadians called it – in order to swell his income, and if he allowed dignity to limit his actions he knew that he would be lost. He loved and treasured his dignity – and hated it because he regarded it his greatest enemy.

"What do you want to see me about?"

"Ah working at de gas station, sir. Wid Mr Millan."

"You? I've never seen you there."

"Ah turn on to work day before yesterday."

"And what's it you want?"

His gaze averted, Mungalsingh said: "Ah lil' short of cash today, sir, and Ah come to ask you to help me out."

Mr Benson thought quickly. Mr Millan's gas station supplied the firm's lorries and jitneys and delivery vans with gas. Mr Millan and Mr Benson had a very private arrangement whereby gas was supplied to Mr Benson's car and the cars of a number of Mr Benson's close friends who paid Mr Benson for it at the rate of one-third the cost of a gallon (Mr Millan collecting a flat sum from Mr Benson every month). This gas was all charged to Essential Products or the Tucurapo company as having been supplied to the lorries, jitneys and delivery vans. Here now was this man who said he had been taken on to work at the station. Could it be that by some odd chance he had discovered the bub-all that was being practised and had come to capitalize on his knowledge?

"Look here, tell me your name," said Mr Benson, who knew it already.

"Mungalsingh."

Where had he heard this name before? When Horace had mentioned the name of this man to him Mr Benson had accepted it as he would have any other name. It was a common East Indian name in Trinidad. Hearing it spoken by the man himself now, however, caused him to reflect. He had a first-rate memory. But for his memory he might not have been Chief Clerk today… Suddenly he remembered. He had seen the name in the newspapers beneath a picture of this man – yes, he was the same – published by the police on an occasion when he was wanted. He had a long criminal record. He was noted for picking pockets at race meetings. Once he had been mixed up in a big rape case.

"And what made you think you could come to ask me? Why do you imagine I'd want to give you money?"

Mungalsingh was silent, tugging at his chin.

"Get out of here."

Mungalsingh gave a slight smile. He glanced shiftily from side to side. "Ah hear plenty lil' stories in de rum-shop round de corner, chief."

"What stories?"

"You should know, chief." After a hesitation: "About de gas station."

"Get going before I kick you down."

The man went. He glanced back once and grunted.

Mr Benson watched him descending, saw him pause at the threshold. He stood just inside the doorway, the dim shadow of his body on the central facing design of the big door – a ball and two clubs. His left ear was on a level with the deep dent in the woodwork. Then he was gone.

Mr Benson's first action on returning to his desk was to call up Mr Millan. "Got any fellow called Mungalsingh working for you there, Millan?"

"Mungalsingh? Never heard of him. What's up?"

"All right. When I see you."

Mr Benson hung up.

Miss Yen Tip dusted her notebook briskly to call attention to the fact that she was waiting to take a letter.

"I've got to glance through these manifests, Miss Yen Tip," Mr Benson said irritably, waving her off. "I'll call you in a little."

Miss Yen Tip went to her desk, which stood about six feet to Mr Benson's right.

Mr Benson wanted to think. He did not like what had happened. He was not alarmed, he assured himself – though he fidgeted when he assured himself – but, looked at anyhow, it was an attempt at blackmail.

His round face, bent over the Customs manifests stacked before him, acquired new lines around the puffy eyes and the flat, wide nostrils; whenever he was thoughtful this happened.

Something, he decided, must have leaked out somewhere. Nothing to trouble over, of course – he adjusted himself in his chair – but it mustn't be overlooked.

Mungalsingh had mentioned a rum-shop. Rowland's chauffeur was a talkative fellow, and he drank in rum-shops. Why Rowland had to keep a chauffeur always baffled Mr Benson. Sheer swank, because Rowland could drive perfectly.

Mr Benson smiled, and the lines around his eyes and nose melted into the greasy, sallow-olive skin. His face shone like not too brightly polished brass.

He felt safe.

Naturally, this coolie crook could not know that it was he himself who checked and passed all the gasoline accounts sent in by Millan before they were handed to Jagabir. The Tucurapo accounts as well as the Essential Products accounts. Mungalsingh could not know that Mr Benson handled all matters relating to transportation for the two companies and that if there was anybody to question a gasoline bill it was Mr Benson himself. Mr Jagabir, despite his officiousness and supposed omniscience, was completely ignorant on the subject of motor vehicles and their gas requirements.

Mr Benson knew that what he was doing was dishonest, but his conscience – and he had a conscience – had long ceased to be a nuisance on this score. Didn't every businessman in Port of Spain – especially a man in a responsible position – go in for some sort of bub-all? This was what prevented his conscience from being a nuisance. He did not consider himself singular. He felt that what he was doing was an accepted procedure, even though dishonest; almost an unwritten law governed it. Almost, but... Here he stopped his conscience from going any further.

The best in the land, white and good-class coloured, dabbled in these little bub-alls, so why not he, too? Moreover, argued Mr Benson, no true Trinidadian would consider himself self-respecting if he did not devise some method of making money on the side. The man in Port of Spain who was satisfied with his salary, and nothing but his salary, reasoned the Chief Clerk, was either lacking in brains or not a Trinidadian by birth and upbringing. In the first instance he could only be pitied; in the second, well, everybody knew how stupid and goody-goody small-island people were. For, like most Trinidadians, Mr Benson felt that people from Grenada, St Lucia, Barbados and the Windward and Leeward Islands generally could not possibly be as urbane and sophisticated as Trinidadians.

He watched Mr Reynolds, the salesman, who had just come in, on his way to his desk.

There was an example, thought Mr Benson. As salesman, Mr Reynolds had dozens of opportunities of making money on the sly. But no – he was scrupulously honest; had he not been, Mr Benson would have known; there were ways of knowing. Mr Reynolds was Grenada born and a staunch Wesleyan who attended service twice or thrice every Sunday and who did not go to dances because Wesleyans considered dancing immoral.

Mr Benson shrugged.

Anyway, it would be well to look into this matter. He was not at all alarmed – not in the very slightest. But he would still have a chat with Rowland and try to get him to dismiss that chauffeur.

A sense of relief and security (which deep down he knew to be false) had no sooner settled upon him when his gaze happened to rest on Mr Murrain – and at once the stab of shame returned.

That impolite English pig of a woman walking into the office.

Why couldn't he have treated her as Miss Henery had done? Why did he have to cringe and...

Then he remembered that Miss Henery came of a good family. She had been brought up by proud parents and would stand no haughty airs from a person like Mrs Murrain. This made him envy Miss Henery – and then hate her. He hated both Miss Henery and Mrs Murrain.

He stirred in his chair, the old bitterness wrenching at his stomach. His parents had been nobodies – at least his mother had been. He was not even legitimate. His black mother had not been content with the income her sewing had brought her (not unlike himself – the stinging irony!). She had had to hire out her body to these good-class coloured people – young gentlemen who could not afford to get girls of their own class in the family way: it was they who had come to his mother. His mother herself had not been able to say who was his father. Then, as though to pile up ignominy upon ignominy, she had died when be was seven, getting another child. And his godmother, who had taken him to live with her, had never been tired of reminding him of what a character his mother had been. She had taken pleasure in torturing him with the taunt.

At school he had always topped his class (beating his foster-brothers, who generally came tenth and eleventh out of a class of twenty-three), and then his godmother would say: "Get swell-headed now! No matter how bright you is you can't live down de shame your mother put on you!"

The day when he had stolen a sixpence from the dinner-wagon to buy half-share in a sweepstake ticket she had screamed at him between blows: "You can't help stealing! It's de bad blood what your mother put in you! It must come out one day..."

But they had never caught him stealing at the wholesale provision shop in Henry Street where he worked as porter for a year; he had been too clever for the East Indians who ran it. Instead, discovering that he was quick at figures and had an exceptionally good memory, they had put him to work at a desk as delivery clerk and checker... He was on his way up... From there to the big shipping office as tally-clerk. And then he had got his diploma in accountancy through the correspondence school:

a piece of paper symbolizing two years of sleeplessness and brain work under exceptionally adverse conditions – kerosene lamp, children yelling in the barrack-yard until nine at night, then grown-ups quarrelling until midnight and after; his godmother mumbling to herself in the next room, cursing him sometimes at the top of her voice for his meanness and ingratitude in not giving her what she considered enough to feed and lodge him out of his pay and out of the extras she knew he made selling beer and stout from broached cases on the wharf or in the warehouse... Then Essential Products as junior accountant – the post Mr Lopez held today... Up and always up. Intrigue at the office, intrigue at home, too, until he married and was rid of his godmother.

His marriage to Elvira Rogers, the girl from British Guiana, had proved a half-and-half success. They got on well – but she had given him no children. She had had an abortion soon after her first marriage (her husband had died in an accident on the timber grant up the Berbice River where he worked). She had been very ill, had nearly died, and the dispenser who had attended to her – for there had been no doctor up the river – had said that she would never he able to have another child.

She had told him all this before they were married, but he had cared enough for her not to let it stand in the way... Only nowadays he told himself that he ought to have been less impulsive. Now that he had passed forty he wanted to see editions of himself in miniature – a Eustace Benson Junior to top his class in school, a Mary or Kate Benson to grow up into a lady and marry a good-class young man. Already he had crashed his way into the outer perimeter of the good-class coloured strongholds; his children, with the education he could have afforded to give them, would have reached the citadel – especially as Elvira was olive-skinned – kinky-haired, too, but never mind that so much; complexion was the first consideration. His children would have been sure to have inherited olive complexions...

But Elvira was barren.

Mr Benson turned his head and watched Horace. He saw the boy at his desk. He looked very serious and pensive – even despondent. He was staring before him, his hand inside his shirt. Holding a sacred medal, of course, thought Mr Benson. Probably saying a prayer to the Blessed Lady. Asking for her help in his work – asking her to push him up in the world...

A vague, bitter smile passed across Mr Benson's face. These niggers. Why did my mother have to be a nigger?

He stroked his close-cut kinky hair. There were many flecks of grey in it already. From all the worries and all the agony of the struggle to get on top... Anyway, the Catholic Church had helped him in many ways. At one time, he too, used to wear a medal on a chain under his shirt... Through the Church he had made valuable contacts, social and business. He went to mass every Sunday, and was well up in the favour of the priests; he gave generous donations. On big festivals that called for processions he was always sure of a prominent place. Two years ago he had been a canopy-bearer in the Corpus Christi procession. And about a year ago a picture of him kneeling and kissing the Bishop's ring on an important occasion had appeared in one of the big newspapers...

That nigger would get on, too. He was efficient and alert; no fool. Soon he would be throwing his weight around. He was learning shorthand and typing. Who knew if he didn't study accountancy, too, at home?

But socially he will never get far. That black skin will always hold him back...

Mr Benson spread out his hand, palm down, on the manifests.

Watch my complexion. No nigger could show a complexion like this.

The thought was comforting. It assuaged his bitterness.

He saw Mr Waley appear at the top of the stairs. He started.

"Miss Yen Tip! Take this letter! Come along! Hurry up!" ...

Mr Murrain rose. His air was so urgent as he crossed the office that several pairs of eyes were turned upon him.

He stopped Mr Waley just as Mr Waley had passed through the barrier-gate.

"I'd like to see you about something rather important, Waley."

"Now?" asked Mr Waley, surprised.

"Yes – at once."

The Salesman; the Key Again.

Miss Henery laughed.

Mr Lopez laughed.

Mr Jagabir looked at Miss Henery with envy. In her place, he told himself, he would have been too weak with misery to utter a word, much less to laugh. They were going to dismiss her – it was certain – and there she was laughing with Mr Lopez as though nothing were the matter. He wished he had her self-assurance; he wished he had come of good class and could afford to be indifferent like that.

He tapped his coat pocket, suddenly conscious of the *roti* wrapped in a piece of newspaper. His lunch. He did not go home at noon for lunch when the office closed for an hour; he remained and ate his *roti*.

Miss Henery lunched at a restaurant – and Miss Laballe – for Miss Henery and Miss Laballe lived out of town. He, too, should have had his lunch in a restaurant, for his home in St James was right at the other end of the city. But he had to be thrifty; a meal at a restaurant would cost sixty cents at the cheapest. These coloured people could afford to be extravagant, but he who never knew where he stood with the firm must save something towards a rainy day. Buying clothes for his wife and children was bad enough, and with this fifth child on the way…

"He must think this is the only office in Port of Spain," he heard Miss Henery saying … See that! She could get another job in any office. But *he*…

"Murrain is a joke," grinned Mr Lopez, his black Spanish eyes gazing with a naïve insouciance at Miss Henery's face but, in reality, interested in the division between her breasts visible over the top of her low-cut dress. "Don't take him seriously. How much you want to bet he won't get Waley to sack you?"

Miss Henery shrugged. "I won't take any bet – because I don't care. Really, Rafael! I'll go to Barbados and spend a few weeks and when I come back get another job. It won't trouble me at all."

Mrs Hinckson typed rapidly and with concentration.

Miss Bisnauth, too – but not with concentration. She had put aside the poem for the time being, and was typing minutes for filing. Now and then she took swift glances at Horace. She was wondering why the boy's face looked so anxious and set – almost wild, as though he were planning to commit some terrible deed. It baffled her that he should look like this, because, she reasoned, if it was not he who had written out the love verse and put it on Mrs Hinckson's desk, he ought to have nothing to be worried about.

She did not like to be baffled by people's moods and conduct. It made her feel that she was failing in her efforts to understand human nature. It made her pessimistic as to whether she would ever be a great poet.

Xavier had his hand in his shirt as though he were clutching something. Could it be a love charm? Some of these black people, she knew, believed in *obeah* charms. *Obeah* was very rare, of course. Still… Oh, she knew what it must be! It was one of those Catholic medals. She had often seen big men wearing them on thin chains round their necks – rough, burly men with hairy chests whom you would never dream could bother about religious medals.

What was it they found in religion at all?

Like her parents, she had been baptized and confirmed in the Anglican church. But she never went to church. Her mother did, perhaps two or three times a year; her father not at all.

She was inclined to agree with what Arthur said. Religion as practised by the churches was a retarding influence in the world. Mrs Hinckson believed so, too. It was true. Religion only filled people up with a lot of impractical mumbo-jumbo and superstition. It encouraged people to delude themselves and escape from reality…

She had left out a word. She looked for the eraser, and as she brought it into use heard Mr Reynolds laugh.

The laughter of Mr Reynolds was the only laughter in the office which was unrestrainedly loud and hearty – though it was a shrill, whinnying kind of laughter and could easily have been a female's.

He was speaking on the telephone. Miss Laballe had just put

him through. He had a high tenor voice.

Miss Bisnauth heard Miss Laballe say: "Lord! I wonder *when* he'll be off the line now!"

Miss Bisnauth turned her head and smiled: "It's five to eleven now. I give him until twenty-five to twelve."

"Twenty-five to twelve! Not a minute before twelve o'clock, child! He never stop speaking dere till de Angelus ring: You take it from me!"

"Oh, Laura!"

"I'm not making fun. You wait and see. Who you think he's talking to now? One of his little Sunday School friends."

Miss Bisnauth blushed and giggled. The innuendo was not lost on her. It would not have been lost on anyone who knew Mr Reynolds well.

Mr Murrain had just left Mr Waley's presence. As he moved towards his desk the office seemed to grow chilly with tension.

Miss Bisnauth stared after him – and Miss Laballe grunted significantly.

Horace, at his desk, fidgeted.

Mr Lopez bent lower over the open journal before him than was really necessary, and Mr Jagabir took a deep breath, anticipating unknown terrors.

Mr Benson frowned – and then scowled, the scowl ostensibly directed at Miss Yen Tip who had glanced from her notebook to Mr Murrain.

Mrs Hinckson and Miss Henery typed like statues with animated hands; the most imaginative observer could not have said that they had the slightest interest in Mr Murrain's progress across the office.

Mr Reynolds, who was ignorant of the happenings of the past hour, seemed to sense that something was wrong. He began to glance around slowly and with an air of inquiry. He was extremely sensitive to the atmosphere of a crowd – of any group of people. He astonished Miss Laballe by saying: "Right-ee-o, boy! I'll see you and talk it over with you some time today," and hanging up.

He rose and took the sales-record book to Mr Murrain. "One or two little items you might be interested in here, sir," he said breezily – so breezily that a stranger might have thought that he was going to slap Mr Murrain heartily on the back as an accompaniment to his words.

Mr Murrain straightened up with a jerk. "What? Oh! Yes, yes!" He smiled briefly and tried to pay attention to what Mr Reynolds began to tell him. It did not interest him in the slightest, but he listened attentively. Mr Reynolds knew it did not interest him, but Mr Reynolds knew Mr Murrain's plight and knew that Mr Murrain welcomed interludes like this; Mr Murrain welcomed anything that prevented him from seeming idle, and conversation he welcomed most of all because it was far less jejune than the price-list or a ledger: it occupied him and entertained him, however slight the entertainment might be. Mr Reynolds liked helping out and entertaining people in need.

Mrs Hinckson stopped typing, and, in two or three precise and perfectly coordinated movements of her hands, extracted the sheets from the machine and rested them in the *Outgoing* tray. She took up her notebook and pencil, rose and went into Mr Waley's sanctum.

Both Miss Bisnauth and Mr Jagabir noticed how Horace started, how he stared after Mrs Hinckson until the frosted-glass door closed upon her. A gleam of purpose, of sudden resolve, came into his eyes – though only Miss Bisnauth translated it this way. Mr Jagabir thought it merely an infatuated gleam, and called Horace a silly jackass. Mrs Hinckson can't move a foot, thought Mr Jagabir, but the foolish black boy must be following her round with his eyes.

Miss Bisnauth felt alarmed. She thought: This boy is planning to do some terrible thing. I don't like the look on his face at all. His eyes have a mad glitter. She tried to laugh it off, certain that it was only her imagination playing tricks on her as usual, but the feeling of alarm persisted.

She switched her gaze – and her thoughts – over to Mr Reynolds. She smiled as she watched his gestures and his alive, twitching face. He was still speaking to Mr Murrain.

She liked Mr Reynolds. She did not mind that he was the joke of the office – the one who was always being sniggered about.

She watched him return to his desk, his sallow face with a fixed expression of good humour, a lock of his dark hair drooping over his right temple – hair dead-straight like an East Indian's, though he had no East Indian blood in him.

She sighed and went on typing...

Mr Reynolds's French and English ancestors were responsible for his dead-straight hair, and his Negro ancestors for the nose which was small and bridgeless with wide nostrils. Though taken with the rest of his face – light brown eyes, small, thin-lipped mouth and low cheekbones – it did not seem an obviously negroid nose.

In certain lights, Mr Reynolds could have passed for pure white, especially as a faint pinkness sometimes showed under his sallow complexion – markedly so when he was in a cheerful mood or amused over anything, which was not infrequent.

He was the least racially conscious coloured member of the staff. This was because he had been born and had spent the first twenty-two years of his life in Grenada, an island where the coloured people reign as aristocrats. There are hardly any whites in Grenada, and all the important Government posts are held by coloured men; the sugar and nutmeg planters are coloured; the leading businessmen are coloured.

The coloured people of Grenada suffer from the minimum of inferiority complex in the company of whites. They have their grade-distinctions, as in other islands of the British West Indies, but, with them, it is more or less an academic pastime; it becomes active and bitter only when the question of marriage involves a fusing of two physically disparate "grades" (say, kinky hair and light brown with straight hair and olive or sallow-olive), and even then the acridity and dissension do not spread beyond the families directly concerned.

Unlike Trinidadians and Jamaicans and Barbadians (who have to come up against a much greater number of whites), the coloured people of Grenada have cultivated a self-assurance which gives them, in the majority of cases, immunity to psychological conflict involving racial discriminations. There are no East Indians, Chinese, Portuguese, Spaniards, Assyrians or Jews in Grenada, as in Trinidad, Jamaica and British Guiana. Grenadians are either black (of pure negro descent) or coloured (of French or

English stock – or both – and negro). Only two classes of society exist – peasant black and coloured aristo-middle-class. Transplanted as adults to Trinidad or Barbados or British Guiana where the atmosphere is perfervid with the complicated polemics of class-race hierarchies, Grenadians are still at ease, for they simply merge themselves into one of these hierarchies – whichever will admit them most readily – and continue to behave as aristocrats. And as racial prejudice in the British West Indies is never overt and obtrusive, as in southern America and South Africa, Grenadians receive no ugly jolts to shock them out of the complacency brought with them from their own island.

Mr Reynolds, who had come to Trinidad in 1943 with the intention of securing a lucrative job with one of the American construction companies engaged in building the military bases but, instead, had joined the staff of Essential Products (he was never tired of telling people he had been born to be a salesman), went through life without a thought to race and class questions. Asked, he would have replied: "Race and class discrimination! I haven't come up against such a thing in all the four years I've been in Trinidad!"

On his mother's side he was of French descent, on his father's, English (there was negro slave blood on both sides). His father was the manager and part-owner of a nutmeg estate, and William Reynolds, the fourth of six children – four sons and two daughters – had known a life of ease and plenty from birth. One of his brothers was a doctor; a sister was married to a Scotsman, and, with her husband and three children, lived in Dundee, though she corresponded regularly with her people in Grenada; she was quite happy in Scotland, though she mentioned that some of Roy's (her husband's) people were a trifle crude and uncultured.

Mr Reynolds had just settled down at his desk and was whistling softly the tune of an anthem, *Oh, lift up your soul,* his head moving to and fro in time, when he became aware that Horace was approaching his desk.

"Mr Reynolds, I can have a word wid you, sir?" Horace spoke in a quick murmur.

"A word! Dozens!"

156

But despite his breezy tone, Mr Reynolds fidgeted sensitively. In his manner could be detected shyness, caution.

"Ah don't want to trouble you dis very minute, sir. I mean – I mean if you happen to be going down to your car – I just wanted to say a word to you in private."

Under the desk, Mr Reynolds's hand closed over his thigh. He saw the green beret...

One afternoon, two years ago, he had had cause to come into the office after hours with a young Englishman, a travelling agent, and while Mr Reynolds sat at his desk toying with the office key the Englishman narrated some of his experiences in the blitz. Noticing the key, he exclaimed: "A Peterson & Jason key! Can't mistake it. They were bombed out in the big Coventry raid." He told Mr Reynolds the story of the Jasons – how Thomas Jason was killed in a train smash in France and of the young man who was in his company – a young man wearing a green beret...

Since that afternoon Mr Reynolds had begun to dream at night of himself sitting in a railway coach beside a young man in a green beret. An unendurable ecstasy would possess him just before he awoke.

There were waking occasions, too – like now – when the green beret welled into the focus of his fancy. It was a ghost which, he felt, would haunt him until he died – but he was not so certain that he minded being haunted.

"I won't keep you long, sir," said Horace.

Mr Reynolds rose.

On the stairs, he gripped the boy's arm and chuckled shakily: "Well, what's it? Let's hear your troubles."

"Sir, I didn't want to trouble you."

Mr Reynolds waited.

From the day Horace had come to work at the office Mr Reynolds had made him understand that whenever the boy had any worries he was to come to him... "Don't hesitate. No trouble at all. You're new, and when you're new in any place there must be little things you'll find difficult to get the hang of."

This was the first time Horace had approached him on any matter.

"It's about something I write last night, Mr Reynolds."

"A letter?"

"No, sir."

The boy's discomfiture made Mr Reynolds discomfited, too. It was painful to watch his twitching face and his hand pulling at the fingers of the other hand, one by one. Mr Reynolds gripped his elbow briefly. "Tell me. Fire ahead."

"Sir, it's a paper wid a love verse from Shakespeare."

"Shakespeare?"

"Yes, sir." Horace bit his lip.

Mr Reynolds became aware of the clamour of the traffic in Marine Square. His face was perspiring slightly.

"Go on. Tell me."

"Sir, I write it – Ah copied it out from the book I have at home, and dis morning I brought it and put it on Mrs Hinckson's desk."

"What was it? One of the sonnets?"

"No, sir. A passage from *As You Like It.*"

"I know *As You Like It.*"

Horace was silent.

"Go on," urged Mr Reynolds.

"I wanted Mrs Hinckson to find it, sir, but —" He broke off. He seemed to have reached a point too unbearable.

Mr Reynolds gripped his elbow again. They stood facing downstairs.

"What's worrying you, Xavier?" His voice came out in a croak. He released the boy's elbow. He felt he was going to tremble, but with a supreme effort controlled himself.

"Sir, Ah just did it as – as a joke. I mean —"

Ants were darting about on the treader. Horace tried to crush one with the tip of his shoe. It escaped, but he got it at the second attempt.

Mr Reynolds, too, put out his shoe at one.

"Sir, de truth is, I like her a lil' bit – Mrs Hinckson, sir – and I put dis verse in her letter-tray – but Mr Lorry must go and tell her it was he who write it."

"Oh."'

"That's what happen, sir."

Mr Reynolds frowned and rubbed his neck slowly. "You say Mr Lorry found it and told her he wrote it?"

"Yes, sir – no sir! Mr Lorry didn't find it, but he went and tell her dat he write it – and she believe him." He kept looking at the treader.

"I see."

"Sir, why I ask you – what I was going to ask you was if you could have managed to tell her dat it wasn't Mr Lorry who did it – dat you hear it wasn't Mr Lorry. Don't tell her it was me; sir – please, sir! Don't tell her dat! I don't want her ever to know it was me, Mr Reynolds. But just tell her it wasn't Mr Lorry – that you saw de person who put it in her tray – and dat you know for certain it wasn't Mr Lorry. Dat's all Ah wanted to ask you to do, Mr Reynolds."

Horace was breathless.

A man was coming up the stairs. The chauffeur of one of the delivery vans.

Mr Reynolds patted Horace's shoulder. "I'll do what I can for you. Don't let it upset you."

Mr Reynolds turned as the man came abreast. "Vincent, you took the five hundred cases to Kerstin's?"

"Yes, Mr Reynolds. Ah just drop dem dere."

"I hope you didn't forget to have the book signed this time."

"No, sir. It signed."

"Who are you going up to? Mr Lopez?"

"Yes, sir. I got two accounts here for him."

"Right. Remind him about Redman's account, too."

"Yes, sir."

After the man had gone up: "Don't let it prey on your mind too much. I couldn't understand why you looked so tight and set-faced." Mr Reynolds grinned sympathetically. "I'll put things right for you. I think I understand the position."

… Settling down at his desk, he recalled one particular dream which reached the point where the train was about to crash and he pressed himself with a cry against the young man with the green beret…

His control weakened. He could feel his legs trembling.

Everyone got up and went to the window nearest. Mr Murrain frowned, hesitated, then followed suit.

Mr Waley, too, stopped dictating to rise and move over to the window.

Mrs Hinckson, faint disapproval and irritation in her manner, put down her notebook slowly and joined him.

It was a dock-strikers' demonstration. The strike, sanctioned by the trade unions, was five days old, and these demonstrations had started since the day before yesterday.

A long procession of the strikers with banners, followed by a straggling crowd of spectators, made its way west along Marine Square. The strikers were singing a political song to the tune of a hymn, and the singing triumphed above the rumble and blare of the traffic. The banners, among other things, said:

WE WANT FOOD!
DOWN WITH BRITISH TYRANNY!
NO CARGO UNLOADED – NO FOOD!
WE MUST NATIONALIZE OUR OIL!
BRITAIN IS DOOMED!
WE WANT A FEDERATED WEST INDIES!

Some banners mentioned the names of Government officials and Members of the Legislative Council, adding words and phrases like: BETRAYER, LACKEY OF THE CROWN, HYPOCRITE, STOOGE.

The demonstrators were composed almost entirely of negroes and East Indians, negroes in the majority. They were orderly; the straggling band of spectators gave the police far more work to control.

After they had passed and the sound of singing had succumbed to the noise of the traffic, the office went back to work.

Mr Murrain made soft sniffing sounds, a smile on his face. He said to Mr Jagabir: "What do they hope to gain by such a display?"

"They're stupid people, sir," frowned Mr Jagabir. "Most stupid people. Never satisfied wid de wages they get."

Mr Benson flashed at him: "Because you're drawing a big salary from the white people? They're right. I agree with them for striking."

Mr Murrain gave him a surprised look.

Mr Benson went back to his desk with a feeling of satisfaction. He felt that, in a way, he had vindicated himself for his shameful display when faced by Mrs Murrain. He had won back some of his self-respect.

"Let them keep up the strike," he told Miss Yen Tip. "They'd be fools in give in. These English people only want to come here and bleed us dry. They must get the best jobs in the place. They must live off the fat of the land while we wallow in the gutter."

"You're right," smiled Miss Yen Tip automatically. Labour questions and sociological matters were a mystery to her and did not interest her at all.

In the Manager's sanctum, Mr Waley smiled at Mrs Hinckson: "How does that impress you?"

Mrs Hinckson shrugged. "If you mean do I agree with them, I'd say yes. They're having a rough deal, poor people."

"Oh, I don't know. I suppose, in a way, it can be said they are. But I was thinking more of the banners. Do you agree with the sentiments the banners express?"

"Not with all of them – but one or two said things I'm definitely in favour of. A federated West Indies, for instance. And nationalizing our oil industry."

Mr Waley whistled and raised his brows. "You're really in favour of nationalizing the oil industry?"

"Most certainly! Don't you think it a scandal that millions of our dollars should go into the pockets of absentee proprietors in England and America every year while, comparatively speaking, we get next to nothing?"

"Next to nothing! Do you know how much royalty the Government collects?"

"How much! Not half as much as they should. Look at the dividends the oil companies declare! Fourteen, fifteen, sixteen per cent."

"That may be so – but another point you are forgetting. What about the vast amount of employment the industry provides?"

"Yes – with all the best positions and all the fat salaries going to white men from abroad who live in posh quarters, with posh facilities in a section all by themselves. Haven't you ever been to the oilfields to see how things are run?"

He flushed and laughed. "Oh, there may be a lot of truth in that – yet you must remember the local people are not qualified to hold the top jobs."

"Quite. That's always the excuse. But you know very well, Mr Waley, because you've been out here long enough; even if a local man of colour did secure all the qualifications which are supposed to be necessary he still wouldn't be given a top job." She saw him squirming in discomfort, and added quickly: "Anyway, I'm sure the labourers in the oilfields aren't paid and treated so magnificently as to compensate for what goes into the pockets of foreign investors."

He seemed relieved and grateful that she had left the acutely precarious territory.

"That's a debatable point," he said, lighting a cigarette. He flicked the match out of the window instead of putting it in the ashtray before him; the energy in him expressed itself in various little ways like this.

"Of course, we haven't time to debate now, but when you speak of nationalizing the oil industry, have you considered this question: Where would the Government of Trinidad and Tobago raise the money, and *how* would they raise it, to work oil on their own?"

"That's the old argument. I don't say we'd make as tremendous profits as the foreign companies are making now – at least, not at first – but we'd be able to raise enough capital to get on our legs, I'm sure.'" She realized she was on uncertain ground; she knew practically nothing about big business and economics.

"The point is," she laughed, "we'd much prefer to handle our own natural resources. If we did fail to make them pay as they should we'd be satisfied that we ourselves messed things up. We'd, at least, have our self-respect in that we wouldn't feel we were being persistently exploited by outsiders."

"What a consolation!" He laughed, too – and there was a good-

162

natured ring in it; he was not being patronizing. "I think you should have been a politician, Mrs Hinckson."

"No, thank you."

One of these days, she told herself, as he resumed dictation, she was going to fall in love with him. He was the most human Englishman she had ever known – and she had met a good many, even though she had never been to England.

Of course, he had his queer English ways. For instance, he had made no reference whatever to what had happened a short while ago. Not a word about Sidney Whitmer or the conversation with Mr Murrain. It must have disturbed him, but when she had come in he had shown no signs of it. He had looked up and smiled in his usual brisk, alert way and remarked that yes, they must get to work again on the London mail.

A West Indian – or an American – would have greeted her with: "What's all this been happening in my absence, Mrs Hinckson?" … But she liked him for his reserved traits. They went with him as an Englishman. It would have been uncomfortable – and disappointing – had he lacked them.

She respected his reticence even while it irritated her. For instance, she would have liked to have asked him about Kathleen Henery, whether he had agreed with Mr Murrain that she had been impertinent to his wife. He would not have snubbed her, but it would have embarrassed him; it would have struck a false note in their relationship; she could envisage the slight frown and the evasiveness of his blue eyes, the hesitant tone of his voice.

In the main office, Miss Henery was curious, too, to know what Mr Waley felt on the matter – and more: whether he had decided to dismiss her.

Her air of indifference as she typed the new batch of accounts Mr Jagabir had just handed to her was only assumed. She had been sincere when she had told Mr Lopez that she felt she would get another job without trouble; she was an efficient stenographer, and though her family might not be as influential as Mrs Hinckson's, she knew a number of highly placed coloured men in big firms who would be only too ready to manoeuvre her into a job. In a way, too, she would not be so unhappy about leaving now because it would mean she could spend a longer time in

Barbados with her cousin and her family than the two weeks she had originally planned on. But while this was very pleasant to ponder on, the shadow fell upon her happiness when she reflected that she would have suffered an ignominy. Had she tendered her resignation her pride would have felt no hurt, but to be dismissed would be as good as a slap. An insult…

This was what worried her.

… I'm sure, though, thought Mrs Hinckson, he hasn't decided to get rid of Kathleen. It would be a big shock to me if he has. It would be entirely out of keeping with the man I know. He isn't small and vindictive like Murrain.

She clicked her tongue. "Sorry. Would you mind repeating that last sentence? I'm afraid my thoughts strayed a little."

"Take care!" he said, his tone implying so strongly "Who is he?" that she found herself smiling and getting warm in the cheeks.

The telephone rang, and as he answered it she went over what she had jotted down to make sure she had everything right.

Finished, she watched his fingers; he was still speaking on the phone. He kept tapping his fingers lightly, actively, on a letter with English stamps that rested on his blotter.

The postmark, she could see, was Devonshire. He was a Devonshire man. More than once he had told her about the moors and the lovely undulating scenery. About the large, ancient stones on the moors which – whenever he remembered them – were so nostalgic of his boyhood jaunts. About the mists, too, and of getting lost in the mist; of how when he was twelve he had fallen into a quarry and broken an arm. He had always been of an adventurous nature, and liked dangerous expeditions.

His father had been a greengrocer in a small town – she could never remember the name, it began with a C – and George was an only son. A great-uncle – a brother of his mother's father – had left him a legacy, and it was this that had permitted him to attend the grammar school in Exeter…

"… and from which, by the way, in my last year, I nearly got expelled. Broke bounds one night with two other chaps and didn't get back until one. The gate-porter spotted us, flashed his lamp full in our faces – and we were in the soup."

He had never mentioned what was the object of this nocturnal escapade, but she had conjectured it must have had something to do with girls. Even nowadays he had a reputation for being more than normally keen on ladies. He had married a woman from the Midlands ten years his senior and of some means and who – rumour said – could not possibly satisfy him sexually any more, for she was fifty-one and ailing to his forty-one and robust constitution. He had married her, it seemed, because of her good connections and means, when he was holidaying in England after three years on the Tucurapo estate as an overseer (he had come to Trinidad to work when he was twenty-four).

On his return to Trinidad, he had risen quickly in the firm, and before coming to Port of Spain as Manager of Essential Products had acted as Deputy Manager of the Tucurapo estate.

He took his work very seriously – how seriously had been illustrated only a few months ago during the period everyone in the office had come to know as the Crisis.

The Government had issued a new regulation (one of many echoes of the wartime restrictions) forbidding the export of marmalade and all jams and confectionery containing cane sugar. The order, the Government explained, when tackled by manufacturers, had come from the Crown Office (if there had been no outcry from the manufacturers the Government would have made no explanation). Because of certain economic factors which had arisen, the Home Government thought it wise that the West Indian colonies should conserve their stocks of cane sugar, and therefore only a limited amount of this commodity would be permitted to be exported. There was too high a percentage of sugar used in the marmalade and jams being exported at present, and the Government saw no alternative but to "restrict, if only temporarily, the export of these products and thus halt the drain on sugar stocks". (That this meant the virtual ruin of the industry – for the local market was far too small to support it – did not appear to disturb the Home Government.)

Despite this edict, Mr Waley and the heads of the Tucurapo company showed no signs of discomposure – much to the astonishment and conjecture of the business world.

But the reason was not long in being discovered.

Export licences for shipments of marmalade and jams continued to be granted, as before, to the Tucurapo company and Essential Products. When questioned, Mr Waley simply smiled, became evasive and uncomfortable (Mrs Hinckson always held this to his credit) and said: "Ask the Government, my dear chap. I don't control these things."

To Mrs Hinckson he said in confidence (and a trifle shamefacedly): "We're a big company, you know. Our principals have good connections – and they aren't asleep."

She made no comment. But the explosion came.

The newspapers got on to what was happening, and front page headlines and thunderous editorials ripped the calm.

Letters deluged the column known as the People's Forum in one big paper.

The Legislative Council took fire as though a chain reaction had come into effect. Questions were levelled at the Government by elected members – the quiet, mousy ones as well as the troublesome ones; even Government-nominated members rose to make protests at what was considered "partisanship that is too obvious to be ignored".

An elected member put before the House a motion to create a committee of investigation.

The newspapers began to draw up petitions to be forwarded to the Secretary of State for the Colonies "to call attention to certain flagrant malpractices on the part of the local Government which had been brought to the notice of the public of Trinidad and Tobago, and to state that the Government's explanations have been found unsatisfactory…"

Pictures were displayed prominently on front pages, showing elected members engaged in impassioned debate (one member was shown shaking his fist at the House; another pointing an accusatory finger at His Excellency the Governor).

This, for the office, was the Crisis.

No one could remember seeing Mr Waley smile once. He was a man possessed. He could hardly spend two hours a day at his desk. He was always in consultation with some Government official at the Red House, or at the Tucurapo estate in conference with Mr Holmes and other members of the company executive staff. Mrs Hinckson seldom went home before five-thirty. Cables came and went all day. Most of her time was spent in decoding cables received or putting into code cables to be sent off.

The Crisis lasted eleven days – then the Government issued a statement.

The new regulation in respect to marmalade and confectioneries manufactured locally must stand. Government had gone into the matter "carefully and at great length" but no alternative could be found. "Further, relevant to the question raised as to why Tucurapo Cocoa & Citrus Producers Ltd and Essential Products Ltd had been made exceptions of in respect to the new regulations, Government wishes to point out that these two concerns held large export quotas prior to the outbreak of war and the coming into effect of the Defence Regulations whereas the majority of small manufacturers came into being during the war and are therefore not entitled to the same consideration. Government would also like to call attention to the fact that Tucurapo Cocoa & Citrus Producers Ltd and Essential Products Ltd are responsible for the employment of a large number of agricultural labourers, and should the new regulation be made to apply to these two companies the result would be a sharp rise in unemployment figures."

Mr Waley sighed: "I knew we'd win, but it was all the strenuous fuss and commotion that gave me the jitters."

"Long live Crown Colony government!" murmured Mrs Hinckson.

"What's that?"

She repeated it in a louder voice – and he flushed. And then laughed.

As she waited for him to finish speaking on the telephone she observed his face surreptitiously, noting the thin, slightly upturned nose, the eyes set far apart, the mobile mouth – his most expressive feature after his eyes – and the dimpled chin that was always shiny with sebaceous grease. He was not very hairy, and his chin was almost boyishly smooth. The light-brown hair was thick and bristly, cut rather short so that it looked like a military brush when he had just come from the barber ("Behold the porcupine!" Mr Lorry would remark); at other times it had a semi-damp, unsettled look, as though undecided whether to lie flat or to stand on end.

A feeling of doubt attacked her.

She wondered whether she could be mistaken about him, whether behind this exterior of sincerity there was not a mean, superficial nature. A nature like Mr Murrain's.

She frowned.

What right had she to be critical of him? Was she so sincere herself? Did her own nature lack meanness and shallowness to such an extent that she could afford to condemn other people for possessing these traits? In what did the profundity of a man or woman lie? The answer came at once. Integrity. A rigid code based on one's intuitive conception of the rightness of things. Everyone, she believed, conceived of the rightness of things in one and only one way; it was a stable factor; outward manifestations did not affect it; it was absolute and could not be viewed in a relative spirit as a series of varying facets, each one shaped to suit the casuistic self-vindication of the individual; it existed as part of the calm divinity in every human; the grossest of us possessed it. But only a very few recognized it in themselves and made any attempt to live by its standards. Those were the ones with integrity.

She gave herself a mental shake – but more thoughts came.

She wondered whether his reluctance to discuss the incidents of which Mr Murrain had informed him could indicate that he had decided to dismiss Kathleen Henery. She would be disappointed in him if it turned out to be so. She doubted if she could ever recover from such a disappointment; it might even cause her to resign before long.

I'm being self-righteous again, she thought – and remembered her attitude towards Xavier and the love verse. Xavier was a black boy, which meant that automatically she classed him as her inferior and too absurd a candidate for a love affair with her. Could such an attitude be associated with a person of integrity?

She dismissed the subject.

She tapped her pencil against the edge of the desk, her gaze on one of the two letter-trays… I believe I left that paper in my *File* tray in a spirit of conscious vanity so that anyone passing could take it up and read it. Why didn't I put it into my handbag? ...

... Mr Reynolds smiled as he put it back in the tray again. A smile of understanding, quiet and sensitive.

Mr Benson had sent Horace to the Control Board, or Mr Reynolds would not have strolled across to Mrs Hinckson's desk to read the love verse. He knew that the boy would have been discomfited to see him reading it.

He returned to his desk, his face still with its expression of good humour. He was whistling softly ("a whispering kind of whistling" Miss Bisnauth had once described it to herself). But there was loneliness in him. And the old feeling. The feeling of differentness.

I must see if I can help him in some way, he thought. He seems so upset about the whole thing.

It was his policy to help everyone he possibly could, no matter the inconvenience to himself. He was afraid of himself. He dreaded introspecting, for when he introspected he pitied himself and saw his loneliness as a thing of magnified terror and ugliness – something that would pursue him to the end of his days. Helping people and his work as a salesman were screens against the sight of himself. His church work, too – but he saw through this screen too often and too easily and did not put as much confidence in it as in the others.

He helped people irrespective of their sex because it made him feel that he was capable, despite his inversion, of doing good in a dispassionate spirit and without expectation of reward.

He was a frequent visitor at the home of a girl who had practically no hopes of getting married. She worked in an office in Frederick Street, and lived alone in a small cottage on the outskirts of the city; her parents were dead and her sisters were all married; a brother was in Venezuela, an oil driller.

She was a cheerful, pleasant person, but secretly unhappy and lonely. She was thirty-one and weighed nearly three hundred pounds; she had tried every possible method in an effort to reduce – but to no avail; the doctors had told her it was no use: it was endocrinal.

He visited Delly Winter four evenings a week, and he knew

that his presence gave her solace. They never discussed it, but he was aware that she knew everything concerning him; everyone knew it; it was no secret. But she never let it interfere with their friendship...

... Mr Waley put down the telephone and said: "Good. Now, where were we again? The packing-cases —"

The telephone rang.

"My God! ... Yes? ... Ah! That you, Henderson? ... At last, eh?"

He put his hand over the receiver.

"Mrs Hinckson, it's Henderson with that list."

"What! Oh, Lord!" She rose. "I'm going back to my typewriter, then. That means a solid twenty minutes."

He grinned. "Not less, I'm afraid. We'll have to try again after lunch... Yes, yes, Henderson. Just a moment."

He put his hand over the receiver again, glanced at his wrist watch.

"By the way, when you go out tell Miss Henery to come in and see me – let's say at about a quarter to twelve."

"Very well, Mr Waley."

It was while Mr Jagabir was on his way to Mr Murrain's desk with the petty cash book that he observed Mr Reynolds pause at Mrs Hinckson's desk and take up the paper with the love verse. He remarked to Mr Murrain: "I never see anyt'ing to interest people so much like dis love verse, sir."

"What?"

"De love verse, sir."

"Love verse?" Mr Murrain, in an instant of genuine alarm, thought that Mr Jagabir's mind had become affected. Mr Jagabir pointed with a thumb.

"Mr Reynolds. Look at 'e dere, sir! He reading it now. It's a paper wid a Shakespeare love verse what Xavier copy out and put in Mrs Hinckson's letter-tray dis morning. Everybody in dis office interested in it. You would t'ink it's a cheque for a million dollars."

Mr Murrain's eyes were round. "I'm afraid – you'll really have to be more explicit. Xavier copied out – what are you talking about?"

Mr Jagabir explained in elaborate detail, and with enthusiasm and frillings of his own invention.

"Just fancy," he said in the course of his closing sentences. "A stupid black boy like dat. Dat's why he can't do his work properly. Always staring about de office following de lady wid his eyes. I won't be surprised if he fall in love wid Miss Henery, too. She's de next one he will —"

"That will do now," Mr Murrain interrupted – and Mr Jagabir was baffled at the sharpness of his tone. "Is the petty cash book here in order? You've attended to everything — ?"

"Oh, yes, yes, sir. Ah attend to everyt'ing. It in perfect order. You can look through it and see."

Mr Jagabir moved back to his desk, and Mr Murrain adjusted himself in his swivel chair to the accompaniment of a deep breath. His lips came together in a thin line, and his gaze moved from the price-list before him to the inkstand – then to a *Nuttall's Diction-*

ary. To a point an inch or so above the dictionary which brought his eyes directly on to Miss Henery's right foot encased in a shoe made of transparent plastic straps. His gaze made no further hops.

He watched the small olive foot. The nails were painted carmine. He noted the tension of the metatarsal tendons which caused them to stand out clearly. It was a thin foot, and the position in which it was held must be responsible, he reasoned, for the tension.

Without knowing how it had happened, he found that his gaze had travelled up to Miss Henery's waist.

His chin began to move from side to side in a rapid wobble.

He turned his head quickly and his gaze came to rest on the foliage of a tree in Marine Square. Telephone cables intervened – grey, horizontal lines that marred but did not obscure the leaves. The leaves glittered in the near-noon sunshine. He could pick out separate ones that glittered more brightly than others. The sight of them gave him relief – why he did not know, nor was he quite certain what it was he should feel relief from. He liked the leaves. There was something so – so impassive? Yes, impassive and unshakable... well, the wind could shake them, it was true – but it was a spiritual un-shakableness he meant. A feeling of...

He shook his head, experiencing a sense of failure. He felt he had trodden on unfamiliar ground. He had been on the verge of a revelation – but it had bypassed him, as revelations always bypassed him. He supposed he was not big enough to bring into being anything so – so big.

The scar on his forearm tingled. It had grown suddenly pale.

He felt trapped – trapped in his skin.

He shut his eyes for a moment, and heard the noise in the sky...

... He was dragging along the boy whose foot was injured. A wave foamed around the bare foot – it was bleeding – and the boy whined and swore.

A man wearing a sou'wester kept beckoning. He stood in the rocking boat which seemed about to overturn...

... "Hurry up there, you! Only you two! No more!" ... That was a shout from the other boat about fifty yards to the right...

Mr Murrain's hand trembled slightly as he pulled the price-list towards him. He looked at it and saw the shape of two small breasts under thin cloth through which large, dark areolae were vaguely visible.

A few minutes later, when he was himself again, he wondered (as Mr Reynolds often wondered about the green beret) whether Dunkirk would haunt him to the end of his days. But (unlike Mr Reynolds) he was certain that such a haunting would not be pleasant.

Mrs Hinckson had typed two and a half lines when she heard footsteps on the stairs and glanced up casually.

She saw a short, well-built young man with square shoulders and an austere olive face approach the barrier. He approached not hesitantly but with purpose and self-confidence. He paused and looked about the office, a very faint smile of inquiry on his face. A controlled smile in harmony with the rest of him.

Horace, she noticed, was not at his desk. He must have been sent out somewhere.

She rose and went to the barrier.

"Can I do something for you?"

The smile of inquiry merged into a smile of quiet cordiality as a brown mist might merge into a blue mist; the transition hardly seemed to have taken place – yet it had.

The young man tapped a fat cardboard file case he held under his arm.

"I'd like to see your assistant manager, please."

"The assistant manager? Mr Murrain?"

"I think that's the name – yes. It's about an advertisement for a magazine."

"A magazine?" Her cheeks grew warm as she realized how idiotic she must sound repeating everything he said.

"Sort of. 'Booklet', perhaps, would be more accurate."

"You – you're a writer?"

"Yes." He said it without the smile.

"Have you an appointment with Mr Murrain?"

"No, I'm afraid I haven't – ah! I think this is probably Miss Bisnauth."

Miss Bisnauth had come up.

"You're Mr Barnett?" she asked. She smiled shyly, a faint note of reverence in her voice. "Mr Mortimer Barnett?"

"But you can drop the 'mister'."

Blood darkened her face.

Mrs Hinckson lingered. She knew she ought to retire now, but she could not. It was as though invisible tentacles had stretched out from the barrier and were holding her in a numbing grip.

She heard Miss Bisnauth say: "This is Mortimer Barnett, the writer, Nanette. Mrs Nanette Hinckson."

She ought to have inclined her head and smiled as she had done to how many dozens of them in the past – intellectuals, non-intellectuals, artists, civil servants, engineers... But to this one she held out her hand. A force beyond her compelled it. It was as though a gutter of weakness were being scooped through and through her.

Afterwards she felt certain she had stammered when she said: "Well, I think I'll leave Miss Bisnauth to attend to you," as she turned off to return to her desk.

Miss Bisnauth told him to be seated a moment, and went to Mr Murrain, hurrying in quick, awkward steps.

Mr Murrain said: "Why, yes – by all means. I'll see him." He said it with such eagerness that he feared Miss Bisnauth would misunderstand. She would think it was because of his idleness alone that he welcomed the interview with this fellow. She would not know...

He drummed with his fingers on the desk a devil's tattoo...

... she would not know the other need for distraction.

His brain completed the thought as though in malice against him.

He winced. He was suffering.

Miss Bisnauth resumed her seat before her desk, her face still warm with elation.

That's a high soul, she told herself. I can see it in his movements, in his way of smiling. His voice shows it. I'm sure he's going to be famous one day. The world will recognize him. Everybody treats him now as if he's a silly crank, Arthur says.

They say he's mad. Because he's individual – and has ideas they could never hope to have. It's always the way. The minute people find you're different from them they snarl at you. They think you a criminal for standing alone, for not doing as the herd does.

A sorrow came upon her. It was a sorrow for the world. After all, she thought, human beings could not help being human beings. What was the use of railing at their incapacities? It was terrible that individuals of supreme worth like Mortimer Barnett should be spat on and ridiculed, but that had to be expected. To change that you would have to change the chemical composition of men and women.

She felt an abrupt hopelessness. She saw the world around her as a disgusting place. So disgusting that it would not have troubled her if she had known that tonight she was going to die.

She heard the drone of an aeroplane.

Of course, men had achieved great things. Aeroplanes, wireless, radar, *King Lear,* the Eroica… She heard the wailing, awesome noise in the Venusburg music. Music that compelled you to hold your breath and wonder at the genius that could have made it possible. It was Arthur's favourite music – and hers, too. Arthur said that Wagner, if nobody else, recognized the heroic stature of man. She agreed.

Inspiration flooded her. She began to look about her agitatedly for the completed first draft of her poem…

… "How are you getting along, Nanette?"

"Not too bad. How about you?"

Mr Reynolds shrugged, his hands fanning out in swift gestures meant to express happiness and insouciance. "Trying to make the world go round with me. Only thing you can do. Make the world go round with you."

"And how is that done?"

She had lost all urge to work. Her hands felt so limp that she was sure she would not have been able to strike the keys had she made the attempt. She was glad for Mr Reynolds. She wished he would remain indefinitely and talk to her.

"It's done by being brazen. You set your face and ignore the lightning and thunder and the rain. You push your way blindly through the storm. You get wet but you don't take notice."

He laughed – but it was an empty sound. He knew it sounded empty.

"And do you necessarily reach your destination?"

"I didn't say anything about destinations, did I? I said you make the world go round with you."

She looked past him, her eyes wide and vacant.

"Some of us may get dizzy and fall doing that," she said. "If you don't adapt yourself to the motion."

"Don't you think it a little sickening always having to adapt oneself to something?"

He nodded – and now all the laughter and good humour had gone from his face. "You don't have to tell me that."

He fingered his tie and began to whistle softly. It sounded mournful. He said casually: "I was reading this love verse of yours. Hope you don't consider me very inquisitive?"

"Not at all. In fact, only a little while ago I was thinking how I must have left it here out of deliberate vanity so that everyone could read it in passing. I don't mind admitting I'm vain."

"*Ecclesiastes*," he murmured. He began to whistle again. He stopped and asked: Who's it so desperately infatuated with you?"

She told him.

"But I thought —" He laughed.

"What is it you thought?" Her eyes moved past him...

"I don't know what should have given me the impression, but I sort of – well, what I mean is I had an idea it might have been Pat Lorry. I thought you believed it was he who had done it."

"I did believe so – until I learnt it wasn't. You seem interested."

"I'm only on an errand of mercy," he said, flushing.

"You are?"

What could be the matter with her? She spoke as though she were saying a part in a play. And her gaze kept roving past him...

"Considering you know already it's he who did it, I don't suppose it would be dishonourable of me to explain." So he told her of his conversation with Horace on the stairs. "He seemed pretty desperate, poor lad. I was really sorry for him."

"I'm sorry for him myself."

He saw she meant it, and felt foolish. Irritated. It was as though by saying she was sorry for the boy she had robbed him of some privilege exclusively his own.

"Funny world," he mumbled.

"What did you say?"

"Just being philosophical," he grinned. He thrust his hands into his trousers pockets and said he must be moving on.

He collided with Mr Benson, who was going towards the Men's Room. He clutched the Chief Clerk's shoulder briefly to steady himself.

"Sorry, Mr Benny!" He laughed.

He was flushing. In his fancy he saw the green beret. As he went towards his desk he reflected idly how one's private images could be traced back to, and linked with inanimate objects. The office key – the story behind the key – the young man with the green beret in the story. One shadow behind another, telescoped backwards to infinity…

Miss Yen Tip, taking advantage of Mr Benson's absence, skipped across to Miss Henery.

"Child, what happened? Murrain reported you to Waley, na? Nanette told you what Waley said?"

"She says he wants to see me at a quarter to twelve."

"Murrain is a dog. And that wife of his – one of dese days I must put a banana skin on de stairs for her to walk on."

Miss Henery laughed. "Olga, look, I'm not in the mood for jokes!"

"Who say I'm joking?" said Miss Yen Tip, glancing at the door of the Men's Room. "It will be a shame if they dismiss you. Oh, hell! Lemme go back to my desk before dis man Benson come out and catch me. See you later, child!"

She skipped back to her desk, for she knew what an avalanche of disapproval would have descended upon her had Mr Benson come back to find her gossiping with Miss Henery.

But for Mr Benson, felt Miss Yen Tip, life for her would have been one long joy. "Just one long joy, in spite of every t'ing else." (Like most Chinese in the West Indies, eight times out of ten she was unable to pronounce her dental aspirates.)

Mr Benson seemed to take such deliberate pleasure in catching her out in instances of negligence and slackness that she had almost come to feel that no matter what efforts she made to give satisfaction (and she knew that she tried her hardest and was efficient) she would always, in Mr Benson's eyes, be grossly incompetent.

Had she, like Miss Henery, been able to answer back, he would probably have been less exacting; he would have respected her more. But she was, by nature, of a peaceable disposition. And she valued her job. The salary of ninety dollars a month she received virtually supported herself, her aunt and her two younger sisters who were still at school. Her aunt's sewing brought in very little.

Miss Yen Tip was not a wealthy Chinese like her cousins, the Graingers. Her mother and father had been fairly well off in their day – her father had owned a provision shop. But it was seven years since her parents had died, and nine since the shop had been foreclosed on by her father's creditors. Her father had had one virtue in too great excess – liberality towards his indigent compatriots.

Mr Albert Grainger (in his younger days, just Tai Kong) was her father's first cousin, but he and his family were too wealthy and high up in Trinidad Chinese society to recognize Miss Yen Tip and her aunt and the two children. They would readily have extended financial aid if circumstances had grown straitened. But Miss Yen Tip and her aunt would have been too proud to accept it.

"I'd prefer to die dis minute," Miss Yen Tip often told her friends, "dan accept a cent from dose people."

Miss Yen Tip was a creole Chinese who could not speak Chinese. Her outlook was the outlook of a westerner. The outlook of all British West Indians. Like her parents, she had been born and brought up in Trinidad. China was a country as foreign to her as it was to any English child in Surrey or American child in Nebraska. Together with her negro, East Indian, Portuguese, Spanish and coloured school companions, she had grown up with the *Royal Reader, Gentle Jesus, meek and mild,* Sir Walter Scott, and *Drink to me only with thine eyes.*

Only her grandparents, who had come to Trinidad from Hong Kong in the last century, could have spoken Chinese, and thought like the Chinese.

In the West Indies, Chinese are of two main divisions – those who are the descendants of the immigrants from Hong Kong, Canton or Peking who arrived in the latter half of the nineteenth century: descendants completely creolized, even to the extent of knowing not a word of Chinese (some to the extent, like the Graingers, of assuming European names), and those who have arrived within the past ten or fifteen years, as imported cheap labour for the chains of provision shops owned by their wealthy creole compatriots, and who can speak very little English because of their cramped, clannish mode of life.

Mr Grainger owned one of the longest chains of provision shops in Trinidad. He paid the imported Chinese who ran the shops for him about a fifth of what he would have had to pay creoles, and as a result he had grown immensely wealthy. He and his family lived in a three-storeyed residence on Queen's Park West, facing the Savannah, and drove around the Savannah every afternoon in two Packards.

Miss Yen Tip, at twenty-two, was not in any way embittered because of the affluence of her cousins in contrast with her own barely comfortable circumstances. Her nature was too ebullient; she was too gay and extroverted. When she happened to meet her cousins accidentally anywhere (by mutual desire, they had not been on visiting terms for years), she greeted them as cheerfully as though she had entertained them to dinner the evening before – and her manner was sincere; she did not know how to be a hypocrite.

That she was not invited to functions at the Chinese consulate troubled her not at all. She had her own friends – Chinese as well as coloured middle-class – and there were at least three young men, extremely eligible husbands, very much bent on marrying her (though she was determined not to get married before she was twenty-four; life unmarried, she had decided, was too lovely). "What more dan dat," she would say, "I could want?"

She was five feet one, but slim in proportion, with a figure immature but in proportion, too, to the rest of her. Her slightly projecting teeth were considered by some people her most attractive feature.

She dressed with excellent taste, and as her aunt made all her clothes this problem did not affect the budget as seriously as it might otherwise have done.

She had inherited her father's generous spirit. Her aunt often commented that if they were rich Olga would fling around money to poor people with the same casualness and freeness as her father had done.

The telephone on Mr Benson's desk rang...

"Tell him it's Millan at the gas station."

"He's not – oh, yes, wait, Mr Millan! He's coming now!"

"Who's that now?" scowled Mr Benson, just back from the Men's Room.

"Mr Millan at de gas station."

"Millan? What Millan wants with me?"

As she yielded the instrument to him she noted the frown of uneasiness that came to his face.

She turned off, smiling.

Something to do with one of his bub-alls, she thought, her confidence in herself rising as she returned to her desk. The farther away from him the more her self-confidence increased.

A hell of a man! One of these days he's going to get caught out. Let him go on!

"Mungalsingh?" …

"… Came round there to you and created a disturbance?" …
Click.

Miss Laballe, from long practice, had learnt how to make it soft
and unobtrusive, but Mr Benson noted it, for he had been on the
alert for it.

"… No, no! Don't bother to go into details now, Millan. When
I see you… What's that?"

"All right… Yes, I did suspect Rowland's chauffeur… When I
see you. We can't talk about it now."

Mr Benson hung up.

A slow panic spread in him. For the first time in his memory
he experienced lack of confidence in himself as a schemer.

Mungalsingh had gone round to Millan, too, and made de-
mands, and when Millan had ordered him off he had got nasty.

Mr Benson had not foreseen this; it was outside the pattern of
things as the pattern had appeared in his mind. He grew saturated
with a feeling of the bizarre, as though he had just entered the
office and found Mr Waley sitting at Mr Jagabir's desk and Mr
Murrain at Horace's. Nothing had ever gone wrong with his
schemes before. He had never suffered a hitch – at least, no hitch
worthy of consideration. Could this, at last, be the major blunder
that would bring about his downfall! It *was* a blunder, because he
had heard about the habits of Rowland's chauffeur and had done
nothing about it – and here it was the fellow must have gone and
blabbed something to this East Indian.

He put out his hand to the phone, the inclination strong in him
to ring Millan and get the details, find out exactly what and what
the man had said when Millan had ordered him off.

He restrained himself. That Laballe girl listened-in to every
word that was spoken on the wires. He could not take the chance.
He must wait until lunchtime.

He glanced at his watch. Twenty-five to twelve.

He scowled impatiently.

What did this man have to turn up for to mar the smoothness of his undertakings? What gradual evolution of events and circumstances had built up towards his advent on this particular morning with this particular crooked mind and in this particular mood?

Since he was a young man, Mr Benson had been reading books on philosophy. Like Horace, he had considered reading one of the means of improving himself and of accelerating his rise in the world. He had come to love philosophy, and, in quiet moments, it gave him pleasure to sit and try to unravel some complicated theory of his own or of one of the authors whose books he read.

A dark East Indian with shifty eyes. Mungalsingh. A pickpocket, a seasoned criminal. And he the Chief Clerk of Essential Products Ltd. The collision of the two lives could be blind accident; it would be rational to conceive of it as so. Yet, why could there not be an unprobed force that marshalled lives and events – even objects – into a set and prearranged sequence? A train of related pictures stretching back, one behind the other interminably?

(Mr Benson would have considered it an incredible coincidence could he have known of Mr Reynolds' idle thought concerning the green beret only a few minutes ago and of what Mortimer Barnett was at this very instant discussing with Mr Murrain.)

Mr Benson shook his head.

The old idea of predestination. However, it was still fascinating to think that behind every human being an innumerable disregarded or forgotten host of event-trails branched away, touching innumerable other lives and innumerable objects... A human being, viewed in entirety, was a coalescence of all the other lives, all the objects and all the events involved with his past.

He suddenly remembered a book of Santayana's he had got from the library a day or two ago. He must dip into it tonight.

Horace was coming towards him.

"Got them all right? Why the delay?"

"The clerk said they weren't sorted out yet, sir. De Controller passed dem since yesterday afternoon – but they didn't reach – they didn't reach de outer office until about an hour ago."

Mr Benson watched the boy going to his desk.

Why did he have to stammer like that? Something queer in his manner this morning. As if he was excited or anxious…

… something very queer, thought Miss Labelle. I believe this Mungalsingh is the same man who came in to see him a little while ago. One day he's going to get into a big mess over his bub-alls – and then he's going to come down with a big flop.

Her smile was malicious.

… Mr Murrain's was friendly and pleased.

Mr Murrain rocked backward and forward in his swivel chair. Talking to this young man made him realize more forcibly than ever that he had never been meant to be on the staff of an office. During the past few minutes he had forgotten even Miss Henery. He could laugh naturally and speak without self-consciousness.

"It's a very interesting experiment," he said to Mortimer Barnett, who had just told him about telescopic objectivity. "But it seems to me you're giving yourself an awful lot of work. What I mean is this. You start out, you say, by writing about a group of characters. Good. Now, I can understand you painting in their backgrounds with a certain amount of detail, but if you've got to pause every now and then to go into the stories of objects that surround your characters or objects in the past lives of your characters, don't you think you'd find yourself eventually en-gaged in a sort of unending labour of Hercules?"

Mortimer Barnett shook his head.

"Selection," he said, "will limit the extent of your labours. Remember, it isn't *every* object in a room that bears a significant story *and* a story related to the past of one of the characters present. It isn't every stain on the wall or crack in a saucer which carries a trail of related and significant events in its wake, much less a trail related directly to a character's past. Take that scar on your arm. It may or it may not act as stimulus to your major thoughts and major emotions. It may or it may not conjure up – what's the matter? Have I —?"

"No, no! Nothing at all! Go on. I'm interested."

"I didn't mean to be personal, but a pronounced scar like that is a pretty, shall I say, pregnant 'object' – some circumstance involving violence must have brought it into being – that's why

I planked for it right off. The events which resulted in the injury that caused it are likely to have left a deep impression on your mind, if not on your active imagination as well. Of course, I may be quite wrong; perhaps you've forgotten all about it and what caused it. You see, it's up to the artist," continued Mortimer Barnett, pretending not to notice Mr Murrain's fidgetings, "to *know* which object to concentrate on and which to ignore. That's why his task isn't necessarily a Herculean one.

"We always have to assume, of course, that a writer, in respect to the creatures of his imagination, is omniscient. It must be supposed that no detail of their present or past is hidden from him. Therefore *he* must know best what objects to examine and explore in his effort to achieve a telescopic reality. It must be taken for granted that if he selects one object for investigation and ignores another he is acting out of the fitness of his knowledge of his characters. It must be assumed that he is sincere when he implies by his disregard of the other objects present that he knows there is nothing vitally influential to his characters' lives in these objects."

Mr Murrain nodded and smiled. This interview was delighting him.

"But," he said, "there's another aspect which has struck me. Couldn't the influence of an 'object' be shown to affect a character's future outlook?"

"Certainly. Some 'objects' are static in the present – what I mean is they've influenced the character's past, but in the now with which we may be concerned they have no 'active' significance. But there may be dynamic 'objects' which may well continue to shape the character's life in the present as well as in the future. It's up to the artist to indicate any future developments or consequences…"

… The clock said twenty-two minutes to twelve when Miss Laballe glanced at it. She was hungry, and her hunger was a consequence of her having had only one small object for breakfast – a banana.

Some mornings she did not even bother with the banana. Her mother was always warning her that her health would break down if she continued to eat in this fashion… "And look how frail and thin you is awready!" To which Miss Laballe would reply: "But what you want me to do if Ah don't feel hungry in the mornings, Ma!" And her mother would shrug and say: "Awright, me dear. You is a big woman for you'self. You must know best."

It was only since Laura Laballe had given birth to the child she had had by an American soldier that her mother had begun to refer to her as a big woman for herself. All along she had pampered Laura and called her her little girl.

Laura herself was illegitimate, but Teresa Roheiro had had hopes that her daughter Laura might have done better. When Laura had followed Teresa's example Teresa had been disappointed but had had to make the best of the situation and take consolation in her blond-haired, blue-eyed grandson. Blue eyes were a rarity for Teresa, for Teresa was a Portuguese. It was because she was a Portuguese that Karl Laballe, the father of Laura, had not married her.

Karl Laballe was the son of a French creole family which had fallen on modest times. But modest times had not reduced the pride of the Laballes, and Karl was, by nature, weak and tractable; he had yielded to pressure at home...

"A common Portuguese girl! Karl, are you mad?" ...

"You may marry her, but you won't set foot in this house again..."

Portuguese, in the West Indies, are not looked upon as white. Like Jews and Spaniards, Portuguese are just Portuguese. They came from Madeira, the great majority of them, in the latter half of the nineteenth century when the Chinese and East Indians were also flowing in. They came as pedlars and worked their way up to the top strata of commerce and finance. One or two remained poor, like Teresa and her father and mother, but most of them grew wealthy off rum-shops and pawnbrokeries.

The English-whites, the French creoles and the coloured middle-class look on creole Portuguese as inferior people – people on a level with the Chinese and East Indians – the argument being that the Portuguese are descended from peasant immigrants; they lack a background of ladies and gentlemen; the only creole West Indian ancestors they can show are greasy pedlars and greasier salt-goods-shop-keepers.

Karl Laballe had married a respectable French creole girl with money, and lived now with his family in an ornate house facing the Savannah. He had allowed Laura to bear his name (for he had loved Teresa), and he had supported mother and child until Laura was old enough to go to work.

Miss Laballe regarded the young man in the advertisement on the back cover of *Woman's Home Companion*, and smiled. He reminded her a lot of Jerry Burhoff. Jerry had had light-brown hair like this young man's – and the same blue-green eyes and even teeth. If only she could find out what had happened to Jerry. He had gone on to the Pacific after his stay in Trinidad, and, for all she knew, might have been killed.

He had never written her, but she held nothing against him for it – nor did she regret having had a child by him. It had been such a lovely affair while it lasted.

He used to take her every night to the Rock Garden – and some nights when there was moonlight they would pick out the tree with the darkest shadow to lie under.

The memory of it was enough to excuse everything that had followed, everything bad that might happen to her now; it was as though her life had been fulfilled and completed during that affair with Jerry; what she was living now was a kind of aftermath. She would get married, of course, if some chap she liked came along, but if she remained single for the rest of her life she was sure she would not mind...

She turned her head as she heard footsteps on the stairs. Her gaze met Mr Lorry's. Mr Lorry winked.

She sucked her teeth and tossed her head... Most fresh man! Don't know what women can find in him...

Mr Lorry moved towards his desk, but looked at Mrs Hinckson's which was vacant. He asked Miss Bisnauth who had just emerged from the Ladies' Room: "Where's Nanette? Gone home already?"

"No, she's in the Ladies' Room," smiled Miss Bisnauth.

"All right, don't get jittery. I won't follow her in there."

"I should hope not!'" giggled Miss Bisnauth, moving on.

What a boy! He can be so amusing...

She settled down at her desk. She was in a good mood. The

vitalizing work on her poem was going to her liking. The lofty fire had come – all in a flash. She had just changed

> *"Oh, I wish it were mine, this flower,*
> *Just to hold to myself for an hour..."*

into

> *"If, like white-hot steel, this calm flower*
> *Could sear me for but a yearning hour..."*

She glanced up and noticed that Horace had advanced cautiously through the barrier-gate. He was staring in the direction of Mr Reynolds. He hesitated, then turned back and returned to his desk.

Mr Reynolds, too, had noticed the boy's movements. Mr Reynolds frowned, then rose and hurried towards the barrier-gate. Bending confidentially towards Horace, who sat stiffly upright, his gaze on his tightly clasped hands which rested before him on the blotter, Mr Reynolds murmured: "I meant to tell you before I went for lunch. I've fixed up that thing for you."

Horace made no reply.

Mr Reynolds suddenly felt uncomfortable, awkward. The boy's posture disturbed him. He sat so unnaturally rigid; his eyes glittered with such a fierce anxiety.

"You heard what I said, Xavier?"

Horace nodded.

"Everything is all right. She understands."

Horace glanced up. An invisible string might have jerked his head up.

"She understands? How – what you told her?"

"Eh? I – about Mr Lorry not writing the love verse – as a matter of fact, she knew already: She guessed, she said —"

Mr Reynolds broke off. He realized that he had blundered. It was inexcusable, he rated himself. For a salesman, it was inexcusable... God! Why can't I speak to a young fellow privately without seeing that thing in my fancy! The only time I can feel safe from it is when I'm with Delly Winter...

Mr Reynolds was perspiring. He almost recoiled as Horace stood up.

It was like a statue facing him – a statue in clothes, thought Mr Reynolds.

"Mr Reynolds – sir, you don't mean – oh, God! She knows it's me?"

Mr Reynolds patted his shoulder, allowed his hand to linger, though the hand trembled.

"You mustn't upset yourself, Xavier. What's the matter? I didn't even say such a thing. Don't jump to conclusions —"

He stopped abruptly, knowing it was too late. He turned hurriedly and began to move away, calling back softly: "Buck up, there's a good fellow! You'll get over it!" He tried to laugh, but it was a croak that escaped him.

Miss Laballe, who had been observing them with a smile, now shook with sniggers. Only the black holes unplugged saw the malice on her face.

Like Miss Bisnauth, Miss Henery was in a good mood. She had suggested herself into a good mood. She had no doubt now that she was to be dismissed. Mr Waley would not have asked her to go in to see him if he did not intend to dismiss her. In her fancy, she already heard him telling her in a pleasant voice how much he regretted having to do it. She was a good worker, and, of course, he would be ready to give her a first-class recommendation if she wished it. He hoped she understood his position in the matter. He could not very well ignore his assistant manager if his assistant manager recommended her dismissal.

This would be a very un-English way of dealing with her, but Mr Waley, she reasoned, had been resident in Trinidad long enough to understand the West Indian mind, and would realize that he could not simply tell her in a curt voice that her services were no longer required. Such a course might have for him repercussions of an unpleasant nature: who knew if it might not be taken up in the press? Like that incident in the Civil Service in 1943 when the head of a department, an Englishman transferred to Trinidad from Africa, told a coloured lady clerk to stand when addressing him; the incident had been taken up by the *Civil Service Review* (run by the coloured members of the Service) and had precipitated an indignant furore in the general press; the Government had threatened the editors of the *Civil Service Review* with "disciplinary action", and the furore developed into a pandemonium... No, she was sure he would hand her a cheque for a month's salary in lieu of notice, and be very nice about it. He would know that her pride as a member of the coloured middle-class would make it impossible for her to continue work in the office under notice of dismissal – and, in any case, her continued presence would be intolerable for Mr Murrain.

So certain was she that she was about to be dismissed that she had begun to clear up her drawers of little odds and ends of a personal nature which she put unobtrusively into her handbag, for it would not have been good form for the rest of the staff to see her openly engaged in these winding-up operations.

While she cleared up she told herself that she was glad – glad and relieved – at the prospect of going. She was free now, and could set her mind definitely on her Barbados trip.

She began to picture herself in Barbados on Worthing beach. She paused, her hand on a vanity case she had taken from the left-hand bottom drawer. She gazed at it and projected herself away from the office…

She and her cousin's husband, Gerard Beaton, were walking on the beach, Gerard in play-pants, she in her blue-flowered two-piece bathing-suit. They wore sunshades against the glare (the sand on Worthing beach, she had heard, was white and threw up a painful glare).

Rachel had gone to Bridgetown to do some shopping, and the children were in the house in the care of their nurse. So she and Gerard had at least an hour and a half to themselves.

On leaving the house, they had indulged in a few casual remarks concerning the sea and the glare – remarks which, if overheard, would have sounded impeccably proper. Now they walked without saying anything, Gerard humming a tune.

They came upon a sea-grape tree whose large, saucer-like leaves overhung the beach and made a cool shade from the sun.

Gerard glanced at her, silently questioning, and she nodded.

They seated themselves, and, still silent, played idly with the sand and fallen sea-grapes.

In the tensity of her anticipation, she could hear the sea as a low whirring – not unlike the sound of an electric lathe. When she was eleven or twelve at school, there had been a joiner's workshop obliquely opposite the school, and almost all day you could hear the whirr of the electric lathe. Just so the sea sounded now.

Gerard's hand closed over her leg – her right leg, near the calf.

A shiver went through her. She breathed hard, and sifted sand with intense concentration.

Gerard's hand tightened. It was over her knee now.

There was nobody in sight. The beach was deserted – as far as she could look in either direction.

And the sea whirred – like an electric lathe.

The hand was above her knee. It squeezed the narrow part of her thigh. She shut her eyes and held her breath…

Strange, though, it did not quite feel like Gerard's hand. It seemed a larger hand with a palm rough and calloused. Like some nigger man's hand…

Miss Henery sat rigid at her desk, staring before her.

This was no daydream. There *was* a hand clutching her thigh under the desk. It had her knee pinned hard against the right desk-leg. She wanted to laugh – wished she could – at the absurdity of the thing.

A coarse, calloused hand. What nigger could ever dare… It moved slightly…

She sprang up, her chair crashing backward.

Mr Murrain, looking, saw the indication of dark areolae and prominent nipples. Nipples made prominent by fear.

Mr Lopez and Mr Reynolds had rushed to the rescue…

… "I really can't imagine," Miss Henery was saying. "I thought…" She broke off and laughed, utterly confused.

"It must have been a centipede," said Mr Lopez. He began to look about the floor.

Mr Reynolds had already bent down and was peering under the desk. He had suggested it might have been a mouse.

"Perhaps it was," said Miss Henery, her face red. "I felt it tickle – it touched my knee."

"Lucky it didn't nip you," said Mr Reynolds.

"But how could it have vanished so quickly?" said Mr Lopez. "A centipede moves fast, but not so fast that we shouldn't have seen it. There's no hole in the floor."

"Couldn't it have run into one of the drawers? Didn't you have that drawer open?" Mr Reynolds still believed it must have been a mouse.

"No, it couldn't possibly have got into that drawer. That's on the left. It was on the right – oh, don't bother! Let it go at that."

She sat down, too perturbed to notice that the clock was saying fourteen minutes to twelve…

"… I'm running off now, Mr Murrain."

Mr Murrain extended his hand. "Please drop in again. And I don't say that to be polite. I mean it. I've enjoyed this talk."

Mortimer Barnett said he would drop in again soon. "I'll probably bring you a short story for you to give me your opinion on."

"That will be splendid," smiled Mr Murrain, and felt an unusual elation. For a long time he had not experienced such sincerity and honesty when talking to a fellow human. He knew that every word he had said to Barnett had been free of hypocrisy; somehow, he had not found it necessary to indulge in conventional cordialities. With a shock he realized that perhaps it was visitors like Mortimer Barnett that Sidney Whitmer used to have at the Overseers' Quarters at Tucurapo. Good gracious! But one couldn't object to the company of a person like Mortimer Barnett on the grounds of his colour! …

"… of course. A full page. Come in in a day or two and I'll let you have the wording of the advertisement itself. Probably our marmalade or lime-juice. Mr Waley will decide which…"

Mrs Hinckson, at the door of the Ladies' Room, watched Mortimer Barnett leave. Her eyes were wide. Her hand grasped the door jamb, and the knuckles were white. Her lips were parted a trifle.

"Oh, God!" she murmured, and turned and moved inside, pushing the door shut.

Mr Lopez happened to see the look on her face before she retreated and closed the door. He raised his brows so that his forehead became tightly wrinkled, and scratched his temple with a forefinger.

The first time his Great-uncle Juan had seen him doing this he had commented: "That's a family trait, boy." And he had gone on to tell how Rafael's great-grandfather, a landowner near St Joseph, the old Spanish capital of Trinidad, had had the same way of wrinkling his forehead and scratching his temple when intrigued by some observation. Rafael, with his deep-set black eyes and high, thin nose, was even supposed to resemble Great-grandfather Luiz.

Great-uncle Juan had always been fond of relating tales of the old days, for he had been proud of the family's connections with the former rulers of Trinidad. He spoke the purest Castilian, and believed that there was conquistador blood in him. Cortez and Simon Bolivar were his heroes, and he kept a collection of books locked in an iron canister supposed to have once contained buccaneer treasure – books that dealt with the adventures and conquests of the Early Days.

On his death – aged ninety-three – five years ago, the key for his canister could not be found, and it was said that he had given it into the care of a spirit when he knew that he was about to die so that no one could open the canister and desecrate his books.

His niece, Rafael's mother, had started this tale going, for Mrs Lopez, like most Spaniards in Trinidad, was very superstitious. Rafael, who had been educated at St Mary's College, considered superstition the bane of the family – and was never afraid to tell his parents so…

"You make me ashamed. Supposed to be intelligent people and devout Catholics, and believing in *obeah* and *soucouyant* and *diablesse*. And you're the ones who talk about pride…"

… Miss Bisnauth was wondering about Mrs Hinckson's pride. She had always thought Mrs Hinckson so proud – yet here she was not even trying to disguise how she felt about Mortimer Barnett.

"Is that all the work he does? Writing?"

"Yes, so Arthur said. He used to work for Arthur's newspaper, but he resigned. He said he couldn't be a stooge for the directors. He had to write what came from inside him – and write it in his own way."

"Yes, I could see he has integrity."

Miss Bismuth fidgeted. "Yes, of course," she mumbled.

"You've never met him before, you say?"

"No, never. This is the first time. Arthur rang this morning to say I must look out for him. He wanted this advertisement."

"What a beastly shame!"

"A shame?"

"I mean, his having to depend upon advertisements to bring out this booklet of his writings."

'Yes, that's so. You see, we haven't any publishers in the West Indies who will bring out a writer's work at their own risk."

Mrs Hinckson stared past her in silence, and Miss Bisnauth toyed with an eraser, uncomfortable...

... As a boy in his teens, when the family was living in the country, Rafael's mother had insisted that he should be in the house every evening before darkness. His mother believed that he might be waylaid by a lovely young woman – in reality, a *diablesse* – who, as all *diablesses* did, would lure him into the hills and do him to death. His brothers had had to suffer the same restrictions... When anyone in the house fell ill his mother would call in an *obeah* woman to say "prayers" and sprinkle holy water and rice about the sick-room and burn candles to keep off *maljo* (the evil eye).

Josephine, a married sister of Rafael's, was today not on speaking terms with their mother because Josephine had refused to have rice sprinkled on the ledges and shelves of her new home and chalk-marks drawn on the windowsills to safeguard her house against the *soucouyant,* the vampire woman who was said to come through the night as a ball of fire; she could not cross chalk lines, however, and if she found rice on the shelves or ledges she must first pick up every grain before she could do any harm to the inmates, but in doing this she had to bend low, and, as a result, broke her back and perished.

Josephine, apart from being well educated, was rising in society (she had married a Spanish creole of wealth and real, not sham, gentility), and could not afford to jeopardize her chances of admission into the Country Club...

... How could she have explained, thought Miss Henery, that she had been indulging in a sexy daydream? And to have mentioned that she had actually felt the coarse hand gripping her thigh under the desk was equally unthinkable. For one thing, it would have been obscene, and for another, it would only have given that confounded Englishman the opportunity to laugh at her and call her a superstitious West Indian native. English people and Americans always thought West Indians superstitious, and this incident would have confirmed it in Mr Murrain's mind.

Personally, she did not know what to make of the whole thing herself. She felt convinced that it was not her imagination which had conjured up that hand. She had actually felt it shift along her skin...

She shuddered.

It was an odd coincidence, though, that in her fancy she should have had Gerard fondling her leg... Or could it be that her thoughts and images had been directed by some unsuspected force to serve the purpose of an unseen personage? Oh, nonsense! That was magazine story stuff! Yet...

Yet, from what she had read, there seemed to be a tremendous amount of evidence in proof of the existence of ghosts. She did not agree with these people who scoffed outright at psychic phenomena. Supernatural events were not products of an idiotic or childish imagination, as some thought.

She looked down at the desk-leg, and wondered whether there might not be some strange story behind it. Who was the joiner who had turned it? In what part of the city did he live? Or perhaps he was dead. For all she knew, there might be some sort of psychic plasm adhering to this desk-leg, and by her fanciful thoughts of a few minutes ago, she had unwittingly put herself *en rapport* with the forces allied to this psychic plasm. She had read of such things. Purely by accident she might have produced, by her daydreaming, the right conditions to precipitate a manifestation...

Something else occurred to her. If Gerard ever caressed her leg when they were in Barbados she would remember that coarse hand and shudder in revulsion. Yes, revulsion.

Perhaps this incident, trivial as it seemed, might influence the whole of her future life...

... Mr Lopez was engaged in a perpetual struggle to protect himself against the superstitious beliefs of his parents – especially his mother. He had to struggle, too, to keep in their good graces (for though he did not respect them he loved them) and, at the same time, avoid humiliation at their hands before his friends.

He had many friends – cricketers and sportsmen of all types – among the upper coloured middle-class, but he was generally reluctant to entertain them at his home for fear his father and mother and their friends (many of whom were Venezuelans contemptuous of British ways and the British) should come crowding unexpectedly into the sitting-room laughing, gesticulating and jabbering in Spanish.

Mr Lopez valued his sportsmen friends. They were to him what a collection of fine porcelain is to a connoisseur. He had acquired them with care and discrimination during his past seven years of serious cricket (he had been a cricket star since a schoolboy of seventeen when he had first played for an all-Trinidad team), and he took extreme precautions to protect them from damage; nothing must flake the esteem in which they held him as a sportsman; nothing must so much as scratch their loyalty to him as a friend...

... Mr Lorry kept watching her. Casually, unobtrusively.

Funny look on her face. Wonder what could be up. If anybody had asked him, he would have said that she had just fallen in love. Whatever she was telling Miss Bisnauth was making Miss Bisnauth uncomfortable.

I must have that woman, thought Mr Lorry. I'm going to get tired of her in less than a week, but I must have her. I believe she's in a ripe mood at this very minute...

... Mr Lopez' friends were of little use to him in his career as a cricketer, for in cricket – and all cricket in the British West Indies is non-professional – race and class play no part. Cricket is taken too solemnly. In the newspapers a forthcoming series of matches against the M.C.C. is given the prominence of a royal wedding or the invasion of one European country by another; it is an event discussed and speculated upon months in advance; every detail relating to it is big news. Inter-colonial test matches – hardly less momentous – rank as front page news, and during the two weeks of the Tests every radio set in the islands opposed on the Field blares out a running commentary of the game. Business offices and stores close half-day to permit their employees to attend the matches.

The name Raffy Lopez was known throughout the British West Indies; it was synonymous with "century"; if Raffy Lopez failed to score a century in any innings he was considered to be off colour – and he was rarely off colour.

Under these circumstances, there could be no race and class prejudice in cricket; a superb batsman was a superb batsman, a first-class spin-bowler was a first-class spin-bowler; no one stopped to ask what was his shade of complexion or his position in society; his performance was enough. Was he capable of wiping up the Barbados bowling? Was he capable of mowing down the Barbados wickets? The hero who could answer these questions in the affirmative received recognition and its concomitant privileges without stint or reserve...

... Mr Murrain kept smiling at the price-list. A quiet, contemplative smile.

He felt as though he had had a spiritual purge. Mortimer Barnett's voice still sounded in his fancy... "The artist must know how far to portray his people and their surroundings and significant objects objectively without sacrificing the subjectivity necessary to gain an insight into the minds of his characters. Telescopic objectivity, as I've conceived it, is nothing that must be limited to strait-laced rules..."

For some reason, Mr Murrain, in this moment, felt that in time to come he might yet achieve his dream of writing a good novel. Or a good poem. This young man had given him a sudden wild new hope; he had revitalized something in him – something which had been dying.

Mr Murrain regarded the scar on his forearm, and it did not make him nervous. The trapped-in-the-skin shudders did not come on. The scenes on the beach at Dunkirk failed to materialize in his fancy to plague him.

Good gracious! He believed he was actually cured of all that now. Suddenly and miraculously as a result of that chat with Barnett...

... Mr Lopez could have held a far more lucrative position than his present one as junior accountant of Essential Products; he had been offered jobs by other big firms and by the banks; his complexion was fair enough for a bank (the banks employ only people of fair complexion; they do not object to their employees having negro blood; all they ask is that the negro blood does not reveal itself in pigmentary form).

But, to Mr Lopez, the idea of working in the same office as that in which one or more of his sporting friends was employed was out of the question (and he would have had to do so in any of the other jobs offered to him). He feared that, in some way – it might be a clash of temperaments engendered by the irritations of business; it might be petty jealousy hatched by a reshuffling of the staff – in some way, he feared, he would inevitably have succeeded in damaging that valuable esteem in which he was held by his friends. He could not risk it. He knew his attitude savoured of fetishism, but he could not help himself. His secret nightmare dread was that circumstances would so devolve that one morning he would look up to see one of his precious collection of chums entering the office as a new member of the staff...

...But who can he be glaring at like that? Miss Laballe asked herself, watching Horace...

... Something is the matter with him, thought Miss Yen Tip, whose desk was separated from Horace's by not more than eight feet.

But for the barrier, she would have felt a little alarmed.

The boy's feet made scraping sounds at intervals, as though he were about to spring up and rush at someone. Without glancing at him she could sense the tension in his manner...

... Idly, Mr Lopez wondered what could have possessed Mrs Hinckson to stare at that writer fellow so hard. Was she acquainted with him? Could he be one of her boy friends? He had heard that intellectuals and artists were always attracted to her.

He snatched up a notebook.

Lucky fellow if he's sleeping with her...

He conjured up a breathtaking picture of himself in bed with Mrs Hinckson.

Mr Lopez had had sex fantasies involving every female member of the office staff. He was sex-starved, because he believed in rigorous abstinence as a means to first-class performance on the cricket field.

Next week he would have to play in the matches between Trinidad and Barbados, and for the past six weeks he had had nothing to do with a woman. He had no regular girl friend; he believed, as he always told his friends, that there was "safety in numbers – that's my motto!"

When the tournament was over he would indulge in an orgy that might last a month – then abstinence again, or very moderate indulgence, for three or four months, in preparation for the Cup matches in July and August.

He turned his head as Mr Jagabir's chair scraped. He saw the bulge in Mr Jagabir's coat pocket – and the grease stain. The grease from the *roti* had seeped through...

The contempt that arose in Mr Lopez was abruptly extinguished by a flash of pity. He saw Mr Jagabir as a lonely, too-much-despised figure. His eyes narrowed and softened as he watched him move over to Miss Henery. He could not hear what he said to Miss Henery...

"Look at de time, Miss Henery!"

Miss Henery started and glanced at the clock.

"Ten to twelve!"

Mr Jagabir fidgeted. His face had a concerned look. He seemed as though he wanted to say something sympathetic but the words defeated him.

"I t'ink de clock a minute fast, miss."

"Is it? Good Lord – but time can fly! I never noticed —" She gave a nervous laugh, frowned.

Mr Jagabir hesitated, turned and moved back towards his desk.

"Thank you," she mumbled in confusion, turning her head swiftly.

How on earth had he known, though?

She rose.

She knew Miss Yen Tip was staring at her, and her heart beat fast. But outwardly she appeared composed as she made her way to the frosted glass door and tapped lightly on it.

Horace rose, his hands clenched, his body so rigid that it shook.

For about ten seconds he stood like this, his gaze on Mrs Hinckson's desk.

Then he sat down.

"I agree. I am saying queer things."

"But —"

"I feel different."

"Different?"

Mrs Hinckson nodded. "A change has occurred in me."

"Oh."

"Not half an hour ago I was certain such a man never existed."

"A man like Barnett, you mean?"

Miss Bisnauth watched her.

"I look up – and there he is, a masculine animal – and a writer." Her voice had a far-away note. "The next minute he's going – right out of my sight and my life."

"But why —"

"There could never be anything between us. He wouldn't want me. I'm not big enough for him. He's a giant in spirit. I sound like a cheap novelette, Edna." She touched Miss Bisnauth lightly on the shoulder and moved off.

Miss Bisnauth watched her go to her desk, hesitate irresolutely, then move on and go into the Ladies' Room.

Depression settled on Miss Bisnauth's face. But it was not because of Mrs Hinckson. Her mood had changed again. Not a few minutes ago it had come to her – all in a flash – that her poem was no good. It was idiotic.

She began to sketch figures aimlessly on the cover of her notebook. She remembered Arthur's unpublished fairy tale. Of late, in moments when she felt a failure, she would recall the Jen…

"The Jen began to weep… 'I'm lonely. A great, lonely, dreadful Jen.'"

She mustn't be too down-spirited. It was only fear that got her down. Everybody in the world feared a dreadful bogey. But what you had to do was to face it bravely. If you did that you might discover that it wasn't half as dreadful as you had imagined it to be.

Of course, what Arthur was really trying to do in *The Jen* was to debunk the old West Indian nancy-story. He wanted to show that it was a mistaken idea of certain West Indian cultural groups that West Indian literature and art should be based on these primitive tales. West Indians were not primitives. Only a handful of backwoods peasants were familiar with the nancy-stories that featured such characters as Compère Tigre and Compère Lapin.

Arthur felt that if one had to write fairy tales at all with a West Indian flavour the creatures or characters in them should be very nearly in the European tradition, for weren't the West Indies practically European in manners and customs?

The Burroo Tiger and Burroo Rabbit of the nancy-story represented a mere aspect of the old plantation days of slavery. It was irrelevant (and affected), thought Arthur, to resuscitate them and try to base a culture on them as certain faddists wanted to do.

These faddists had awakened one morning with the sudden idea that the West Indies lacked an individual culture and that it was their business to manufacture one without delay...

Miss Bisnauth glanced up at the sound of footsteps on the stairs.

It was Mary, the sweeper.

Miss Bisnauth rose and went towards the barrier.

Mary was sighing – in relief and happiness. She told Miss Bisnauth that she had dropped in to tell her what had happened in court.

"Ah know you would want to hear, miss, and Ah couldn't wait till dis af'noon when Ah come to make de tea. De magistrate put Richard on a bond, miss."

"You hadn't to pay a fine, then?"

"No, miss. Not a cent Ah didn't have to pay. Ah just had to sign dis bond saying Richard will be of good behaviour for a year. If he fall into any trouble again they can call him up and send him to de reformatory – but he promise me solemn he won't have no more to do wid dese steel bands. And Ah mean to watch him day and night, miss..."

"I'm glad, Mary. Really glad. I know how relieved you must be."

"Yes, miss. I know you would be glad. You such a kind lady..."

Such a kind lady, thought Miss Bisnauth, when Mary had departed and she had returned to her desk.

Am I really a kind lady, I wonder? Or could it be just the sentimental in me that makes me feel a great pity for humanity?

She felt completely negative, desperately miserable. And lonely. She was the Jen.

"Come in!"

Miss Henery went in.

"What! A quarter to twelve already?" Mr Waley glanced at his watch. "Ten to! How time does get away in this office! Sit down, Miss Henery. Make yourself comfortable."

She sat down.

"See this list? Henderson. Twenty-seven names and addresses – and he'll probably be phoning me another lot before the day is out. They've got to be sent off to the London office by tomorrow morning."

Miss Henery smiled politely.

"You've heard we want to start a small factory in Grenada?"

"Oh, yes. I – yes, I did hear something about it."

He gave a sigh of mock gloom. "And you can bet about eighty per cent of the work will fall on my shoulders. Sorry for me, Miss Henery?"

"No. I think you like a lot of work."

He laughed, his face getting red from sheer vitality and good humour. He slapped down the sheet of paper he had been waving at her.

"Well, let's see. This little matter I've got to speak to you about. Now, what was it?" He drummed on the blotter, then nodded as though just remembering.

"How would you like working for me?"

"Working for you?"

"M'm. Doing the minutes and seeing after the files and helping Mrs Hinckson generally. In Miss Bisnauth's place, I mean?" Miss Henery could not help it. She gulped.

"You – do you mean you'd like Miss Bisnauth and I to exchange — ?"

"Exactly. Nothing like a change, you know. One type of work

is apt to get monotonous after a while. I meant to suggest some reshuffling, but I've been so confoundedly busy I kept putting it off from day to day. There you are! Phone again. See the kind of life I lead, Miss Henery?"...

"... after lunch – certainly! ... Miss Laballe, as soon as you return from lunch, do your best to get a call through to New York for me... Yes, Miss Henery, what do you think of the idea?"

"I shouldn't mind, Mr Waley. In fact – I think I should prefer it."

"Good. Of course, I haven't spoken to Miss Bisnauth yet. I wanted to see how you would feel about it first. After lunch I'll have a chat with her. Oh, and by the way! You want your two weeks' leave this month, I've been hearing. You can have it. Going to Barbados, eh?"

"Yes, I was thinking of going there —"

"Delightful little island. Too delightful, I think sometimes." He winked and wagged his finger at her. "Don't go and get into trouble!"

"... The water in the Canje Creek is black, and along the banks the bush is dense; you never knew what might be wriggling in the water besides fishes, and sometimes strange cries that frightened Mooney came from the bush."

"That's how I feel now," murmured Miss Bisnauth to her typewriter. I can see only black water and dense bush around me. I'm afraid because I don't know what might be wriggling in the water besides fishes. I can hear, continued her thoughts, strange cries that frighten me.

The Nightmare Moment gripped her.

Colour seeped out of her dress – out of the trees in Marine Square. Her lungs were two silver bellows in deep twilight. Her breasts mounds of lead.

This time her throat would really burst into flames, and the splinters of ice in her veins would prick her heart into a deathly numbness.

But it passed – as it always passed.

She gave an inward groan and tried to concentrate exclusively on Arthur's fairy tale. Only that way lay comfort...

Arthur said these faddists were trying to dig up everything they could pertaining to Negro folklore in the West Indies: the *cumfa* dance, *shango,* the nancy-story. They were glorifying the calypso and encouraging primitive institutions like the steel band. They had purposely blinded themselves to the fact that if the West Indies was to evolve a culture individually West Indian, it could only come out of the whole hotch-potch of racial and national elements of which the West Indies was composed; it could not spring only from the negro.

These faddists, Arthur had told her, were even trying to whip into life a spirit of aggressive nationalism, forgetful of the misery nationalism had already caused, and was still causing, in the world at large.

Arthur said he was always pointing out that West Indians should remember that they were first of all citizens of the world and only secondly West Indians. The British West Indian colonies were working for federation and eventual dominion status and independence, and the goal seemed well in sight already, but this was no reason, argued Arthur, why West Indians should get aggressively nationalistic...

"Eh? You spoke to me, Laura?"

Miss Laballe hissed: "Child, I believe Benson is in a hell of a mess. He and his bub-alls..."

Mr Benson had not been able to wait for twelve o'clock. He had had to phone Millan.

"What happened? Did you succeed in driving him off?"

"Oh, yes, he's gone. He can't make any trouble for us. He's a fool. No more brain than a caterpillar."

Click.

"You're sure?"

'Quite sure. He doesn't know a damned thing that matters. He came back begging for the price of a drink, as docile as a lamb, and I asked him a few questions. All he picked up were a few scraps of gossip from Rowland's chauffeur. I gave him a shilling and sent him about his business."

When Mr Benson hung up he was perspiring slightly on the forehead. He was relieved, but he felt chastened, too. These last few minutes had been a shudderingly horrible ordeal. He had seen himself disgraced, on the way back to the gutter; he had reached the gutter and squealed and died.

He stared at his inkwell and decided on two things – to put ten dollars in the offertory next Sunday, and to read over Santayana's *Scepticism and Animal Faith*.

Miss Yen Tip frowned.

That boy seems not too right in his mind this morning. It's funny because he's always so level-headed and quiet.

Why must he keep fidgeting all the time like this? And looking so queer and mad?

Getting up and sitting down. And staring before him as if he want to spring upon somebody and bite them. I don't like it at all. I must keep me eye on him.

Mr Jagabir's face assumed an expression of deep concern.

He's only black, but he's intelligent. One day he may be a famous writer, who knows? I must ask him if he's never tried his hand at writing stories. He could begin with simple little tales like *The Jen*...

Miss Laballe, very hungry and determined to go to the Ladies' Room this instant to prepare herself for departure, called to Horace: "Xavier! Come and relieve me, please!"

Horace ignored her.

Miss Laballe looked round again.

"Eh-eh! Xavier, you didn't hear me speak to you?"

No response from Horace.

Mr Jagabir poised himself to rise.

Miss Laballe looked blank. She murmured to herself.

In a loud voice: "Xavier! I spoke to you!"

"To hell wid you!"

It went through the office like a prong of lightning.

Mr Jagabir dropped his pen with a soft clatter on the blotter.

By the safe, Mr Murrain, putting on his coat, paused and turned.

Miss Yen Tip glanced at Mr Benson to make sure that the scowl on his face was directed at Horace and not at her.

"To hell wid all o' you!"

Horace was on his feet. He kept looking about him in jerks.

Mr Reynolds perspired.

"Because I black? You-all not better dan me!"

The door of the Ladies' Room opened a trifle.

Horace strode through the barrier-gate with a crash. He was at Mrs Hinckson's desk in three strides.

Mr Jagabir half-rose from his chair.

Horace snatched the paper from the *File* tray.

"Boy! You gone off you' head!" shouted Mr Jagabir.

Horace sprang round to face him.

"Because I black? It's my paper! I put down de words on it! I got a right to take it back!"

He was trembling all over.

"You hear me? It's mine! Nobody can stop me from taking it!"

He went towards the barrier-gate at a half-run.

He stopped at his desk, gathered up his books – *A Tale of Two Cities,* his shorthand text-book, his exercise books.

"Keep you' job! I don't want it! Keep you' job!" His voice cracked.

A moment later the office heard, mingled with the stamping thud of steps down the stairs, a sound that might have been a stifled sob.

"No need for him to worry," said Mr Reynolds to Mr Lopez as they began to descend. "He's a bright fellow. Must rise in this world. I'm going to get him another job tomorrow – easy as kissing hands."

Mrs Hinckson settled down to do an urgent cable Mr Waley had asked her to get done as she emerged from the Ladies' Room.

She had just put the cable forms into the typewriter when she became aware that Mr Lorry was standing beside her.

"I'm lunching at the Kimling today. I was wondering if I could give them an order for tonight – dinner for two."

She made no reply.

"And after dinner, a little fresh air on the hills."

She was staring at the machine. She raised a hand from her lap and flipped off a speck of lint from her notebook. The hand trembled.

"Very well," she murmured.

Miss Henery paused at the barrier-gate and glanced round.

"Yes, Mr Murrain?"

"Miss Henery, I was wondering – could I give you a lift in my car to your restaurant? It's all in my way."

The rumble and blare of the traffic in Marine Square took on the sudden heightened pitch of noon. Miss Henery heard the Angelus far away.

"Oh – thank you, Mr Murrain."

"Now dat boy behave like dat and rush off," said Mr Jagabir to Miss Bisnauth, "who would have lock up de office now? They ought to be glad I always eat my lunch here."

"Yes, that's so," said Miss Bisnauth.

She watched him make his way towards the lunchroom.

People, she thought, as I've seen them this morning are cruel caricatures of what I conceived them to be yesterday. She covered her typewriter.

Yet, I still don't feel they should be laughed at outright. We ought to see ourselves with ironic eyes, but we should revere the humanity in us. At our worst, we have a dignity and grandeur that no other living things can emulate.

I agree with what Arthur said once. He said that a novelist ought to laugh at his characters – and even at himself – but his laughter should be in respectful undertones.

She sighed and rose, wincing at the thunder of the traffic.

ABOUT THE AUTHOR

Edgar Mittelholzer was born in New Amsterdam in what was still British Guiana in 1909. He began writing in 1929 and despite constant rejection letters persisted with his writing. In 1937 he self-published a collection of skits, *Creole Chips*, and sold it from door to door. By 1938 he had completed *Corentyne Thunder*, though it was not published until 1941 because of the intervention of the war. In 1941 he left Guyana for Trinidad where he served in the Trinidad Royal Volunteer Naval Reserve. In 1948 he left for England with the manuscript of *A Morning at the Office*, set in Trinidad, which was published in 1950. Between 1951 and 1965 he published a further twenty-one novels and two works of non-fiction, including his autobiographical *A Swarthy Boy*. Apart from three years in Barbados, he lived for the rest of his life in England. His first marriage ended in 1959 and he remarried in 1960. He died by his own hand in 1965, a suicide by fire predicted in several of his novels.

Edgar Mittelholzer was the first Caribbean author to establish himself as a professional writer.

CARIBBEAN MODERN CLASSICS

Jan R. Carew
Black Midas
Introduction: Kwame Dawes
ISBN: 9781845230951; pp. 272; 23 May 2009; £8.99

This is the bawdy, Eldoradean epic of the legendary 'Ocean Shark' who makes and loses fortunes as a pork-knocker in the gold and diamond fields of Guyana, discovering that there are sharks with far sharper teeth in the city. *Black Midas* was first published in 1958.

Jan R. Carew
The Wild Coast
Introduction: Jeremy Poynting
ISBN: 9781845231101; pp. 240; 23 May 2009; £8.99

First published in 1958, this is the coming-of-age story of a sickly city child, sent away to the remote Berbice village of Tarlogie. Here he must find himself, make sense of Guyana's diverse cultural inheritances and come to terms with a wild nature disturbingly red in tooth and claw.

Neville Dawes
The Last Enchantment
Introduction: Kwame Dawes
ISBN: 9781845231170; pp. 332; 27 April 2009; £9.99

This penetrating and often satirical exploration of the search for self in a world divided by colour and class is set in the context of the radical hopes of Jamaican nationalist politics in the early 1950s. First published in 1960, the novel asks many pertinent questions about the Jamaica of today.

Wilson Harris
Heartland
Introduction: Michael Mitchell
ISBN: 9781845230968; pp. 104; 23 May 2009; £7.99

First published in 1964, this visionary narrative tracks one man's psychic disintegration in the aloneness of the forests of the Guyanese interior, making a powerful ecological statement about man's place in the 'invisible chain of being', in which nature is a no less active presence.

Edgar Mittelholzer
Corentyne Thunder
Introduction: Juanita Cox
ISBN: 9781845231118; pp. 242; 27 April 2009; £8.99

This pioneering work of West Indian fiction, first published in 1941, is not merely an acute portrayal of the rural Indo-Guyanese world, but a work of literary ambition that creates a symphonic relationship between its characters and the vast openness of the Corentyne coast.

Andrew Salkey
Escape to an Autumn Pavement
Introduction: Thomas Glave
ISBN: 9781845230982; pp. 220; 23 May 2009; £8.99

This brave and remarkable novel, set in London at the end of the 1950s, and published in 1960, catches its 'brown' Jamaican narrator on the cusp between black and white, between exiled Jamaican and an incipient black Londoner, and between heterosexual and homosexual desires.

Denis Williams
Other Leopards
Introduction: Victor Ramraj
ISBN: 9781845230678; pp. 216; 23 May 2009; £8.99

Lionel Froad is a Guyanese working on an archeological survey in the mythical Jokhara in the horn of Africa. There he hopes to rediscover the self he calls 'Lobo', his alter ego from 'ancestral times', which he thinks slumbers behind his cultivated mask. First published in 1963, this is one of the most important Caribbean novels of the past fifty years.

Denis Williams
The Third Temptation
Introduction: Victor Ramraj
ISBN: 9781845231163; pp. 108; May 2010; £8.99

A young man is killed in a traffic accident at a Welsh seaside resort. Around this incident, Williams, drawing inspiration from the *Nouveau Roman*, creates a reality that is both rich and problematic. Whilst he brings to the novel a Caribbean eye, Williams makes an important statement about refusing any restrictive boundaries for Caribbean fiction. The novel was first published in 1968.

Roger Mais
The Hills Were Joyful Together
Introduction: Norval Edwards
ISBN: 9781845231002; pp. 272; August 2010; £8.99

Unflinchingly realistic in its portrayal of the wretched lives of Kingston's urban poor, this is a novel of prophetic rage. First published in 1953, it is both a work of tragic vision and a major contribution to the evolution of an autonomous Caribbean literary aesthetic.

Edgar Mittelholzer
A Morning at the Office
Introduction: Raymond Ramcharitar
ISBN: 9781845231217; pp. 215; May 2010; £8.99

First published in 1950, this is one of the Caribbean's foundational novels in its bold attempt to portray a whole society in miniature. A genial satire on human follies and the pretensions of colour and class, this novel brings several ingenious touches to its mode of narration.

Edgar Mittelholzer
Shadows Move Among Them
Introduction: Rupert Roopnaraine
ISBN: 9781845230913; pp. 352; May 2010; £10.99

In part a satire on the Eldoradean dream, in part an exploration of the possibilities of escape from the discontents of civilisation, Mittelholzer's 1951 novel of the Reverend Harmston's attempt to set up a utopian commune dedicated to 'Hard work, frank love and wholesome play' has some eerie 'pre-echoes' of the fate of Jonestown in 1979.

Edgar Mittelholzer
The Life and Death of Sylvia
Introduction: Juanita Cox
ISBN: 9781845231200; pp. 362; May 2010, £10.99

In 1930s' Georgetown, a young woman on her own is vulnerable prey, and when Sylvia Russell finds she cannot square her struggle for economic survival and her integrity, she hurtles towards a wilfully early death. Mittelholzer's novel of 1953 is a richly inward portrayal of a woman who finds inner salvation through the act of writing.

Elma Napier
A Flying Fish Whispered
Introduction: Evelyn O'Callaghan
ISBN: 9781845231026; pp. 248; July 2010; £9.99

With one of the most delightfully feisty women characters in Caribbean fiction and prose that sings, Elma Napier's 1938 Dominican novel is a major rediscovery, not least for its imaginative exploration of different kinds of Caribbeans, in particular the polarity between plot and plantation that Napier sees in a distinctly gendered way.

Orlando Patterson
The Children of Sisyphus
Introduction: Kwame Dawes
ISBN: 9781845230944; pp. 288; August 2010; £9.99

This is a brutally poetic book that brings to the characters who live on Kingston's 'dungle' an intensity that invests them with tragic depth. In Patterson's existentialist novel, first published in 1964, dignity comes with a stoic awareness of the absurdity of life and the shedding of false illusions, whether of salvation or of a mythical African return.

V.S. Reid
New Day
Introduction: Norval Edwards
ISBN: 9781845230906, pp. 360; August 2010, £10.99

First published in 1949, this historical novel focuses on defining moments of Jamaica's nationhood, from the Morant Bay rebellion of 1865, to the dawn of self-government in 1944. *New Day* pioneers the creation of a distinctively Jamaican literary language of narration.

Garth St. Omer
A Room on the Hill
Introduction: John Robert Lee
ISBN: 9781845230937; pp. 210; September 2010; £8.99

A friend's suicide and his profound alienation in a St Lucia still slumbering in colonial mimicry and the straitjacket of a reactionary Catholic church drive John Lestrade into a state of internal exile. First published in 1968, St. Omer's meticulously crafted novel is a pioneering exploration of the inner Caribbean man.

Wayne Brown, *On the Coast*
George Campbell, *First Poems*
Austin C. Clarke, *The Survivors of the Crossing*
Austin C. Clarke, *Amongst Thistles and Thorns*
O.R. Dathorne, *The Scholar Man*
O.R. Dathorne, *Dumplings in the Soup*
Neville Dawes, *Interim*
Wilson Harris, *The Eye of the Scarecrow*
Wilson Harris, *The Sleepers of Roraima*
Wilson Harris, *Tumatumari*
Wilson Harris, *Ascent to Omai*
Wilson Harris, *The Age of the Rainmakers*
Marion Patrick Jones, *Panbeat*
Marion Patrick Jones, *Jouvert Morning*
Earl Lovelace, *Whilst Gods Are Falling*
Roger Mais, *Black Lightning*
Una Marson, *Selected Poems*
Edgar Mittelholzer, *Children of Kaywana*
Edgar Mittelholzer, *The Harrowing of Hubertus*
Edgar Mittelholzer, *Kaywana Blood*
Edgar Mittelholzer, *My Bones and My Flute*
Edgar Mittelholzer, *A Swarthy Boy*
Orlando Patterson, *An Absence of Ruins*
V.S. Reid, *The Leopard* (North America only)
Garth St. Omer, *Shades of Grey*
Andrew Salkey, *The Late Emancipation of Jerry Stover*
and more...

All Peepal Tree titles are available from the website
www.peepaltreepress.com
with a money back guarantee, secure credit card ordering
and fast delivery throughout the world at cost or less.

Peepal Tree Press is the home of challenging and inspiring literature
from the Caribbean and Black Britain. Visit www.peepaltreepress.com
to read sample poems and reviews, discover new authors, established
names and access a wealth of information.

Contact us at:
Peepal Tree Press, 17 King's Avenue, Leeds LS6 1QS, UK
Tel: +44 (0) 113 2451703 E-mail: contact@peepaltreepress.com